AQUASAPIEN PRODIGY

BOOK THREE

CAROL M. SALTER

Wayside Publications

Published by Wayside Publications

Manston, Kent CT12 5AW
First published in Great Britain in 2022 by Wayside Publications
Text Copyright © Carol M. Salter

Paperback ISBN 978-1-9993528-5-1

Printed and bound in Great Britain.
By Book Printing Ltd

CONTENTS

CHAPTER ONE – SAUDI ARABIA

L EWIS was sick of school. Not just this his current school, which he'd been attending for over two years, but any school. *I hate everything about them. From the stupid Victorian uniform with its unbearable winged collars, to the archaic subjects we're taught. What use is mythology and classical Latin anyway, when we live in a world of computers and iPads?* To emphasize his point, Lewis kicked the obligatory stone in front of him—hard.

He heard the sound of glass breaking before he figured out the stone's trajectory. A window in the quadrangle opened and a balding head shot out.

"Blaine. My office. Twenty minutes!" bellowed the headmaster.

"Typical. Bloody typical!" Lewis groaned, stuffing his hands deeper into his trouser pockets.

Why the hell his mom had sent him to school, in cold boring England, was beyond him. His previous school in Denver had been fine. He had loads of friends, and Katy that cute girl in the year below him seemed interested. But no, mom insisted he learn some English manners. Even suggested he could do worse than cultivate an English accent. Enrolled him in school where he was a good year older than the rest of his cohort too. *Why?*

Thank God this was his last year. Exams almost over, he could leave in July, though his mom wanted him to continue his education at University somewhere. She'd been dropping hints about an English establishment for that too. *What on earth is wrong with her?*

He bet it had something to do with his invisible father. His mom never spoke of him, but Lewis knew. Knew he was English; from something she'd said just before he boarded the plane to come here. Redshaw, his middle name, he'd guessed long ago was his father's last name.

Without realising his feet took him down the usual path towards the canal. He loved it here. It calmed him. It was quiet and restful, almost a park in itself, with its dog walkers, couples and pigeons. He thought about the things Mr Timpson taught in history. Before trains and roads, the waterways had been the backbone of English transport. Lewis imagined himself at the tiller of his own narrow boat plying his trade between Cambridge and London. He liked the sound of that, being his own boss.

At nearly nineteen, Lewis Blaine wanted to travel, leave academia behind and see the world. He was going; he just hadn't built up enough courage to tell his mom yet.

Maybe I'll just leave, do a secret gap year. That appeals, he thought, warming to the idea. He sat on the edge of the canal, dangling his legs over, watching a moorhen, its black plumage and red bill bobbing about, the colours a sharp contrast to the green duckweed. *How's that supposed to be camouflage?* Leaning further forward he spied six, tiny black fluff-balls, that were her chicks, bowling along on the top of the water behind their mom.

It was a degree too far; maths were never Lewis's strong point. He fell face down into the canal, dropping like a stone wearing his heavy backpack in the manner of school kids everywhere. The weight of his books, sportswear and shoes were against him. He struggled to free himself becoming more entangled for his efforts.

He'd always been a good swimmer. Prided himself on his ability to hold his breath for the longest time at swim club. This was different. He wasn't in a sanitized pool prepared. He panicked, losing valuable oxygen in the process. He thought he'd managed to free himself for a moment when he pushed

2

up against something firm behind him. Then realised to his horror he'd signed his death warrant. It turned out to be a dreaded shopping trolley, probably submerged for years in the canal. It snagged his backpack straps anchoring him firmly in place below the surface. He twisted and turned, but the trolley was part of the canal, embedded deep into the muddy bed.

He thought of his mom in those final seconds. Replaying the last time they'd seen each other. They'd argued in the airport even as he headed towards the plane bound for England after the Easter break. He'd never get to say sorry for those angry words, spoken in the heat of the moment. Words he regretted uttering now.

His heart was beating like an African drum in his ears. He had to breathe. Needed to breathe. He couldn't hold his breath any longer. A thin stream of air bubbles forced themselves over his lips. They rose mockingly upwards to freedom and the surface mere feet above.

Lewis was saddened that his life would end here, now, with so little accomplished. And then, he let go emotionally, accepting his fate. *The Head will be furious when I don't turn up.* The thought brought a bizarre grin to his face. More bubbles escaped. *I'm losing it.* He watched the moorhen's red feet dart across the wet sky above, not noticing that he shouldn't be able to see them through the murky water. *Something has scared her.*

A pressure wave brushed past his legs, then vanished inside the cover of the canal. *What was that?* He stared down resisting the urge to squeal in terror. *Does England have crocodiles or water moccasins?* He'd heard stories in America of locals putting baby alligators and pythons down the sewers. *Do they do that in England too?* Whatever it was, passed a second time, a blur of motion and bubbles.

Then Lewis was rising. His backpack left behind, tethered to the trolley below. He burst to the surface like a cork from a bottle taking great gulps of air. His neck hurt like crazy. *Must have strained it somehow.* His head swam with dizziness. Without his usual finesse, Lewis swam to the nearby concrete slipway and flopped out on the slope like a beached dolphin.

Raising his head, he stared back at the water. No one followed him out. No saviour rose like a saint, instead, a thin line of bubbles headed south downstream. He watched the moorhen and her chicks fast-tailing it at top speed in the opposite direction, away from the mysterious happenings. *I must have imagined it.*

"You're late, Blaine," the Head grumbled, without looking up from his papers. When no answer was forthcoming, he raised his hairless head to inspect the troublesome boy. "…and wet," he added, noticing the boy dripping water onto his precious Iranian carpet.

"Sorry, Sir. Had a bit of an accident. Fell in the canal and got stuck." The Head stared astounded, as Lewis Blaine dropped unconscious onto his expensive rug.

In a desert somewhere in Saudi Arabia, north of Riyadh, three men hunkered down behind the barren sand dunes. They'd been dropped off in the early hours of the morning by the Spade, their all-purpose Tiltrotor aircraft. It was dark when they arrived, and cold. They passed the time busying themselves; completing weapons checks, making sure the comms were working, then sat in a huddle waiting, watching the sun rise. The burning disc, the size of a dinner plate on the horizon, rose, lighting the red dunes on fire.

Soon as it was light enough, they rose from their meagre place of concealment and began to walk, heading purposely in the direction of the compound. It was difficult terrain to traverse stealthily. Although it undulated with rocky crags and crevices between the dunes, cover was sparse. They made good use of their camo-netting, unrolling it from their backpacks to cover their equipment, pulling it over their heads too like see-through ponchos.

Their mission, a relatively easy one, promised T-cut the mission lead, involved the extraction of a mother and her two children. Relatively easy that was, provided no unexpected complications arose.

The woman and her children were English. Married and divorced, Samantha Khan, nee Dudley, had somehow become enmeshed in the complicated politics of a prominent Saudi family connected distantly to their Royals. The result being, she'd brought the children on a three-week holiday to see their father, and four months later, they were still all here, unable to leave for reasons unknown.

Their client, the woman's father, Norman Dudley, was an ex-forces colleague of Jeff Johnson, the former commanding officer of the Unit One team. Unit One, or U1 for short, was an elite independent military-style organisation. Others might have called them mercenaries, and in reality, they were, but they didn't take just any job for money, they had a unique code of honour that set them apart.

The client had requested a No-Blood-Shed contract. For this mission, they'd utilise the tranquilliser rifle designed by Johnson a few years earlier. Use of the Johnson rifle was Standard Operating Procedure in most missions these days, and always part of their weapons cache for any missions involving innocent civilians.

"Bloody foot's gone dead again," whispered Davidson in T-cut's earpiece. T-cut, whose real surname was Mason, had called a halt to their advance twenty-five minutes earlier, despite nothing moving for five clicks in any direction, except an elderly camel spider climbing erratically over the nearest dune to their right.

"You should move a bit more when we stop, flex your feet. I've told you before not to stay in one position. It's our age, grandpop." Davidson, U1's second-in-command, growled at

T-cut's ageist comment. He was only a year older than T-cut's forty-three years, and in no way could either of them be described as grandfather material.

T-cut smirked as he glanced behind. Davidson was doing a reasonable impersonation of Elvis Presley, as he shook his left leg in an effort to improve his circulation. Once he could feel the tingling rush of blood to his foot, Davidson breathed a relieved sigh, and stomped off across the sands to catch his teammates up who'd deliberately continued without him. *This is becoming a habit.* He cussed under his breath, thinking about his circulation, rather than the fact his two comrades had left him behind—again. *Something I'll have to investigate, not with Doc though.*

Doc Williams was Unit One's medical officer. In his late seventies and semi-retired, he remained one of the most sought-after plastic surgeons in the world. With full responsibility for all the team's health, he could pull Davidson off active duty in a micro-second. *No, needs to be somewhere private. When we touch land for R & R again.* He closed the gap on his teammates. *With someone who won't blab about any health issues they might find. I'm not ready for a care home just yet.*

They hiked the remaining few miles, covering the ground at an easy pace, as Davidson mulled over his options. The shortest member of the mission, Yin, who'd been with U1 three years, despite being only twenty-two, bought up the rear.

Unit One was an extremely active team, its members, men at the height of their physical prowess and in peak condition. Davidson wanted to remain part of that organisation for as long as possible. They weren't just his teammates; they were his brothers—brothers-in-arms.

At approximately seven a.m. local time the team arrived within visual range of their target. They stopped on the far side of a low hill some distance away. From their current location, they could observe the compound and the single road that led in and out, without being detected. There was no activity outside, no one seemed to be up and about yet, which was surprising.

T-cut rested his elbows on the rocky sand. Using high-spec binoculars he surveyed the compound's interior. To the casual observer, there wasn't much to see; a stone wall ran six-foot high around the perimeter. In the centre, sat a large detached concrete building, with two smaller rectangle buildings at right angles to it, set slightly forward. One seemed to be currently used as a garage, judging by the cars in front of it, the other was some kind of workshop. Behind, and to the right of the detached house, four outhouses existed, these were built out of African wood, local wood being a scarce commodity. They looked like somewhere the hired help might live if not allowed to stay in the main house.

On closer inspection, the place had the appearance of an oasis, compared to where they were currently crouched. There were several palm trees, date palms, citrus fruit trees, and they could hear the trickle of running water playing its endless tune, so a low fountain or ornamental waterfall must be somewhere within the property. T-cut surmised whoever owned it was wealthy, judging by the gunmetal grey Rolls Royce, and two brightly coloured Lamborghini's sitting inside within the long garage.

Although they had received intel on the property before leaving base, experience had taught T-cut to always complete a visual survey. It had saved the mission on more than one occasion. Lowering the binoculars T-cut started his report.

"Okay, there's one main entrance providing vehicular access at the front of the property."

Yin, returning from his recon of the perimeter added his information.

"Two smaller side doors in the walls, one on the left nearest us and one at the back. Both doors are bolted from inside."

7

"It's the wall then," replied T-cut despondently.

"Yeah. It's always the bloody wall. Why doesn't anybody leave a door open these days?" Davidson grumbled. "It would make our job so much easier."

Okay, which wall?" Yin asked, eager to be getting into some action. The walk had bored him to tears.

"Well, not the front wall that's for certain. Bound to be under surveillance. We go over the wall with no door in it," suggested Davidson, hoping T-cut would agree with his assessment.

"Roger that," replied T-cut. "Good idea, since there'll be less activity around anything without doors." Or so they thought.

The three of them made their way from the left-hand side of the main entrance, around the back, to the right side. Quickly and quietly, they uncoiled the grappling hook, expertly lobbing it over the wall. The odds were on their side, as nobody was up, no one noticed the small 'clang' of the hook as it caught and tethered on the other side. Luck stayed with them as Davidson, then T-cut, climbed the wall, and jumped down. Releasing the grappling hook, T-cut secured it in reverse for an extra avenue of escape—if they needed it. In reality, they were going to leave via one of the side doors, seeing as they would be herding two young children and their accompanying mother.

Yin had watched the two older men straddle the wall in disgust. Proficient in parkour, he positioned himself in a straight line facing the wall and ran at it. With first his right foot striking it, then his left halfway up, he literally ran up the wall. Reaching up with his right hand, his fingertips grazed the lip and tightened to grab hold. Hauling himself to the top, Yin swung his legs like a pommel-horse Olympian, landing silently inside the compound next to T-cut.

"You two are getting old," he teased quietly, in his strong Cantonese accent.

"I'll give you old," muttered T-cut, his voice barely above a whisper. "Wait till we get back to the Bucket, I'm going to thrash you in the dojo."

"I'd like to see you try. How many times is it now, sixteen? You still haven't beaten me," chuckled Yin.

"Everything comes to those who wait," answered T-cut philosophically. "Experience is everything."

"Well, if you wait much longer you'll be stood down first," said Yin smiling evilly. Yin knew that the older members worried about being dropped from active status. They talked about it all the time and he wasn't going to make their life any easier, despite knowing they'd lay down their lives for each other if it came to it. Sureswift had. It was the only way to get into Unit One, the classic Dead Man's Shoes.

The team always memorized the layout of target areas from plans before missions began, but nothing was ever the same as it looked on the computer screen. Yin took the lead, tiptoeing into the cover of the buildings like a butterfly strolling across rice paper, leaving the other two to follow.

He raised his hand suddenly, signalling a halt. Flicking two fingers towards his eyes and then pointing up at the buildings, he highlighted two security cameras, one nestling within the trellis running up the rear of the main building. The other was secreted under the eaves of the nearby outhouses which they were currently huddled behind. Fortunately, neither were positioned in such a way to record their entry. Whoever installed them didn't know a thing about surveillance, or the equipment had been tampered with. Finding two cameras meant there were bound to be more covering the complex.

T-cut deftly removed the jamming device from his back-pack, extending the small aerial and placing the item on the bottom of the first outhouse back wall. It was a shame to leave such valuable equipment behind, but on the plus side, because it contained explosives, he could detonate it via remote control if needed.

Cameras suitably blinded throughout the premises, each was now transmitting feedback loops of their last image, courtesy of T-cut's ingenious invention. A moment of sadness touched him as he remembered, with fondness, the hours he and Sureswift had spent inventing their gizmo's. This baby was one of many patented by them. T-cut missed his friend and oppo every day.

Something made a noise. The men froze. The sound came again. They edged passed the imported soil of a pristine vegetable plot to join Yin at the far end. T-cut spared a glance at the soil, it wasn't local dirt, that was an orangey-red, mostly sand. This was a brown earthy loam with its own expensive irrigation system. *Someone likes their veggies fresh,* he mused.

The buildings were freshly painted too, a glaringly, almost obscene white. The team huddled behind one of the single-storey wooden huts. *Some kind of garden or maintenance shed*, T-cut concluded, peering around the corner. The source of the water sound? A trickling Moroccan-style fountain in tiny blue and white mosaic tiles inside a small, paved courtyard. On the far side, was the main house, the building where U1 assumed the family were being held.

All seemed peaceful, nothing moved. The sound they'd heard earlier re-started like someone chopping wood, or somebody banging something on wood. A continuous beat or rhythm of notes, three fast, two slow, three fast, 'SOS'. Both men behind Yin acknowledged the Morse code, someone was brave, if foolhardy, to think anyone would hear or take notice of it. It wasn't coming from the house either. It was coming from the building they'd assumed was a workshop. A low building with two windows in the front, its door facing the detached house. T-cut decided they should investigate to exclude it.

He was about to signal his teammates, to move around the outhouse towards the single-storey building door, when a man appeared out of the main house. Dressed in western clothing and swearing in Arabic, he strode angrily towards the source of the noise, slamming the door behind him. It seemed the signal had attracted the wrong kind of attention.

The beat stopped. The sound of a hand making contact with skin rang out. Followed by a child's sudden cry. This quickly lowered to a trembling whimper. A raised voice was heard berating the instigator of the noise, threatening more violence to the child if it continued. The conversation was one-way. The man re-appeared, grinding his half-smoked cigarette into the sand under his shoe like it offended him. He headed back to the house apparently appeased.

"That's good," whispered T-cut. "We won't need to enter the main house and now we know there's no guard in this building here, where the family are being held."

"Roger that," answered Davidson.

"Drat," replied Yin. "I was looking forward to some fun." He grinned when the other two men rolled their eyes, and to annoy them further, proceeded to go through a series of head and shoulder warm-up movements.

"Never mind, I promise I'll spar with you when we get back," smiled Davidson, always happy to fight.

"You're on," answered Yin.

"Yin, you take point again," ordered T-cut, bringing them back to the mission. Yin was gone the moment the command left T-cut's lips. He didn't need telling twice. Checking the route was clear Yin crossed the courtyard as silent as a cat stalking a mouse. Peering in the small window by the door, he gave the coast clear sign to his teammates. Together the three men entered the unlocked building. Their adversaries, it seemed, were not expecting anyone to enter their isolated lair.

Despite their battle-hardened countenance, scenes involving families always took the team members' breath away. The mother and her two children were bound and gagged. To add to their misery, the children were restricted in movement, their ropes anchored to butchery hooks inserted into the ceiling

11

beams. The girl's heels were red raw where she'd banged them repeatedly on the wooden floor.

Their mother, bound to the bed for obvious reasons, sobbed with frustration at not being able to comfort her children. All of them were covered in red marks, swelling and bruises. The children sported cigarette burns and small lacerations, of the sort commonly caused by strikes from signet rings and the like. The girl had a man's bright red hand-print on her cheek, the victim of the recent slap. Obviously, the children had been used to get their mother to acquiesce and behave herself.

It was a pitiful sight. The boy was unconscious. The girl was whimpering. Her dirty face was streaked with tears which dripped down her cheeks into her long knotted hair.

The woman watched warily, her eyes wide, as the men stole through the door and crossed the room. Initially, she thought as they neared her bed, that they were more men coming to pleasure themselves with her. She gasped with relief, then cried silent tears as T-cut removed her filthy gag.

He was saddened by what he saw. The horror people continued to afflict on others appalled him. *Does it never change?* He wondered, wiping away a tear of his own. *Is it always a case of the powerful inflicting their will on the weak?* He guessed it was.

"Release them," he signalled to Davidson and Yin, pointing to the children. Gently they held a child each, expertly reaching—without needing to look—for their commando knives secured at their waists.

The children sagged in their arms, as the ropes parted. They groaned as their protesting joints moved from their enforced positions into their natural state, the boy's eyes flickering open briefly. Meanwhile, T-cut freed the woman.

"Your father sent us," he said simply. She nodded, unable to say more. She stood, and stumbled forward, wanting to embrace her children, but too weak to move further. T-cut lifted her in his arms, and they left the confines of the building.

Why is it I'm always rescuing damsels in distress, and still haven't managed to keep one for myself? "Fulwood nabbed the only girl I ever fancied," he mumbled, not realising he'd said the words out loud in the heat of the moment. A slip that shouldn't have happened.

"Problem?" Davidson signed a question, rather than speak due to them being back out in the open. His load was considerably lighter than T-cut's though not by much.

"No problem," he signalled back one-handed.

They headed towards the compound's rear door without a hitch. Yin, on-point again with the girl in his arms. T-cut lowered the mother gently to the ground motioning with one finger of his lips for them all to keep quiet. The females nodded. The boy hadn't roused fully yet.

Yin reached the door, padlocked, but this didn't stop U1. Davidson stealthily extracted and opened a small plastic box from his pocket, removing a tiny tablet that looked like play-dough. He poked it into the mechanism.

This innovative form of gelignite, manufactured by U1, exploded within seconds of coming into contact with metal, remaining inert otherwise. Its innovation came about following a review of U1 missions. The team encountered most problems with metal objects; locks, hinges, bars, vehicles, handcuffs, not to mention guns and knives. The scientifically-minded team members worked on finding a solution. A few mishaps occurred. Johnson now sported one less finger, a result of trying solutions on himself whilst in handcuffs. He felt the sacrificial digit worth it.

Every U1 member carried the explosive—just in case. If they were captured the tiny plastic box was overlooked, especially as it had been transformed into four little tablets resembling the angina medication, glycerine trinitrate. U1 affectionately dubbed the chemical 'Johnsonite.' Its final formulation, too complicated to remember, and known only to Johnson and a chosen few, proved to be invaluable. The explosive would have made any one of them a billionaire, but Johnson's men were loyal through and through.

The locking mechanism gave a slight 'pff' as the surplus Johnsonite dissipated. T-cut's instinct told him that in moments the heavies would be coming out to check on their prisoners. He called the Spade, their aerial transport, via his earpiece, requesting immediate evac to their sub-cut tracker location.

They were outside the compound, moving fast on foot, when they heard the first sounds of an alarm being raised. Shots rang out as their escape was telegraphed around the compound. The wind carried the sound of raised voices near the door they'd just vacated.

"Where's that bloody pick-up?" Davidson muttered under his breath. The wind changed direction, moving from behind them—where the sound of pursuit was coming from—towards the welcoming commotion of rotor blades clipping the air. Over the rise loomed the Spade, its SMG loaded and aimed.

The new improved Tiltrotor crested the dunes, creating a mini-sandstorm in its wake. It obliterated the landscape till it resembled a scene from a science fiction movie. Heads down, the U1 team ran towards it. The twang of decelerating bullets falling short into the sand behind them was equally terrifying and reassuring. The Spade replied in kind, the steady rattle of the clip discharging, a comfort to the ears of the men, but unsettling to the woman and her children. The rounds, not aimed to kill but to frighten and impede their pursuers.

The twenty-eight-year-old pilot, José De Silva, nicknamed Hutch, was a veteran of countless rescue missions but was still considered new by the team, until recently. The flack he used to get had thankfully moved to the latest U1 newbie, Yin. Yin clambered aboard last. The boy in his arms asleep despite the racket of the blades and the gun.

"You took your sweet time," Davidson mumbled, scowling at Yin. Yin grinned in reply. He savoured the ribbing from his comrades, it made him feel part of the team.

T-cut signalled 'away'. Hutch nodded. The Spade screeched vertically up into a cloudless sky.

✦ ✦ ✦ ✦ ✦ ✦ ✦ ✦

Frank Fulwood was in the Ready Room aboard the Bucket, the liner that U1 called home. It had been his command for the last ten years. Ever since Jeff Johnson, the founder and first commander, handed over the reins of this high-pressured, high-adrenaline position to his second-in-command. Johnson had left to run their new land-based facility in England, codenamed uninspiringly, Unit Two.

Unit Two was situated on the South-East coast in Kent, a stone's throw from France. Its precise whereabouts was on a need-to-know basis since it couldn't operate and move around as freely as U1, who were based in international waters.

U2 carried out techno-missions. Missions which didn't always include people as the major target. These missions often involved the acquisition of documents and computer software. Stealth and calm was the code, rather than adrenaline and action. Their prime aim, not to alert the target to the fact they were compromised. The U2 team was smaller, comprising currently of only three agents, as Johnson preferred to call them.

Currently, they were on assignment in Southern Ireland. Covert techno missions required intensive recon of weeks or even months. Hours were spent assessing and planning before the mark was even identified as viable. In this case, U2 was infiltrating a company double-dealing in arms selling. Irish government agencies hadn't been able to get close.

CHAPTER TWO - RUE

"IF you ever, ever, do that to me again Lewis Redshaw Blaine, I'll, I'll,..."

Lewis woke to find his momma, Victoria Blaine, sitting on the edge of his bed in the school infirmary. Her voice trembled with emotion, but despite her anger, he was pleased she was there. He couldn't quite figure out how she'd managed the sixteen-hour journey so quickly. However, it didn't seem important at that moment.

"I'm sorry," Lewis mumbled, opening his dark brown eyes—so like his grandfather's—to smile at her, before dropping back into a restful sleep.

Victoria Blaine tousled her son's hair, and wiping her own eyes with relief, turned her head slightly to look through the glass door panel. She nodded to the man waiting outside. He smiled, turned, and left.

It had taken all Lewis's powers of persuasion to prevent his momma from transporting him back home to Denver, Colorado. He'd assured her again and again that he was fine once he'd been discharged from the infirmary. He needed to carry on with the pretence that his school studies here were important, so that she would leave him in England. In reality, he wanted to be in England so he could disappear quicker, going by tunnel, ferry, or plane into Europe.

Where was he now? Sitting in Geography looking out of the window bored to tears. Okay, geography would be useful travelling around the world, but he couldn't see how knowledge of crop rotation systems in the mid-west of America would be of any use, unless he decided to take up farming. If it had been something like border control crossings or important phrases he could memorise, maybe he would have sat up and listened. Even taking footnotes on customs and currency exchange would have helped. But no, they'd been studying the mid-west, the very place where he'd been born, since the previous term. It didn't look like Mr Underhill, his teacher, was any closer to changing the subject this term either.

The lesson that surprised him and had been the most helpful was citizenship. In it they'd learned about cultures, about how to interact with people, but still no languages he could use. He had two options, travel to countries where English was spoken, or wing it.

Winging it appealed the most. He'd be harder to find. No one would expect an inexperienced teenager to go to a country where English wasn't spoken. He'd leave a note for his momma naturally. Didn't want her to worry, though he knew she would. He didn't want her to think he was unstable or something like that. *It's just that I feel more grown-up than an eighteen-year-old boy. I can't explain it, maybe my father has something to do with it.* Thinking about his father brought Lewis's mind back to that day by the canal. *What did I see there?* He wasn't sure. *A fish, a blur. Whatever it was, it saved my life that's for sure.* He still had nightmares of drowning strapped to the old shopping trolley, waking in a cold sweat in the middle of the night. Yet here he was alive and well, and contemplating running away.

"Blaine? Are you listening?"

"Yes, Sir," answered Lewis, brought back to the present.

"Then kindly describe to the class the seasonal rotation for Arizona's wheat fields please." Several students sniggered, knowing he'd been daydreaming again.

"Err," stalled Lewis. It was going to be one of those days.

Lewis sat in detention later that afternoon, considering his future. He still hadn't come up with a plan of when, where, or how he was leaving. He was going, he just needed to get more structure around the idea he'd been thinking about for almost two years. For some reason, almost drowning in the canal had focused his thoughts, making it more imperative he act. He needed to get practical; work out possible destinations, how much money and clothing to take, things like that. Before he knew it, his sanction for daydreaming in geography was over.

As he sloped off after detention, Lewis happened to notice a poster depicting a map of Europe on the wall in the humanities corridor. Moving over to read it, he couldn't believe his luck. It almost seemed too good to be true, and if it was to be believed, solved his problems about getting to Europe, providing him with a departure date. A date that made his desire a reality.

During term five, there was a yearly retreat organised by his school. Lewis's momma supported him going on the trip, when he mentioned it to her during their weekly phone contact the following evening. Victoria Blaine was pleased her son was finally taking an interest in his schooling and gave her consent at once. The retreat was in France. The location made leaving a lot easier for Lewis. He hadn't been able to figure out how to cross the English Channel alone without his passport—the Head of House held all documents for safe keeping. The school would do all the organising, meaning Lewis just needed to make sure he was included.

Approaching Mr Carfax, the head of languages, was a bit tricky after he'd just sanctioned Lewis's earlier geography detention, but he seemed delighted Lewis was interested in going on the retreat—despite the short notice—they were leaving in four weeks. It was Mr Carfax's second home. He regaled Lewis with tales about the wonderful time the students had last year. After their conversation, Mrs Blaine emailed Mr Carfax her consent and transferred the necessary monies.

18

Once settled at the retreat, Lewis planned to leave a note in his hotel room, telling them that his momma had met up with him and taken him back home to Denver, due to a family emergency. That would work; people did it all the time. He started organising the finer details; wrote a list of the clothes he'd take, then realised there were too many to carry, crossed it out and started again. He didn't know what the temperature would be like in many of the places he planned to visit. He wrote the list a third time.

Money was never an issue, he always had sufficient funds. His momma, being the daughter of a famous senator from a wealthy family, made sure he never ran out. The main problem was he wouldn't be able to use his Visa card anywhere because the minute he activated a cash machine, or purchased something from a retailer, they'd know his location. He planned to get casual work where he could, but he had to have some money to keep him going until he got employment.

Every few days in the four weeks up to leaving, Lewis started taking cash out of his account until he'd got several hundred Euros stashed away. Clothes were sorted, the date was sorted, and soon enough money would be sorted too. Next, he needed to consider where. *Where should I go from Rue?*

Lewis didn't have any specific direction, he just wanted somewhere nobody would know, or find him. He supposed that meant countries where communication was poor and the internet unreliable. He didn't fancy Africa, far too hot, too dry, and too many nasty creatures, same with Australia. He liked temperate zones better. China would be good. It was big enough, with lots of different temperature zones, and also a long way from France. Apart from him sticking out like a sore thumb because he obviously wasn't Chinese and couldn't speak Mandarin or Cantonese—yet.

He'd have to sort out the route first. If he wasn't careful his money would be used up travelling, leaving him nothing to live on when he got there. That was another point, he had to be able to come back again. He had to have enough money in reserve to do that, or at least be able to call his momma to wire him money to return, if things got difficult. That meant leaving his precious iPhone six behind and buying a burner phone which couldn't be traced. His momma would be furious and terrified for him, and she knew people who could track phones.

As time progressed, the romantic notion of running away started losing its appeal. *Maybe it isn't such a good idea,* Lewis reasoned. He had this innate urge to go, but it got really complicated when he started figuring out all the variables and hurdles he'd have to cross. Children ran away all the time. He was sure they didn't go through all this uncertainty when they did it, they just grabbed a bag and took off.

Maybe that's what I should do? No, I can't do that! Not to my momma. His momma always told him, "Whatever happens Lewis, be as prepared as you can be." She also said, "Strange things happen to you when you least expect them." A saying he'd never figured out.

No, I'll follow momma's wise words and be prepared. Lewis felt better after reaffirming his decision. The next thing he needed to do was plan his route to China.

A few afternoons' later, Lewis found himself in the sixth form study room with nothing to do. He casually flicked on Google Earth and wrote China in the search line. On Google maps, it was a long way from Edgbaston, near Birmingham, where he currently sat, and then he realised he wouldn't be in Edgbaston. He'd be on retreat in Rue, France. It was now less than two weeks away. After seeing how far away China was, Lewis realised he might need more funds. *I'd better increase the amount I'm withdrawing out of my account from tomorrow.*

So, from Rue in France to China then. He clicked on the maps looking at what countries he'd need to travel through. China looked easy enough to get to, as it was all over land. As he looked at the world map, and was zooming back out, his eyes caught on the Caribbean Islands. They looked remote

20

enough too, and for some reason he couldn't explain, interested him. Admittedly, they seemed much harder to travel to. He wasn't sure how he'd get across the Atlantic, or the Pacific for that matter. It depended on which route he took, but something drew him to them, and he didn't know why. Shaking his head to clear his thoughts Lewis re-focused his attention. *China first, Caribbean second then.*

He glanced out of the window watching the students heading home at the end of the day—not everybody boarded like Lewis. He saw Lucy Bywater crossing the quadrangle. She looked radiant. The sun shining behind her lit up her auburn hair like a halo of gold.

"God, she's gorgeous," he murmured, unable to tear his eyes away. "What I wouldn't give for half an hour alone with her."

Lewis watched spellbound as Lucy strode confidently across the court like she owned it, a fresh-faced, maturing young woman with pouty pink lips. He felt his body grow hard, thinking about her luscious mouth on his own. He was thankful he was alone in the room. He wasn't a man yet, or anywhere near being one. Yes, he'd had urges. He had thoughts about kissing Lucy and laying with her, but for all his wants and desires Lewis remained a boy in body and soul.

Maybe this adventure will help me grow up, change me, turn me into the man I know I can be. Lucy vanished into a doorway across the far side, but not without treating Lewis to a very deliberate sway of her hips, and a coy glance over her shoulder. Some sixth sense must have alerted her to the fact she was being admired. *Somewhere out there is my life, and then the Lucy Bywater's of this world better watch out.*

The retreat students had been staying in a small town in Picardy called Rue. It wasn't a very important town; it had

21

nothing to commend it. No products or inventions, no notable sons of Rue. It was a provincial town with few assets, apart from its well-run War Museum, and its proximity to the World War I site of the Battle of the Somme.

The school had utilised accommodation in and around the town for several years. This retreat location was reinforced after Mr Carfax co-incidentally purchased a holiday home on the outskirts of the town. He claimed his family originated from the area, but Lewis didn't believe his teacher. He didn't look French or speak French well, and he hated escargot which Lewis believed all French loved. Still, it was a good opportunity for Lewis to practice his French and the locals seemed friendly enough.

The trip to Nantes couldn't have been a better cover. A tour of the dark underground city would provide excellent camouflage to aid his departure. He'd slip away unnoticed soon after the tour started, so he'd have plenty of time to make good his escape. Mr Carfax had tried to make him leave the large rucksack behind in his room before the day trip started, but Lewis insisted his momma had made him promise to take his money and personal effects with him wherever he went, or there'd be trouble!

He'd considered leaving the night before, getting an eight-hour head start, but he had to share a room with two other students. His sneaking out in the dead of night was bound to be reported. Lewis rationalised that he could get further away in a shorter time, if he left whilst on the tour. He'd made sure he was the last person out of their room and left a note on top of his pillow for his momma, so she wouldn't worry unnecessarily. It was a few weeks shy of his nineteenth birthday and he realised, as he wrote, it would be his first birthday without speaking to his family.

It had been easier leaving the tour than Lewis thought. No one missed him when he disappeared on the pretence of needing the toilet. Outside, he jumped on a local bus going into town. Once there, he got on a bus heading towards Abbeville, not really sure what route to take, but knowing he needed to get across France and over the border fast before they raised the alarm.

He reckoned, after a few hours, they'd start searching Rue and maybe Nantes, figuring he'd got bored with the tour and wandered off. They'd step up the search once Lewis failed to re-appear after several more hours. When that happened, they'd start watching the borders, the barriers would be down, making travel through harder. Fortunately, he'd secured his passport from Mr Carfax's room whilst he went to wash. As their designated first aider, Mr Carfax had been forced to stay in the same pension as the boys, regardless of him having a home nearby. He wasn't happy with the new Health and Safety rules.

Knowing most western societies had good communications—since the advent of the Internet—Lewis planned on travelling through countries where government-endorsed technology was limited, unless one had money. He knew his momma would eventually send someone to find him. It was uncanny how easily she seemed to know where he was.

He thought back to the time he went missing as a kid. He'd made headline news locally and enjoyed some notoriety in school for a short while after. He remembered the incident like it was yesterday. His grandfather had taken him campaigning around Estes Park, North of Denver.

Despite being six years old, and not the least bit interested in politics or the dramatic scenery—he thought that was for old folks—the Rockies in all its splendour overwhelmed him. He loved them at first sight. The wide-open pastures with slow-moving oxbow waters. The snaking roads leading below the snow-capped peaks. The majestic conifers stretching for miles towards the snowy tree-line. One moment he'd been following along behind his Granda, the next, he was lost. Even at six, he knew he was in trouble. He'd grown up with his

Granda telling him of the dangers of the Park area; of mountain lions, grizzlies, aggressive moose, and elk.

The sun dropped from the sky like a bullet. Night closed in, and still Lewis couldn't find his way out of the vast forest of trees. His voice was hoarse from shouting, his feet ached, the skin rubbing off inside his sneakers. He was cold and hungry and frightened. He knew bears were able to climb trees and he couldn't, at least not very well. A sound behind him, made him jump. He struggled to hold back the tears threatening to fall down his cheeks, knowing he needed to find shelter, and fast. In abject terror, regardless of bears, he climbed the nearest tall tree. He climbed higher and higher, till the branches beneath him trembled and bent under his weight.

There he cowered, in an intersection where two branches met, too frightened to sleep, listening to imagined sounds of Big Foot stamping around far below in the undergrowth. Lewis was so high up, as the wind got up, the branch he clung to waved back and forth despite his minor weight. Twice, he almost fell as he sobbed himself into a stupor.

As he huddled there against the tree, cold and fearful, he could hear one of his Granda's sayings. *You're not properly dressed without a belt young man.* In desperation he took his belt off, thankful that his Granda had insisted he wear it that morning. He looped it around the thin branch and under his arms. In this position, he fell into an exhausted sleep, missing the human seekers as they panned out across the forest floor below him.

They searched every fallen log and all the dimly lit hollows for the senator's grandson but couldn't find him. Not once, did the rescue parties consider a six-year-old capable of climbing the massive evergreens which dominated the area. The search moved on, leaving Lewis behind high up in his arboreal refuge.

The next morning, aching from his upright sleeping position, and red raw from where the bark and belt had rubbed his skin, Lewis half climbed, half slid down the tree. Unknown to Lewis, the seekers had moved on and were five miles north of his current position, as he struck out towards the rising sun in search of food and water. Stumbling like a newborn deer through the bracken, he found a small stream. It smelt peaty and tasted of earth, but it was wonderfully refreshing.

Watching several birds scoffing red berries on a nearby shrub, Lewis decided they must be safe to eat. He'd devoured a large number of berries before he began to feel unwell with a stomach ache. He spent the afternoon vomiting, as his refined digestion rejected the avian fare. In the end, he was retching on nothing but bile, his tummy long since emptied of its contents. The excessive vomiting had dehydrated him. He felt weak and tired from the exertion. When the night sounds began anew, despite his weakened state, he climbed a second tree, tying himself to the uppermost branches again, and immediately falling into an uneasy sleep.

That's where Unit One found him. Using thermal imagery and flying overhead, the Spade easily located the lost boy, nestled like a large pigeon in the empty treetops. Lewis never knew U1 existed, nor that his momma had connections with them and had called in a favour to find her son. She never mentioned the men who found him. She hugged him close, crying softly into his dirty torn T-shirt as she rocked him back and forth. Her reason for living had been found. His Granda' fell to his knees, as they arrived by Tiltrotor, celebrity-style, on the back lawn behind the senator's home. Cried more than momma, Lewis noted. He also noted the silent pilot of the helicopter-type plane from his position in the cab smiling at him, and saluting him like a professional soldier, as he and his solitary team member lifted off.

The family, too focused on Lewis's homecoming, failed to acknowledge the pilot's gesture. But Lewis saw it. Watched the aircraft rise over his momma's shoulder. Lifting swiftly into the night sky, in seconds it was no more than a star-like speck. Lewis always remembered the insignia, a capital letter U and the number 1 on its cab door.

Funny how his family never mentioned the men who found him, the pilot, and the smiley short man, who abseiled down into the tree and fed him chocolate and coke. He'd never been allowed coke before. It made him burp which made the smiley man laugh.

Lewis smiled at his recollection of the memory. *Will my mystery plane appear this time I wonder*? When he was ten, he finally plucked up the courage to ask his momma about being lost. She hadn't replied straightaway. She told him they were from another state, requested by the Estes Park police to assist as they had a rescue plane. He pestered her. As a small boy, anything aeronautical fascinated him.

"It was a special plane wasn't it?" His momma sighed but responded.

"It was more like a helicopter than a plane. That's all I know."

Lewis remembered its bright searchlight above his head. It hovered high over him. Aeroplanes didn't hover, helicopters hovered, but it wasn't a copter either. Needing to resolve some of the facts surrounding his unusual rescue, Lewis began researching aircraft categories. It took a few weeks for him to identify it as a Tiltrotor plane. He'd used his school library, wading through countless books without success. He finally found one like it on the town library bookshelves. Once he'd identified it his interest waned. He returned to his academic studies, all thoughts of hovering aeroplanes moving over to make way for more important things, like girls.

Lewis was interested in girls at an early age. His momma seemed relieved and worried simultaneously, but he couldn't figure out why. Relieved, he supposed that he was proving to be heterosexual, and worried that his desires at thirteen were far too early to be interested in, the opposite sex, as she called it. He suspected it was one of the reasons for the transfer to schooling in England at an all-boys private school. His momma didn't know it had gone Co-Ed until she visited.

A sudden lurch in the bus's progress brought Lewis back to the present. While he'd been reminiscing, the bus had filled with other passengers. Sitting in the second row from the back, he was able to view the other occupants. None stood out as unusual, but he smelt a strange scent he couldn't identify. There was a couple in their fifties holding hands, several elderly women clutching stuffed shopping bags. A gang of loud teenagers chatting and laughing in French, naturally, and taking the Mickey out of everyone else on the bus and each other. A mother with a sleepy toddler scowling in their direction, and some single men in various fashions from navy work jeans to business suits. Each looked bored and uninterested.

At the very back of the bus, in the far seat, leaning against the escape window was a single teenage girl. She appeared roughly Lewis's age. The scent came again. This time he inhaled a deep breath, drawing it in through his nose. Without realising it, he opened his mouth to enhance the capture of pheromones. He turned in her direction and caught her quickly looking away. He smiled, and knew, like Lucy Bywater, that she was interested in him.

He'd never experienced anything like it before. For some reason, her presence captivated him. She was ravishing, schoolgirl pretty, fresh clean and virginal. He felt himself harden at the thought and moved his backpack onto his lap to cover it. *What is happening to me? I can't believe every man gets a hard-on when they look at a pretty girl.*

Lewis didn't have anyone to ask this type of question to, and he certainly wasn't going to discuss his increasing urges with his family. He could imagine their response. He would be sent to a therapist—again. He'd been there once, after he went missing that time because his Granda felt there was, "something wrong with him." At least that's what he overheard when they were discussing him that first night home, after they thought he'd gone to bed.

The girl got off at the next stop. It was all Lewis could do not to leave with her. On the step, she paused, and turned back for an instant to look at him, as if to say, "You coming?" He half-rose from his seat, until an older man, likely her father, appeared in the doorway apparently irritated by her delay. It seemed he'd been waiting for her late bus to arrive. Lewis caught pieces of the verbal exchange between the two, and then received a glare of such open hostility directed at him from the man, that he sat back down. The girl shrugged her shoulders and left, throwing one last parting glance at him, as his window drew level and passed her on the pavement.

Lewis nearly threw himself off the bus. His head was in turmoil. His hormones appeared to be going crazy. He sat confused and sad at an opportunity missed.

The bus swerved a few seconds later, throwing everyone on the bus back and forth. The driver narrowly missed a stray dog crossing the road, he swore in fluent French. Lewis's schoolboy French couldn't keep up with the rapid vocabulary. He shrugged his shoulders in defeat, then noticed the lady sitting opposite. She was smiling demurely at him.

She must've got on at the last stop. Whilst I was ogling the girl. Stylish taste in clothes. Good figure. Long tapering fingers with manicured nails in a soft pink nail varnish, very feminine. A confident woman, not a girl. Nice.

Lewis dropped his gaze to her finely tanned legs. *Stockings*. He approved. A sixth sense told him he was being observed. He lifted his eyes, meeting her gaze upon him. He could feel the colour rise up his neck at the acute embarrassment. To his amazement, she smiled and invited him to join her, by patting the empty seat next to her. He glanced about. No one was taking any notice of their exchange. She patted the seat again. He was caught like a fawn at the entrance to a trap, unsure what to do. If he declined her invitation she might make a scene. Attention was the last thing he wanted. She might report him when she got off the bus. She seemed nice, her smile gentle and kind, almost motherly. Gingerly, he rose to join her.

"Enchanteur," she murmured. Lewis stumbled over his reply. She switched smoothly into English. "We will speak English, no?"

"No," he started. "I mean yes, please."

"Yes, it is easier, and fewer people will overhear our conversation, yes?" She replied.

"Yes, I mean no," he blurted out. She laughed, trilling like a beautiful canary. *What a sound*, he thought, captivated by her voice, and enchanted by her nearness. He inhaled her light flowery perfume.

"Good, you relax," she said, noticing his posture ease. "I thought you might flee in terror." Lewis was irritated by the suggestion of this unmanly attitude and sat upright. She sensed his annoyance by his sudden change in body posture.

"I have annoyed you," she stated apologetically. "I meant no harm. My English is not very clear. Yes?"

"Better than my French," he replied, relaxing again at her words.

"You have far to go?"

Lewis only nodded. He didn't want to be drawn into that conversation.

"The service ends soon," she added, nodding her head in the direction of the driver, and diplomatically ignoring his reluctance to discuss his travels. "You have somewhere for the night?"

Lewis shook his head. Looking out the window he saw the sky darkening. She followed his gaze.

"You will stay with me, yes? I have a spare room."

"I don't have much money," he answered honestly, as his mother had taught him.

"I have no need of money," she responded, her neck blushing red like his had earlier. "Some company is all." He nodded, thinking he understood—he didn't.

They disembarked together at the bus terminal. This time a few eyebrows were raised. Lewis insisted on carrying her bag of shopping and followed behind. They walked the quiet country lane in silence. He watched her hourglass figure sway back and forth. It was hypnotic. The trees were black silhouettes against the deep blue, by the time they reached her small cottage.

The exterior was neat with swathes of herbs growing in the front garden. Inside, it had that cottagey feel, its thick walls plastered white, with low black wood beams which threatened to take Lewis's head off. Lewis removed his shoes in the small hallway, following her example.

In the front parlour, a huge brick fireplace complete with wood-burning stove sat empty and hungry for wood. She fed it, then lit it expertly. Soon a golden glow suffused the room. A chintzy overstuffed sofa, vied for position with two arm-chairs to be nearest the fireplace.

They sat down to a simple supper in her farmhouse-style kitchen, cheese, fruit, bread, ham, and wine. She apologised for the basic fare, saying she would have brought more had she'd known a guest would be staying. He apologised in return for imposing, making her laugh delightfully. She poured him a glass of wine, a local red—his first alcohol. In America, the minimum age was twenty-one, and with his Granda being a senator there were standards to uphold. His English friends had offered him cans of cheap lager, but so far he'd refused the temptation. Here, he felt it would be an insult to do so.

He found the wine harsh and bitter, full of strong flavours, an acquired taste. She insisted he'd try it with the food, saying wines tasted better with certain flavours. He began his first-ever wine-tasting session and discovered she was right. This wine tasted much better with fruit. He'd expected the wine to go with cheese, like his momma and Granda had it.

The bottle emptied quickly. He was sure she'd had more than him. She brought out a second, a white. Initially, he refused saying he'd had enough, but she pouted adoringly.

"It's only to test the cheese, my petite escargot." She poured them both one glass each and stoppered the bottle in a dramatic flourish. "There! No more wine for you."

He smiled up at her as naive as a puppy waiting for castration. Finally, his glass was empty, as empty as the second bottle which now stood upside down in an ice bucket. After the first glass, Lewis had insisted on testing it with every other food in her home until the wine ran out.

They sat on the tiny sofa side-by-side in the parlour, watching the flickering firelight in the woodstove. There was no TV, no distractions. She smelt wonderful. He lay back, his arms wide along the sofa, his legs stretched out, crossed at the ankles. No thoughts hindered his mind. She snuggled up under his arm as if it was the most natural thing in the world, like a kitten looking for warmth. He smiled lazily down at her.

One slender, pink-polished hand rose to stroke his face, feeling the fine stubbly fuzz. He hadn't shaved deliberately, wanting to appear older. Her fingertips lingered over his lips, tracing their outline. It tickled. One fingertip drew a line down his arched neck onto his chest.

He must have dozed off momentarily for he missed her next move, rousing as he realised she was unbuckling his belt. He knew he should say something, do something, but it felt natural and somehow right. She pulled the black leather band out slowly and threw it in a lazy arc across the floor.

Part of him knew he should stop her advances, but his body responded easily to her touch. She unzipped his jeans and encouraged him to lift so she could lower them and his pants to his ankles in one smooth action. Common sense fled. Before he knew it, she was kneeling on the carpet between his knees, bestowing him with his first ever blow job. Her expert fellatio touch was the most amazing thing he had ever experienced in his entire life. He laid there watching her head bob up and down, marvelling at the whole situation.

He'd pleasured himself many times alone, like most adolescent boys. Never in his dreams had he imagined a mature woman becoming the instigator of his deflowering. He thought his first sexual encounter would be with an equally inadept amateur teenager fumbling about in the dark. Not this apparition before him with the lights on, letting him revel in every glide and suck.

Without a word, and seeming to know he was near climax, she stood, removed her panties, and straddling him, took him deep in one long thrust. He gasped at the intense pleasure it caused both of them, judging by the expression on her face. He felt her body hot and yielding, yet her sex was firm and embracing. She squeezed his cock till he moaned in pleasure, the moment of his release imminent. She leaned forward and whispered into his ear.

"Next time, you will have to work for me." The image this provoked was his undoing. He tipped over the edge and reaching forwards, grabbed her buttocks, hugging her close as he came deep inside this beautiful stranger. She rode him to her own climax as his pulsing cock slowed. She sagged against him moments later, her release obvious. A light sheen of sweat shone across her brow and cleavage. She looked glorious, an Aphrodite of womanhood.

Afterwards, they lay close together on the sofa, without words. She smelt wonderful, earthy, and sexual. Lewis breathed in deep, trying to capture the memory of his first lovemaking with all his senses. Her scent seemed to increase, raising his cock semi-hard again. She felt it nudging her hip and looked at him.

"Your turn to work young one," she said huskily. "But first come with me."

"I thought I already had," grinned Lewis stupidly, feeling mellow and relaxed.

"Naughty boy," she admonished, pulling Lewis upright, his trousers and pants still around his ankles, a comical sight. She laughed, putting a left foot expertly in the crotch, encouraging him to step out of them or fall over.

Naked except for his ACDC T-shirt, Lewis followed her up the creaking spiral staircase to the main bedroom. She pulled his T-shirt off, and her remaining clothes, then pushed him into a small shower cubicle. She washed him. The warm soapy treatment, another first, was heaven. By the time she'd finished, his cock was rigid again. Not once did she touch, or even acknowledge its existence. Lewis was even more aroused as a result—if that was possible.

Ignoring his condition, she gave him the soap and insisted he wash her next. He'd never touched a woman before, except his momma, let alone washed one. He wasn't sure where to start. Her breasts were amazing, simply begging to be fondled, but he followed her actions and avoided her erogenous zones. It was excruciating. She accidentally, on purpose, brushed past him while bending over as he soaped her firm buttocks. He almost shot his load over her, the sensation so overwhelming. He groaned out loud. Noticing his discomfort, at last, she took pity on him, and taking his hand, led him over to her large white linen bed.

Both were dripping wet from the shower, yet she made him stand, facing her at the end of the bed as she climbed onto it. She deliberately crawled slowly towards the pillows, so he could receive a full view of her swollen wet sex. His hand moved unconsciously towards his cock. She wagged her finger at him.

"No, no, no, it's my turn now." Lewis wasn't sure what that meant.

Settling herself amongst her many pillows, she smiled at him standing literally to attention at the foot of the bed. She opened her legs wide. With her fingers, she separated her labia and began playing with herself. Lewis couldn't stop himself this time, he stroked his cock as he gazed spellbound. He'd never seen anything like this, not even in his dreams. The thought of any girl, let alone a woman, being interested in him enough to invite him to bed was out of this world. For that person to open themselves to him, for his frank inspection was unthinkable. He knew he'd wake up any second and discover it was just another wet dream. Things like this didn't happen to him.

His semen spurted out, hitting the edge of the pristine bed linen, drops of it hit the valance and bare floorboards. He watched its progress, then looked up at her like a school boy grinning apologetically.

"Oops!" He exclaimed, sounding like a schoolboy too, one who'd been caught doing something naughty.

"No matter," she replied as if it was the most natural thing in the world. "Come." Lewis laughed, a slight edge of hysteria in his tone.

"Done that," he smirked. "Again." She was not amused.

"Come," she repeated, more urgently this time. He climbed naked onto the bed, and she introduced him to a whole new world of taste, touch and ecstasy.

Lewis left three days later. They made love countless times in different positions and places throughout the cottage, the garden amongst the herbs, and the woods behind her house. He couldn't help wondering if people were watching. He had an acute sense they were, but she ignored them all, telling him to enjoy the moment. Lewis was a fast learner and his lover, Madeline, an excellent teacher.

On the third morning of their time together, he found his clothes washed, and ironed, together with his backpack by the front door. He'd told her he needed to move on, but he didn't expect her to be so efficient.

Madeline knelt in the cramped hallway and unbuckled Lewis's belt one last time, a kind of going-away present she advised him. His trousers dropped to the floor with practised ease, and he stepped out of them. He leaned against the front door for support. He giggled at the absurd image of the postman arriving and trying to push the mail through the letterbox that his buttocks were rammed up against. *Imagine Postie's surprise,* he mused, as he pictured the flap lifting and his buttocks pressed against the opening facing the man.

As if echoing his thoughts, the doorbell rang, making both Madeline and Lewis jump. Madeline ignored it and finished delivering her excellent gift.

She'd already told Lewis she believed nothing was as important as sexual congress. Lewis struggled trying to maintain his composure. He knew someone stood on the other side of the door not three inches away. He almost laughed out loud, clasping his hands over his mouth in horror. The sudden frisson of excitement at being caught doing something erotic sent his mind over the edge. His release followed, and Madeline accepted it.

Madeline Marnier rose gracefully. Wiping her mouth and placing Lewis's clothes and backpack into his arms, she shooed him into the left-side reception room. With the door firmly closed behind him, she threw open the front door, welcoming her new caller, and apologizing for her tardiness.

Lewis listened through the door as he put his trousers back on. Madeline made some excuse about being occupied. He grinned. When she smoothly ushered the person into the right-hand reception room on the other side of the cottage, instead of the room he was currently standing in, Lewis was stunned. He pulled the door open slightly and watched in disbelief as Madelaine followed the unknown caller into the room and closed the door behind them both. She completely ignored Lewis's presence.

CHAPTER THREE – CARDIFF BAY

Lewis re-attached his belt, and like the school boy he was, unwilling to believe what he'd just witnessed, left the room. He peered through the keyhole from the hallway, scrutinising the unwelcome caller in the opposite room. It was a man. He guessed in his early forties judging by the clothes he wore. From his view at waist height, he couldn't focus on anything except the man's obvious erection, and Madeline's slender hand caressing it tenderly through the trouser fabric.

Lewis's emotions were in turmoil. Part of him had known it was too good to be true, that a refined experienced woman such as Madeline could care for him. *Maybe the man is her husband.* But the fact he didn't let himself in, and the way she was fondling a stranger's cock, told Lewis what his heart didn't want to admit. Madeline was the village whore, not a lonely woman besotted by his good looks and company. He felt betrayed.

Money, he thought hurtfully. *She'll have wanted money.* Hurriedly, he searched his possessions, relieved when he found his money safe and sound. He looked up guiltily; he hadn't noticed the other door open. She was gazing at him, a melancholy expression on her face.

"I do not steal from children," she said, her voice holding a tinge of sadness. That stung, Lewis was anything but a child, now. She saw the hurt look in his eyes and shook her head.

"I'm sorry. I did not mean it like that. I was hurt by your action is all." Lewis was at a loss what to say or do next.

"Do you need any money?" He asked, after a long pause. This time his tone was respectful.

"No. What I did with you, I did for enjoyment, not work," she answered stiffly, sitting down in the nearest armchair.

"I should go?" He asked, knowing it wasn't really a question but a statement.

"Yes, I think so," she answered, but her tone suggested she wanted him to stay. "Work calls." She flicked her head towards the other door.

As he followed her gaze, the implication of what she'd just said hit him. Her punter, a John, or whatever they were called in France, was waiting in the next room. He saw her troubled look and went to her.

"It's ok, I'll be alright. I want to thank you for... everything." What could a boy say who'd become a man? She smiled. Took his hand, her captivating body leading him to the front door and waved him goodbye.

It was a quiet, thoughtful young man who sat next to the anonymous German lorry driver heading towards Amiens. The rain pelted down on the windscreen as Lewis played back the previous three days in his head. He was amazed, now he reflected on it, how naive and stupid he'd been. How he took it all in, thinking she was smitten with his youthful looks and manner. He'd wondered whether it was his American accent that appealed to her. All along she was tutoring him, grooming him in the ways of sexual prowess like some erotic schoolteacher. He'd never met any sort of teacher like that before!

Regardless of her motives, Lewis couldn't think bad of Madeline. She'd taught him more about sex in their intensive three days, than he'd known in his entire life. He reckoned on his own, it would have been years before he attained the wealth of experience she'd shared with him. He was still thinking of his lover Madelaine, when the driver nudged him brusquely, asking whether this was the stop Lewis wanted?

Hans was somewhat disgruntled with the boy he'd picked up en route. He often picked up hitchhikers, despite it being against company policy, especially if they were young and interesting looking. Not that he had any unsavoury motives, he had children of his own, but their company was useful in helping Hans stay awake, and he felt he was keeping them safe, for a short while. Another person in the cab usually promoted conversation.

Lewis's contribution to the conversation during the journey had been minimal, he'd hardly said two words in the last ten kilometres. Hans was beginning to think it'd been a mistake stopping to pick him up, but he looked so sad standing on the country road in the middle of nowhere. His expression was of someone who'd won the Euro millions jackpot and lost the ticket. Hans was big-hearted. He always imagined his own children when he saw strangers by the road. He hoped if his son ever did anything so foolish, someone kind would step in, like him.

Hans didn't want to pry but was experienced enough to accurately guess that the cause of Lewis's sadness was woman trouble. He knew all about that! His ex-wife was still hammering him for maintenance. *What does she think I am, a millionaire? Maybe I should do the Euro lottery? No. She'd want a share of that too.* He frowned at the thought. They could've shortened Hans's long journey, talking about women and the trouble they caused. The boy wasn't up for it, looked like he might cry any minute. *A typical case of first love unrequited.* Hans remembered that feeling. He had married his first love, and now look where he was, divorced, broke, and holding down two jobs to make ends meet.

Lewis climbed out of the cab on the outskirts of Amiens—where he'd asked to be deposited—without a backward glance. He walked over to the nearby bus stop and sat down on the stone bench next to it, putting his head in his hands. It was starting to rain again. Hans watched the boy in his wing mirror, shaking his head in sympathy as he pulled away from the kerb. There wasn't any more he could do without coming over as inappropriate. He'd assuage his growing guilt by spoiling his children the next time they came to visit.

Lewis remained seated, long after the lorry had disappeared into the distance. The sudden downpour left him soaked. His hair, plastered to his face, dripped cold drops into his eyes. His coat, a shower-proof fabric, couldn't cope with the deluge. Water seeped in through the seams and where the hem finished, his trousers were soaked through. He could feel his left sock becoming wetter around the toes, as his fashionable trainer, not made for such punishment, gave up its fight. It might be designed to walk miles but those miles were in sunshine or inside, in the comfort of a leisure centre, not on French country lanes.

Despite his sadness, Lewis wasn't completely disheartened. He never minded the rain, enjoyed it in fact. Which was a good job seeing as how it had rained ever since his departure from Madeline. He wondered if it was an omen, a comment on his journey. Deciding it was time to find cover, no matter how much the rain didn't bother him, he looked around. Across the fields, he could see some barn-like buildings in the distance.

On closer inspection, they appeared derelict. He peered around the fourth barn door, knowing what he'd find, the same state of disrepair he'd found in the last three buildings. The right door hung precariously on one hinge. It didn't look promising. The chances of finding clean straw bedding for the night were highly unlikely. Lewis had hoped to remove his sodden clothing to dry it. He couldn't spare money for lodgings, needing the small amount he had left for food. He'd definitely have to find work in the next town to replenish his funds.

He settled down in the far corner of the barn—at least its roof was intact—furthest away from the wind rushing in through the broken door. It was going to be a cold uncomfortable night. *It's ironic, I've become a man, but at this moment, I feel less like a man than at any time in my entire life. I miss my momma. Maybe I should go home?*

Not yet, something answered in his head. *Almost there.* For some reason, those four words settled him, and Lewis Blaine fell into a peaceful rest despite the appalling weather beyond the door.

The next day rose sunny and warm. Lewis found a small lake close by, where livestock, now long gone, quenched their thirst, judging by the numerous hoof prints set in the clay soil. Like the barn, Lewis spied a derelict stone farmhouse hunkered down in the long meadow grasses beyond the lake.

Pulling off his clothes, he left them scattered like overlarge leaves in the tree branches surrounding the water's edge. Taking a deep breath, Lewis leapt straight in, without any concern for his safety. He scared thirty or so frogs in the process. They jumped in all directions; he'd never seen so many before. He laughed hysterically as they collided with one another in their haste to escape him, till he realised, frogs meant food.

More hilarious than the panicked frogs, was the sight of a naked youth leaping around frog-like in the long grass, chasing after the speedy amphibians and doing a fair imitation of them. Lewis caught four large ones, judging that he'd need at least that many to make a decent meal. He was starving. Their baleful black eyes stared back at him out of his backpack, causing his nerve to fail at the thought of killing them. Securing them inside his pack, he re-entered the pond to finish washing. *I'll think about their future later when I'm cleaner.*

Victoria Blaine was verging on hysteria after Lewis's school in England phoned to say he was missing.

"Normally," the Head continued, once he was sure her

breathing had calmed. "We would have visited the home in person but with Lewis living so far away, I had no alternative, but to phone you." He hoped Mrs Blaine understood.

Was that an undertone of criticism she heard in his voice? She wondered if students went missing often, considering the Head's 'normally visited the home' comment. She missed the next sentence trying to make sense of his English accent.

"What are you doing to find Lewis?" She asked, interrupting him, her voice choking with emotion at the mention of his name.

"Everything we can, I assure you, Mrs Blaine. Of course, things are slightly more difficult, seeing as how he disappeared on the field trip in Picardy." The Head sighed loudly over the line as if to emphasize the problems he was experiencing communicating with the French authorities. He didn't speak French.

"We won't stop till he's found," he added, noticing for the first time it was silent on the other end. "Mrs Blaine, Mrs Blaine?" The line was dead. He received no reply to his call, unsure whether she'd left him hanging, or simply fainted.

Victoria Blaine was no fainter. She was a strong determined individual, as her family knew only too well. She'd dedicated the last eighteen years of her life, assuring her son lacked for nothing. He was her world, just as she was to her father.

Victoria Blaine had changed her title to 'Mrs,' despite not being married after she became fed up with the raised eyebrows and whispered comments whenever she was introduced as 'Miss or Ms'. She'd thought times had moved on, that people were more accepting in mid-west America these days. She was wrong. Despite media coverage of celebrity lifestyles, closer to home, folk were less forgiving. She could have bared her soul and told them Lewis was the product of rape, but she couldn't do that to him. She let him believe, along with her relatives, that his father was one of her many lovers. She'd

41

been a reckless teenager, a fact her father always took pleasure in reminding her, so the lie was easily believed.

She'd never seen or spoken to John Redshaw again, after their one meeting on Angel Island, in San Francisco Bay, eighteen years ago. He'd tried to apologize; told an incredible unbelievable story of a man metamorphosing into… something else.

It terrified her. She was worried for a long time, plagued by nightmares of Lewis turning into some kind of Sci-Fi freak, an alien, hated and persecuted by mankind.

Over the years, the terrors lessened, thankfully releasing their hold on her sleepless nights. She relaxed, became a good mum, insisting on doing everything herself. Despite her early fears, Lewis grew into a great kid, loved by friends and family alike.

There'd been one scary moment when he was six. He went missing then too. She'd panicked. Rung the U1 international helpline number she'd used previously to track down John Redshaw. With access to Police communications and the latest search and rescue equipment money could buy, U1 accepted the mission, found Lewis, and brought him home to her while the locals were still searching five miles in the wrong direction. Victoria had left a message of gratitude but received nothing in return, U1 was like a phantom, and now Lewis had vanished again.

This time she promised herself she wasn't going to panic. This time Lewis had vanished deliberately for his own reasons. She sat in her father's favourite armchair, remembering her last conversation with Lewis. He'd told her he didn't want to be schooled in England. Told her he'd had enough of education, that academia wasn't his thing. It wasn't going to be his career, he was destined for something more, different. He could feel it in his bones, he'd told her. She should have listened to him.

Thoughts of John Redshaw flicked through her mind.

She'd didn't think the French Police would find Lewis if he didn't want to be found, but she also knew he could get into trouble alone. She hadn't told her father, despite his network of contacts that might be able to assist. He was too ill to be bothered by this, especially if Lewis could be found quickly.

A few years ago, Senator Samuel Blaine had suffered a major heart attack and Victoria didn't want to scare him into another one. He loved his grandson deeply. Lewis was the son he never had. She could see a lot of her father in Lewis, both independent and determined. They liked the same things, from fishing and tennis to the same rock music. That active fit father she remembered from her childhood, was now a frail, thin shadow of a man.

No, she wouldn't tell her father just yet. Save him the heartache. Tell him when, and if, Lewis needed their help. If he was found safe and well like last time, her father need never know. However, she wasn't going to sit around waiting for news. She'd take action.

Jeff Johnson was rifling through his never-ending post when the alert sounded on his computer. Glancing up, his attention was drawn to the two keyword metatags highlighted—Lewis Blaine. He switched to a news channel.

"News just in," read the newscaster on the twenty-four-hour news station.

"Lewis Blaine, grandson of Senator Samuel Blaine who initiated the First Nations Rights Bill in Congress last year, has gone missing whilst on a field trip in Picardy, France."

Johnson's attention immediately diverted from his endless paperwork. Over the top of his reading glasses, he watched as the news item continued, theorizing on possible outcomes, whilst moving to a French reporter on the scene in Nantes, where Lewis had reportedly disappeared. When the item finished, Johnson reached over and brought up the search engine source, a police report in Nantes. His interest roused further, he read the internet report with growing concern, then sat a few moments considering the situation. Decision made. His fingers danced over the keyboard with years of practice as he tracked Victoria Blaine's movements.

Johnson had guessed what Victoria's plans would be before she left Denver, identifying that she'd already purchased a Virgin Atlantic flight direct to Paris—she hadn't called U1 for an assist this time. He'd taken a keen interest in the boy's progress over the years but didn't know the reason for Lewis's current disappearance.

Regardless, the U1 boss, felt responsible, possibly because John Redshaw had left him and his mother without a word. Not that he could blame Redshaw's lack of contact entirely, considering the circumstances surrounding the boy's conception.

Jeff Johnson had married Vivienne Oakwood, the research professor assigned to U1, fourteen years ago. They produced two children. One of them, Joel, attended the same Edgbaston school as Lewis. Joel, now aged thirteen, with his mother's piercing blue eyes and father's physique, was an obsessional computer nerd, much to his father's joy, and his mother's slight disappointment.

Lewis had secured a place at the same school, not a co-incidental choice on Victoria Blaine's part, as she imagined, but some behind-the-scenes string-pulling by Johnson. An obligation he felt he owed his missing U1 operative. When he found out Victoria Blaine was thinking of sending her boy to school in England, Johnson had put a word in the senator's ear about a good school in Edgbaston, near Birmingham. The same school where his son Joel, boarded.

Johnson sat for a few moments reminiscing about his old friend John. In the early years after his departure, he'd missed Redshaw's company, his humour, and his brotherhood. Since then, he kept most of the U1 operatives at arms-length, not wanting to feel the sorrow he experienced when John Redshaw threw himself over the side of the liner and vanished into history.

Where is he now? Is he even alive? And if he is, I hope he's happy? And what about all his children? Did he ever visit them? Did he want to see them? John Redshaw left with too many questions unanswered, and too many lives fated by his touch. Lewis Blaine was another such life, and Johnson wasn't going to stand idly by and do nothing.

To say Madeleine was surprised at her morning sickness was an understatement. A professional woman for many years, she was thorough about her methods of contraception and family planning, never trusting her clients' promises of sterility or vasectomy. Currently, she employed both the implant and the coil to give her complete confidence and satisfaction that all the bases were covered.

Her outward composure controlled; she stroked the soft skin on the underneath side of her left upper arm. Feeling the shape of the implant embedded there, reassured her that it hadn't somehow mysteriously vanished. Despite its presence, Madeline was fairly certain she was pregnant. She'd performed the obligatory home test. Thankfully, not receiving so much as a raised eyebrow from the staff behind the pharmacy counter at her purchase. She was glad she'd decided not to buy the equipment locally, ensuring gossip was kept to a minimum.

Now she sat in her doctor's waiting room trying to fight the impulse to bite her nails, as she had done as a child. Once, long ago, the doctor here had been a client of hers, before he met his wife and had three adorable children. Her thoughts were a jumble as she straightened her already immaculate pleated skirt for the tenth time. *Will he ask me who the father is? God, I hope not.* Frankly, Madeleine hadn't got a clue. *He could be any one of a number of men who patronise my services.* She covered several regulars, so it was most likely to be one of them. Then there was the boy—Lewis. His face jumped into her thoughts. She smiled at the memory of him. *Yes, perhaps the boy.*

She shook her head. It was no good reminiscing. She had a business to attend to, being pregnant would seriously cramp, if not liquidate all her savings. Madeline was Catholic, though not enough of one to prevent her from employing prophylactics, but certainly to exclude abortion.

Could I keep a baby, a child? Do I want to? The best solution would be to secure a private adoption. These were delicate matters she needed to discuss with someone she trusted—her doctor. He was more than her medic, he was her counsellor, confessor, and married to her younger sister.

Doctor Jacques Emard looked out into his surgery waiting room and saw the well-dressed woman in her mid-forties, waiting. He smiled warmly. Whatever physical relationship they'd enjoyed years ago was long since over. He knew Madeline Marnier to be a kind, intelligent, thoughtful woman. She dressed immaculately, and though he observed a few fine lines around the corners of her outer eye and above her upper lip, she was still stunningly beautiful. It made his heart leap. He'd never told his wife about their relationship, there was no need, he loved Arianne. He doubted Madeline would breach her professional ethics to comment either.

Lewis spent four weeks travelling across France. From Nantes, he moved in a south-easterly direction. After Amiens, he passed uneventfully through Soissons, Epernay and Troyes. Along the way, he met women who were welcoming, offering him food, lodging, and several joining him uninvited in bed.

Lewis recognised that his chances for survival alone were improving. Women appeared to enjoy his company, or more specifically his body, and he had no qualms about that. He'd gotten pretty good at catching frogs in lakes and rivers along the way too. His fear from his near drowning incident earlier in the year seemed to have lessened. On the outskirts of Dijon, he stopped to swap several more frogs for some cooked chicken from yet another friendly, if a bit intimidating, farmer's wife.

As Lewis drew near the farm, she appeared in the doorway, formidable in her homespun blue pinafore dress with shiny red cheeks, her roughened hands more used to strangling chickens than needlepoint. Her smile was kind enough and grew wider as she listened to Lewis's appalling French. She laughed out loud at one point, as he requested to barter the frogs. He guessed he'd got his words muddled up, judging by her dirty laugh.

"Enough, enough," she grinned, using English. "Stop before my ears bleed at your terrible accent, and I am not giving you my breasts for frogs." The last phrase she uttered in seamless English. Lewis blushed. She'd took him inside and fed him to bursting in the big farmhouse kitchen, attempting to ply him with the same coarse red wine Madeline had drunk. She then offered him a bed in the house for the night. Shades of Madeline reared their head. Lewis swiftly declined the kind invitation, knowing where it would lead. However, he was unsure how to leave without upsetting this woman, who up until now had been as gracious as any hostess. Instead, he begged permission to take his rest in one of the out-buildings, hoping she wouldn't feel slighted by his preference of the pigs over her boudoir.

After Dijon, Lewis's travels took him east. He'd always wanted to visit Germany, a country he'd heard so much about whilst growing up, from his tutors at school, to his grandfather re-living his war memories.

Realising he couldn't continue drifting like a hobo across the world forever, Lewis stopped in Stuttgart, his mind intent on getting a job and staying a short while. His arrival coincided with the week of their famous wine festival, the *Stuttgarter Weindorf.*

Lewis managed to secure a temporary job serving in one of the many marquees and stalls around the event. At the end of the festival, with nowhere to go again, one of the stall holders, Hannah, took pity on him and welcomed him into her permanent bar, where she employed him to serve drinks.

Lewis's nineteenth birthday came and went without celebration. He was hard at work, wiping down the tables and counters after a long evening shift. He knew Hannah would be waiting for him, as always, if he felt like visiting her apartment.

Probably, because he remembered it was his birthday, Lewis couldn't find the motivation or interest to climb the stairs to her door. His birthday at home was usually a big affair. Both his Granda and his momma going all out to provide him and his friends with a good time. These were the things he missed; being with his family, surrounded by love. In such a melancholy mood, he didn't think he would be good company for Hannah tonight.

"Drink up," he mumbled in broken German, to the last remaining customer. "Closing time," he added, pointing to the clock on the wall.

The man at the end of the bar seemed too far into his drink to care. He'd been sat there most of the evening, apparently drowning his sorrows. He was casually dressed, but there was something about his clothes that didn't fit. Without being obvious, Lewis regarded his customer in more detail. Clean-shaven, hair recently cut, his outfit clearly labelled as Ted Baker, the British designer.

Hold that thought. Rewind. Okay, it's possible for a German man to like Ted Baker's clothing, it's not a crime. Perhaps, I'm just being overly suspicious? I need to get a life.

Still intrigued, Lewis moved closer to the man, in the guise of wiping down the main bar. The man, a thirty-something individual, raised his eyes from his half-empty pint of beer, and stared unblinking at Lewis with deep diamond-blue eyes. The man didn't say a word. Lewis, feeling the tension mount, moved swiftly away. He had the distinct feeling he'd just escaped with his life for some reason.

Fortunately, he wasn't the only member of staff in the bar late that night. Gustaf came over and repeated Lewis's request in fluent German. The man nodded, downed the rest of his beer, and glancing once more in Lewis's direction, rose and staggered over to the door. On the way, he fell across one of the tables. Lewis rushed around the counter to help the man up. The man mumbled his thanks and appeared to unintentionally grasp Lewis around the back of the neck, as he attempted to right himself. This frightened Lewis. He froze temporarily as he felt a sting of pain, then raised his hand to the back of his neck, removing the stranger's fingers.

Once upright, the man disappeared through the door and out into the night. Gustaf and Lewis watched him walk calmly down the road like he hadn't been drinking at all. Lewis shuddered. He didn't know who the man was, and he didn't want to meet him again any time soon. He gave Lewis the creeps.

An insane thought occurred to him. The stranger could be waiting for an opportunity to jump him when he finished work. His neck still hurt from where the man had grabbed it. Seeing the worried look on the boy's face, Gustaf came back over from where he was ringing up the night's takings, to check that Lewis was alright. He'd noticed the stranger had ruffled him. Lewis nodded, and waved Gustaf's concerns away. He didn't tell his work colleague that he felt as if he'd been violated in some way.

"Get a grip, Lewis," he chided himself, once Gustaf was out of ear-shot in the cellar. "It's your birthday, nothing's going to happen on your birthday." Needing more reassurance, he turned and faced the optics and made his decision. Selecting a very exclusive single malt whiskey, he poured himself a shot.

"Happy birthday Lewis," he said, saluting and raising his glass mockingly to his reflection in the mirror behind the bar. He downed the whiskey in one go without a sign of coughing, demonstrating that this wasn't his first taste of strong alcohol. Gustaf stood in the cellar doorway grinning, as Lewis put the money for the shot in the till.

Lewis trudged along the midnight roads to his temporary digs. Hannah had secured a room for him in someone else's house. As he put the key in the lock of the front door, he thought he heard a sound behind him. He didn't know why, but he didn't want the person who was following him to know, that he knew, he was being followed. He suspected the man from the bar. He opened the door and without looking back, locked, and bolted it behind him.

Usually, he would have put the hall light on. Instead, he left the hallway in darkness and clambered quickly up the stairs to his room. Once inside and feeling safer, he approached the window stealthily like a thief. Ensuring he stayed well back, he scanned the road outside the house. Five doors down he saw him. A shadowy form stood in a doorway, undoubtedly sporting a Ted Baker jacket.

Travis leaned back into the shadows. He wasn't sure if Lewis had made him, but it didn't matter now. He'd found his target and applied the microdot tracker—mission complete. He had located Lewis because the boy had used an Internet café in Stuttgart to email his mother, so she wouldn't worry about him. He'd done the same before he left Amiens. It didn't take Travis long doing the rounds of the bars to find him. Lewis Blaine was a good boy, Travis realised, even paying for his whiskey on his birthday. He hadn't seen too many good people during his years of military and SWAT service.

Travis St John had found his way to Unit One after being

pensioned out of the police force early at the age of thirty-six. It still rankled him that after fourteen years in the army serving on active duty, he'd never been injured once in all the high combat situations he'd endured, then two years into the police force and he gets shot in the back.

The bullet lodged so close to his spinal nerve was irretrievable—according to several eminent surgeons—they were unable to operate to remove it without paralysing him from the waist down. He would end up in a wheelchair, they advised, likely with a urinary catheter too.

He could have stayed in the force in a desk job, but Travis was a literal action-man, skilled in numerous styles of fighting, including the Filipino martial art, Kali. Both the forces and the police turned him down for active service after his injury, their insurers unwilling to take the chance that his injury might affect him, or more importantly jeopardize their missions.

Unit One didn't have any such qualms about taking on a man with a bullet in his back. Doc Williams had offered to remove it on more than one occasion because he was sure he could do it without any ill effects. Travis explained to Doc that he had come to terms with it, decided it was part of him, and he wouldn't be separated from it. In truth, Travis was too terrified to face any surgery after what the other surgeons had told him, and he didn't know Doc well enough to trust him at his word.

Doc never understood the reasoning behind the men Jeff Johnson selected for U1. It was a permanent bone of contention between them. In his eyes, Frank Fulwood, by employing Travis with a bullet in his spine, was repeating Jeff's mistakes. Especially, since the man refused to let him remove it. *They might have exteriors as strong as diamonds, with enough military experience to survive the worst scenarios, but on the inside, they were all soft mewling kittens.* Though he'd never say that to their faces.

After he had assured himself of the location of Lewis's

digs, Travis, or Swoop, as the team insisted on nicknaming him, headed towards the local airport and his pickup point. Fulwood, his new boss, didn't want the boy apprehended at this point. It was a babysitting role and Travis hated it.

On board the Bucket, T-cut, the unit's second-in-command, and communications guru was already monitoring the Intel from Lewis's tracker. Travis would be sent out again should the tracker fail, or their commander want the boy brought in. With Lewis successfully corralled, and under T-cut's watchful eye, Travis could return to the active missions he loved.

Despite his years of service and training in surveillance, Travis failed to notice a second set of eyes watching him from the darkness, as he walked back to the taxi rank and his rendezvous with a certain tiltrotor, and its exceedingly annoying pilot, José De Silva.

Unit One had evolved over the intervening years. It now consisted of two teams, or units, their missions often running concurrently. It took a lot more planning and a massive amount of communication between Jeff Johnson and Frank Fulwood, the two unit leads—although Johnson still held overall command. Whenever possible they met up for face-to-face meetings, and when the Bucket was halfway across the world they video-conferenced. It was a masterclass in logistics, keeping both operations flowing smoothly.

Frank Fulwood had turned out to be a good choice as the new CO of Unit One. He knew his men well and the new members he'd personally selected suited the team. Johnson was pleased with Fulwood as his choice. His one regret, that Doc Williams refused to consider joining him in the land-based offices. Despite his advancing years, the Doc's heart remained with the people. He lived to serve not only their organisation but the lives of those less fortunate around the globe, through his extensive knowledge and surgical prowess. Interns constantly begged him for placements, and institutions offered him senior consultant and professorship opportunities. Whilst he did concede to occasional land-based locum positions of a couple of weeks here and there, he never stayed long, preferring to return to his home on the Bucket.

It was a great cover for the Bucket and the U1 missions, a wealthy semi-retired consultant living aboard his luxury liner. Jeff Johnson knew the only way Doc Williams would ever leave the job would be in a body bag.

CHAPTER FOUR – LIVERPOOL

Aᶠᵗᵉʳ completing the successful mission in Saudi Arabia, returning the mother and her children to safety, Yin and Davidson were transported to London Heathrow. Their new orders; to assist in a mission which Unit Two were currently spearheading. T-cut, his expertise needed on another mission, headed back to the Bucket.

Johnson decided this mission required a two-pronged approach. Preliminary investigations by U2 uncovered evidence of a trafficking ring which started in Asia, entered Great Britain via Southern Ireland, and spread across England from Wales. Yin and Davidson were to tackle the activity occurring in and around the tourist attraction of Cardiff Bay, whilst U2 operatives would tackle the Irish connection.

Davidson sat in one of the many pub restaurants on the quay, overlooking the picturesque bay, close to the impressive Welsh Assembly building. It was early afternoon and filled with retired day-trippers with grey hair and big handbags taking tea. Davidson was the odd one out in day-trippers heaven.

The two of them had decided that Davidson would meet their contact. Yin, being Chinese in origin, was much too recognisable and unforgettable. Yin had argued that with his thick Cornish accent, he was as British as Davidson, who was French by descent. However, Davidson had his way. An aggrieved Yin sloped off on the pretence of scoping out the gift shop in the second most impressive building on the quayside, the Millennium Centre.

What is it with all these monuments and statues? Davidson wondered as he waited, staring out at the Welsh works of art dotted around the quay in front of the man-made freshwater bay. He had to admit the majority were good. The last one, opposite his window, had him flummoxed. It was an open-ended metal ring. He didn't have time to go down to the lower-level dock and read the inscription he was sure was there. *Another time maybe if they're still here.*

Looking out over the heads of two, seventy-plus women, deep in conversation, Davidson saw his contact striding towards him. The person carried the signature bunch of white roses and a bottle of Prosecco. Johnson always insisted that team members carry these items, so they could recognise their contacts. Davidson's contrasting red roses were propped up on his table next to the sparkling wine.

"Bugger me," inhaled Davidson, those words saying it all. *Yin is going to be so angry.* He grinned at the thought. He rose from his seat in the manner of all good gentlemen to greet the newcomer. The contact was female and Chinese. She was as pretty as an Asian angel too. Davidson pressed his lips closed in order to stop his tongue lolling out in admiration.

She wasn't your stereotypical Chinese babe either. She was tall, very tall, despite her obvious oriental ancestry. His eyes travelled from her expensive red stiletto heels, up her incredibly long legs, halting briefly at the hem of her white minidress where it seductively rode up her thighs as she walked. Her hands interrupted his view when they covered her hemline and jerked it down from where it had risen, aware of his gaze.

Davidson didn't get any further in his lusty appraisal because as she reached his table, she leaned forward and promptly kicked him in the shin—hard.

"Ow! What was that for?" He complained, rubbing his leg, though he knew darn well why she'd kicked him. He grinned sheepishly, while her expression and one hand resting on her tilted hip said, *finished drooling yet?*

"I thought your team were supposed to be highly profes-sional," she flounced, drawing up the chair opposite, and putting her flowers and wine on the small table.

"We are. I am," he replied, attempting to reassure her. Her eyebrows rose into her cute fringe in disbelief, and he was lost again. "I'm sorry, I was distracted, I didn't expect anyone so..."

Suddenly, the chair next to him moved and Yin dropped into it.

"What my inept colleague is trying to say, is that Unit One is a team par excellence." And then with a gleam in his eye, Yin ruined it for Davidson by launching into fluent Mandarin. Within a few sentences, Yin had her trilling in reply in a sweet bird-like way. Davidson was besotted. Her laugh was hypnotic. He didn't even know what they were speaking about. *Probably me,* he guessed astutely, by the way she kept glancing in his direction, in between Yin's explanations.

"I think we'd best continue this conversation in English, Xiaoniao," Yin suggested, inclining his head in Davidson's direction. "For the sake of the locals," he added mockingly. Davidson scowled at Yin, and Xiaoniao trilled some more. *Great! That's all I need,* thought Davidson catching on, at last, *Yin's introduced me as the village numpty.*

Xiaoniao had never met men quite like the ones listening and watching her so intently—especially the English one. They took the information she provided seriously. The concern was clear on their faces, and at odds with their hardened physiques and Yin's schoolboy tomfoolery about his colleague.

In an attempt to calm herself, and re-focus her emotions, Xiaoniao opened her handbag. After a brief skirmish, she removed her Guerlain Diamond pink lip gloss, applying it accurately to her lips without recourse to a hand mirror.

Davidson could never figure out how women managed to do that. He watched entranced, as the pink stick travelled the contours of her plump kissable lips. He was sure if he ever tried, it would end up across his face and up his nose. Xiaoniao composed herself and began her sister Xiaodan's story.

They were following up the lead given to them by Xiaoniao in Cardiff—cleared by Fulwood—regarding her missing younger sister. Xiaoniao had received a hurried call from her the previous week, after Xiaodan managed to get her hands on a phone for a couple of minutes. Xiaoniao heard her sister gasp, she explained, as the phone was snatched away. A loud slap followed, and the phone went dead, but not before Xiaodan divulged that she was being held in the Chinese quarter of Liverpool and the house overlooked a large square lawn. The only such lawn near China town was Great George Square.

Davidson glanced at his watch for the eighteenth time. It had been agreed he'd pretend to be out on an evening stroll, but now he'd been around the same block, completing several laps. He was worried that he starting to look suspicious. He was also beginning to regret agreeing to Yin's suggestion of no ear comms. He'd explained that they would have stood out, been too easy to spot on the street.

"Where is that damn China man? He was supposed to be here ages ago. I said we should have brought a dog. At least if I had a dog, I'd have a reason to be wandering about. Not standing here like a muppet getting noticed."

Davidson's worrio-meter ratcheted up another notch, as he detected the same blacked-out Mercedes circling the block for the third time. It looked like it was following him. He was going to have to move on soon, or someone was going to make their presence known. He wasn't sure at this point whether it would be undercover cops or the gangs' hard men. Either way, it would spell trouble.

Wondering how to let Yin know without alerting anybody else, Davidson walked to the other end of the road. Despite him being in charge of this part of the mission, it had made sense for Yin to do the recon because he was Chinese. It also made sense now why the initial U1 request had been for an Asian operative. The Chinese gangs hung around the Chinese quarter in Liverpool. Davidson would have stood out like a penguin at a barbecue. It didn't stop him worrying. Yin was good, but good didn't stop a bullet.

He was deciding whether to walk back up the road or get out of the streetlights when he heard footsteps running down the street towards him. Yin was holding a young girl's hand, tugging her along.

"Car," was the one word Davidson heard. He didn't need any more. He sprinted to where he'd parked the black BMW series three earlier, further down Nelson Street. Reaching it before the others, he flew into the driver's seat and started the engine. Yin and his passenger were moments behind, and the car was gone before the inquisitive Mercedes turned the corner at the end of the street for the fourth time.

"What happened to the recon part of this mission?" Davidson asked, bemused and irritated at the same time.

"Improvisation," answered Yin, trying to catch his breath.

How far has he actually run? Davidson wondered, knowing Yin's extensive fitness regime and martial art status wouldn't normally result in him becoming breathless.

"You okay?"

"Yeah, just getting old I guess," replied Yin, knowing full well he was over a decade younger than Davidson. He grinned at his own joke, then turned to the young girl they'd rescued to help her with her seat belt.

Davidson reckoned Xiaodan didn't look any older than ten, despite him knowing from her sister that she was twelve. He was dismayed that trafficking had altered so radically in the last five years. U1 were well aware of people trafficking, usually from countries where poverty and destitution were the norm, like Vietnam and Albania. Becoming vulnerable and beholden to criminals, people were purchased by affluent Western families wanting cheap live-in servants. Davidson hadn't realised that people trafficked were getting younger, nor that they could be trafficked within a country like Britain.

The girl sobbed quietly in the back of the car, and though Yin wanted to put his arm around her to comfort her, he refrained, in case she thought ill of him. Instead, he spoke in Mandarin reassuring her she would see her sister soon.

At the start of their reconnaissance mission, a suite had been booked for Yin and Davidson at their favourite hotel in Liverpool. The hotel's interior was impressive, with a huge atrium extending from the reception area and ending in a stunning glass roof. The place had a good gym which Yin appreciated, and king-size-plus beds which Davidson at six-foot-four loved. Though his initial skill set in U1 had been as a pilot and explosives expert, over the years thanks to the numerous missions, Davidson had added many more skills and abilities, till his CV equalled that of veterans of the special forces.

Their accommodation had two en-suite bedrooms. Because of this, and the fact it was already nighttime, they agreed the girl would be better off remaining overnight in one of the rooms and be taken to her sister the following day.

Yin settled Xiaodan into her room after arranging for her to speak to her sister on the phone. He gained her assurance that she would stay put, while they headed downstairs to the bar for a well-earned drink.

In reality, they needed to call Frank Fulwood without the girl present because they didn't want to distress her further, she'd been through enough. Davidson would advise Fulwood of the change of plan, from recon to extraction, after the two of them had debriefed each other first. Their report wouldn't go down well. Davidson could hear Fulwood cursing down the phone already.

"At least the mission had a successful, if early, outcome," Yin reflected optimistically, as they walked towards the White Bar.

It was a new building attached to the hotel like a limpet. The designer had had a drug-induced brainwave, that a Georgian-style house, glued onto the side of a high-rise hotel would look just the ticket. Out of habit, they chose a position that provided excellent coverage of the entrance to the hotel and bar. Their arrival didn't go unnoticed, as a server appeared within moments asking whether they would like anything to drink. Settled back, with a whisky each, the two operatives reviewed the mission.

"Okay, what happened?" Davidson asked. "I thought we were doing recon this afternoon in prep for going in tomorrow night."

Yin nodded. Taking a large swallow of his single malt, before answering his comrade. He felt the burn all the way down his throat. He wasn't a whiskey drinker, preferring instead his ancestral tipple of Baijiu, a type of Chinese vodka.

"I know, that was the plan," confirmed Yin, struggling not to cough like a wimp in front of Davidson. "But plans change," he stated philosophically.

"I see." He didn't, but Davidson trusted his team member. He did, however, need to know all the facts before he put in the call to their boss advising that the mission was completed ahead of schedule. Davidson waited. He could see Yin was struggling to regain his composure after taking the huge mouthful of whiskey. He covered his grin, by picking up his glass.

"There was no other way," Yin admitted, finally getting his swallowing reflex under control. "I overheard them saying they were moving her out tonight."

"Tonight?"

"Yes, tonight. If I hadn't freed her when I did, she'd have vanished to god knows where." He stared Davidson in the eye daring him to disagree. "I couldn't live with that on my conscience. Could you?" Davidson shook his head.

"I guess your action was right," he agreed, not sure how he was going to put that fact across to Fulwood.

"Damm straight," answered Yin, only just holding back from slamming his empty glass down on the coffee table as he chugged back the last of his drink.

Davidson was in the process of reaching into his pocket for his phone when Yin swore.

"Lā Shǐ!"

Davidson didn't need to understand Mandarin to guess what Yin had said. The way he spoke the words was sufficient. It was unheard of for Yin to swear. Something to do with respecting his ancestors he always replied when his teammates teased. If he was swearing, Davidson didn't need to ask why, and he had a fair idea of who, seeing as they had just rescued the girl.

"Where?"

"Heading into reception."

Davidson turned his head casually to confirm what he already feared. Two Asian men were waving their arms about and shouting at the terrified reception staff who were nodding frantically. Fortunately, the staff member who served them whisky wasn't manning the desk, so they had breathing space.

"You get the girl. I'll get the car."

Yin nodded and was gone, using the inside fire escape stairs, rather than risk crossing the lobby, and potentially coming face-to-face with the angry men. Davidson heard the heavy fire-door bang shut, telling him that Yin had made it to the stairs. He was about to leave when their server joined the two on the desk and pointed directly at him. The men followed her trembling finger and stared hard at him through the atrium glass.

"Shit!" Davidson swore, adding his own swear word to Yin's.

He couldn't blame their server for re-directing the hostile men's attention away from her work colleagues. In another life, he might have done the same thing in her place. The bulges in the side of their jackets told him everything he needed to know. He finished his whisky in one swig. *No point wasting good booze.* As they continued to stare, he rose, leaving the bar by the external door, desperately hoping they'd follow him. The men were after Davidson like cats spying a mouse.

He made it around the corner, then sprinted fast down the side of the building. He needed to lose them before he could go back and retrieve their car which was thankfully in a public car park. At the back of the building housing the bar, he ran towards the next building. It sported a huge sign announcing that it was Her Majesty's Passport Office.

Davidson vaulted over the six-foot grey gate and legged it down the side passage, ignoring the close circuit cameras. T-cut could fix them later—if need be. His plan, to do a complete circuit of the block and head back to the car park for the Beamer.

Halfway down the side of the building, the passage widened, and an unloading area appeared. He couldn't quite see why the passage required a gate when the other area was open-ended with an access road from the dual carriageway beyond. He didn't have time to consider it further. As he poked his head out around the corner, the black Mercedes he'd seen in Chinatown, pulled into view crawling along the street. Clearly, the opposition had radioed ahead and told them to be frosty. It's what he would have done.

Glancing right, he thanked the god of lucky people everywhere, for sending him to the exact location of the hotel's external fire escape. He needed to get to it and be gone by the time the car reached the dead-end, or find a hiding place, like yesterday.

The Mercedes neared the loading bay. Its two occupants scanned the area including the fire escape, turned the car around and went back the way they came. Hearing the vehicle speed off, Davidson hauled himself out of the green industrial waste bin. The luck god was still with him because it was a recycling bin and not household waste. It still smelt like a cat had died in there, but he'd had worse. At least he wasn't covered in three-week-old fish guts like last time.

Entering the hotel premises from an unknown area, it took Davidson a moment to re-orientate himself. The stairs he took only went up to the second floor and they were on the fourth, he didn't have time to '*fanny about*' as T-cut put it. He was forced to descend and head back outside.

By now, Yin should have the girl down on the ground floor secreted somewhere safe.

As the Mercedes had gone back the way it came—there was no road onwards—Davidson went in the other direction. The hotel buildings ended, and he was forced to walk through a landscaped art installation, a great place to booby-trap someone.

"Davidson."

"Yin?"

"Yeah."

"You got the girl?"

"Yeah. Where's the bleeding car?"

"I'm on it, stay here."

"Roger that."

Crossing over the road, Davidson walked down Old Hall Street. It was one-way for part of its length, so collecting Yin and Xiaodan wasn't going to be easy. At the point where the road became two-way, he checked the intersections for any sign of the Merc—nothing. Crossing back over he walked passed the next building and turned into the multi-storey car park situated behind it.

They must have realised the hotel didn't have much parking. The only place, the nearby public car park. Either that or the hotel staff informed them where to park a car.

The bullet missed him by a hair. The shot, hitting the concrete wall instead, sprayed him with shrapnel. A tiny piece smacked him in the temple. He felt the blood trickle down.

Ducking low behind the card barrier, the only cover available, Davidson withdrew his baby, a Beretta 92. It would be mere moments before someone alerted the police about the sound of gunshots, by then he hoped he'd have this sorted out.

The key in the game of cat and mouse is waiting. Most people aren't good at it. Davidson wasn't good at it either—he excelled. It came from understanding explosives and to some extent, jets. People could never wait. They always jumped or moved too soon. The mouse moved. The cat waited. Davidson waited and waited. It was only a few minutes, but to his opponents, it probably felt like a lifetime. They knew the cops would appear in minutes. Davidson waited.

The first man, made his mistake when he moved his foot, giving Davison his location. Then he stuck his head up, holding his handgun at arms-length. Davidson waited. Without needing to line up on the man, Davidson swung out from his crouched position and shot the man clean through the head. He dropped like a sledgehammer had hit him and in a way it did, the back of his head a complete mess. The parked car behind him, sporting a new two-tone paint job as a result.

The successful hit put the other man at a disadvantage by levelling the odds. Davidson heard his adversary swallow loudly. Davidson stepped out, this time on the other side of the barrier and ended the man's life in a nano-second. He didn't feel bad for shooting both men, they would have shot him too. He also didn't believe in dragging out a person's life, no matter how bad they might be. Cruelty was for criminals in his book.

"Get in," he called to Yin and Xiaodan from the car, after he'd secured the Beamer and driven it along to their hiding place.

"What took you so long?" Yin muttered, climbing in the back with the shivering Xiaodan by his side.

Davidson looked at Yin in his rear-view mirror.

"Blasted one-way system..." he replied like they were

taking a Sunday afternoon drive because he didn't want to freak the girl. "...had a couple of silly Sunday drivers." Yin nodded at Davidson in the mirror, acknowledging the blood on his face. Davidson nodded back. Their non-verbal comms saying much more than words ever could.

Leaving Xiaodan to sleep in the back of the car, Davidson and Yin, took turns driving until they reached the secluded manor house in east Kent which was Unit Two's base. Johnson opened the door, accompanied by a mature plump South American woman. Taking in the woman's appearance, Davidson deduced she was likely Johnson's housekeeper. He wondered briefly about Johnson's choice; his recent mission having heightened his awareness regarding the trafficking world. However, Jeff Johnson was a man above reproach. He would never be involved in such shady dealings as trafficking. As if guessing the progress of Davidson's thoughts, Johnson spoke.

"Of course, you haven't met Camila. She's one of Lola's aunts. She has joined us from Scotland, where she lived until her husband passed away recently." That statement confirmed what Davidson had already guessed, making him feel slightly guilty about his previous thoughts no matter how brief.

"I thought you might like to freshen up," Johnson suggested thoughtfully, addressing Xiaodan directly since he knew she spoke English. He treated her like an adult and not a young twelve-year-old child. Johnson had surmised she'd probably been through enough in recent days. Showing her respect would go some way to making her feel valued once more. Xiaodan nodded soberly, and followed Camila, once introductions were made, up the wide central staircase to a first-floor bedroom.

Without another word, Davidson and Yin followed Johnson into his study. Davidson hadn't seen Jeff Johnson for many months. It was Johnson who had hired Michael Davidson originally, and to whom he felt beholden for such a fabulous career. A part of him wanted to give Johnson a welcome man-hug, but his huge admiration, together with Johnson's status prevented him from taking that step towards informality. Besides, comrades were more than friends, they were family, and they didn't need man-hugs to remind them of that.

"Problem?" Johnson questioned, getting right down to basics. That single-word query was all Davidson needed. He knew when Johnson reverted to single words, his professional curiosity was aroused.

Yin, on the other hand, had never met Jeff Johnson before. Fulwood had recruited him direct after finding him in Italy, a loose cannon with no direction. His abilities now almost rivalled that of their old colleague John Redshaw, with three black belts to his name by the age of nineteen.

Yin had heard a lot about Johnson, more than a lot. He seemed to be hero-worshipped by the older members of U1. Yin had no such feelings. He saw a grey-haired old man—at least old to his lively twenty-two-year-old point of view—as he lowered himself carefully into his chair behind an ornate oak desk, placed his elbows upon it and steepled his fingers waiting for Davidson—the mission lead—to explain further.

While Davidson debriefed Johnson about the mission in Liverpool, Yin surveyed their surroundings from his seat in a Victorian wing-backed chair. Opulent fabrics and furnishings throughout, enough books on the shelves to begin a county library. Outside through the double doors, he observed lawns sweeping away towards formal gardens and unstructured woodlands beyond. *Yes, Johnson has it right,* Yin decided, slightly envious.

"And you Yin, what was your assessment of the situation?" Johnson asked, almost catching Yin off-guard. Despite this, Yin reeled off his response. *Is that a twinkle in the old man's eye?* Yin wondered after he finished. *Did he notice me jealously eyeing up his assets? Probably.*

They left the girl in the care of Johnson. He would make sure she found a new home, somewhere her sister could find her, and she would be safe. That's what U2 did. In Davidson's opinion, they weren't real operatives in U2, they took the soft approach, working intel, recon, and espionage cases rather than anything involving bloodshed and mayhem. The real work was done by U1 from the Bucket, currently at anchor in the Med.

It was where they were headed now unless Fulwood redirected them to another mission. Without new orders, they drove to Heathrow in the Beamer, handing it back to the hire firm, and taking a direct business flight to Naples. The Bucket was moored in Naples harbour just off the new Marina Road. It docked there when service overhauls were due on various parts of the engine, hydraulics, or navigation systems. It was the latter system, which was currently under review. Gone were the days of compasses and reading the stars, today's modern ocean-going ships were more likely to have ring laser gyros, accelerometers, and navigation-grade inertial measurement units. Due to the vast amount of global traffic on the waterways, ships required platforms with high global positioning accuracy, and continuity of performance to enable them to function at the level required for mission success.

The non-stop flight was uneventful. They fast-tracked through the beige, glass, and marble airport building. Heading outside into the heat, they hailed a taxi to take them down to the Bucket's berth. In addition, to debriefing with Johnson, they now had to do a full debrief with Fulwood as well. Davidson knew that both men had already communicated with each other, their second debrief was merely protocol. As Yin was new it was possible Johnson was using the mission to assess his performance. Davidson hadn't been happy with Yin taking the initiative and removing the girl ahead of schedule, but he agreed it was a case of now-or-never. He guessed Yin couldn't live with the 'never' scenario.

It's great to be back home. Davidson sighed with contentment, lounging on his cabin bunk prior to debriefing. He had lived almost permanently on-board ship for nearly eighteen years and didn't regret a single day. He was forty-three, an age when most men would have been married with teenage children. Brought up in the care system that failed him miserably, Michael Davidson had long ago decided never to have a permanent relationship or children. What would have been a hard decision for others, was no decision for him. He had seen his own family torn apart. Then watched a multitude of other children move, like him, from foster home to foster home with no roots, and in many cases, no love either. It was a cynical way to look at the world, but it was the way Michael Davidson had learnt to survive. He'd finally found a family he wanted to be part of—Unit One.

Fulwood watched as the two men left his Ready Room after the debrief later that day. The mission had been successful despite Yin's unilateral action to remove the girl, and Fulwood couldn't blame him. The boy had come a long way since Fulwood found him in Rome. Yin, or rather Fan Yin came from a historic line of ancestors dating back centuries. That was of little interest to the boy fighting for his life in the back streets of the capital. Fulwood worked out that Yin had been sold into slavery at an early age. From conversations with him, he was probably around three or four years old at the time. When he discovered Yin fighting grown men using a small three-inch blade in a street fight, he felt it was time to even the odds and step in.

Fulwood had saved Fan Yin from the streets when he was eight years old. Without anyone's knowledge, he had transferred Yin to a monastery school, paying for his tuition and lodgings until he was old enough to make his own way in the world. It shouldn't have surprised him that he ended up at the Bucket's door, or rather gangplank. In addition to regular schooling, Yin had received training at the boarding school in several martial arts including Aikido, Shaolin and his old friend's favourite style, Kyokushin. Yin had re-established the old U1 karate school when he joined the team. It was good to hear 'Osu' sounds reverberate around the decks like old times.

"Come in Travis," called Fulwood, recognising Travis St John's brisk knock on the outside of his door. Doc Williams was scowling in his habitual chair in the Ready Room, supposedly enjoying his morning coffee. He still insisted on china crockery, but the old glass cafetiere had been changed to a modern red espresso machine. Doc disparagingly described the coffee units as pellets, rather than capsules as they were called. He also harped on about preferring a cup of quality coffee, but it was obvious he wasn't going to get any in the Ready Room—the glass cafetière had been relegated to Doc's private quarters.

"Ready to report," stated Travis, coming forward to stand at ease in front of his commanding officer. Fulwood nodded, and Doc Williams perked up. Travis took this as his cue to begin debriefing.

"The assigned target is in Stuttgart. He is working as a barista at a local bar. He has rented a room down the street from the bar. The owner, female, likes to indulge herself with his company on occasion."

Fulwood and Doc exchanged a look. They knew exactly what indulgence Travis referred to, and considering Redshaw's history, they were both hoping this wasn't a repeat episode.

"How old is he?" Doc Williams asked brusquely. Travis turned slightly away from Fulwood to answer Doc's surprise question. Doctor David Williams was an institution aboard the

Bucket. He had been on board for as long as anyone could remember. If he was sitting in the Ready Room, it was recognised that he was included in any briefing and able to ask questions, or interrupt as he chose. When Johnson was commander this was normal procedure. Fulwood quickly realised Doc's value when it came to seeing things from a different perspective, and he allowed the practice to continue.

"Nineteen last week," answered Travis smoothly, wondering at the reason for Doc's question. He was about to turn back to face Fulwood when he stopped mid-turn and instead added.

"Not short for any company, even though he's just nineteen."

Fulwood was on him quicker than a rattlesnake on a rat.

"What do you mean by that?"

Travis wondered if he might have overstepped the mark. He figured they were closer to the target than he realised. He wondered why a nineteen-year-old youth would need following to the extent that he required a tracker. There was something they weren't saying. Travis had a feeling they already knew this boy from somewhere else. He could ask the question, or he could wait until they decided to share it. It wasn't any business of his what his boss did, or didn't tell him, and that included Doc too by the sound of it. He searched for another suitable answer in case his flippant comment had been inappropriate to them.

"The time that I watched him, he was seldom alone. There was always female company around, and several seemed almost eager, like his boss, to spend time with him. However, on the night I placed the tracker, and his boss had invited him back to her place, he declined, going home alone instead. That was unusual for his MO."

Doc let out a deep sigh of relief, and never the one to remember confidentiality opened his mouth.

"Well, thank goodness for that!"

Fulwood gave Doc a look this time that Travis couldn't

70

miss. His boss was renowned for his non-verbal comms, and the cliche 'a picture tells a thousand words,' could have been written especially for him. His eyes clearly said, 'What did you have to go and say that for?'

Travis smiled inwardly. Both men were so easy to read. They were never any good at playing poker with the team. He could have raked in thousands off them if he'd been heartless. He left the briefing wondering what interesting nugget these men knew about Lewis Blaine. There was nothing like a good piece of gossip aboard the Bucket and there was always one person on board guaranteed to have the answers to anything.

Terence Mason, a.k.a. T-cut, was the ship's techno-wizard. Now at the ripe old age of forty-four, he too had never met a woman to settle down with. Correction, he would always tell everybody, who wanted to listen that he found the love of his life, and she was stolen by a rogue, in the form of Thomas Seamark. Seamark was a former member of U1. He'd been the team's marksman, forger and second pilot until he met Lolita de Silva, or Lola as she was known to T-Cut.

T-cut would go on about Lola for hours if people let him. About how he met her on a mission in Egypt. How it was love at first sight, until that evil villain swept her off her feet and married her. At this point, T-Cut would sigh dramatically and raise his eyes to the ceiling before dropping his head, eyes downcast to the floor. It was such a regular performance that the younger members could ape it perfectly. Maybe, it was time for T-Cut, to consider retirement they whispered, but only amongst themselves.

Once Travis had left the Ready room, and they were sure he was well out of earshot, Doc and Fulwood began their earnest discussion.

"You're not thinking what I'm thinking, are you?" Doc asked. Fulwood did an abridged version of T-cut's acting role, adding a shake of his head at the end.

"I bloody hope not," he replied, running his hands through

his greying hair in a subconscious effort to wipe away the thought. Doc wouldn't let it lie there.

"Runs away. Attractive to females. Can get any woman he wants. This time at only nineteen. Need I say more? You know what they say."

"In this situation? No. I can't say I've ever experienced this situation before, except maybe once, with a certain ex-U1 member."

Doc smiled, but the smile didn't reach his eyes. He had a feeling of Deja-vue, and it didn't feel good.

"They say," he continued, regardless of Fulwood's hard stare. "The fruit doesn't fall far from the tree. You know Jeff is going to worry about this."

"So, we don't tell him yet," Fulwood answered, ignoring Doc's raised eyebrows. "Don't give me that look. I'm the commander of Unit One and it was a Unit One mission."

"Requested by Jeff," reminded Doc Williams, seemingly not finished with playing devil's advocate. He rose from his new armchair and made himself another cup of coffee out of the hated machine. Fulwood didn't answer.

Travis didn't get very far with T-cut either. Bizarrely, his team member was close-lipped and refused to speak on the subject, which made Travis even more intrigued than before. There was nothing he liked more than a good mystery and he planned to get to the bottom of it. Now though, he felt the need for exercise and headed to the Bucket's dojo to practice some blade work before dinner.

Travis had been practising the Filipino martial arts Kali, or Eskrima, for over two decades and he was more than good. If word got out to the ship's crew that he was training, pretty soon he'd have an audience because it was like watching an expert demonstration of knife skills—which it was. Travis started during his early days in the Army. He continued because he liked it, because it was useful in armed fighting, and adding a knife, machete or stick beat any un-armed combat in his view. It involved a lot of footwork and work against resistant, uncooperative combatants. There weren't many on the Bucket willing to practice with him. Fulwood had finally agreed to the purchase of a couple of combat dummies to enable Travis to train effectively. He had an assortment of blades which included several Filipino swords, a couple of Kris daggers and a large collection of Karambits, which because they were small were easy to hide. He usually had at least four secreted around his person at any one time.

CHAPTER FIVE – DUBLIN

IT was U1 protocol that all weapons were held in the armoury on board the Bucket, except for a few short blades that each member was allowed to keep on their person. Davidson was the Armoury Supply Sergeant now, and despite having several run-ins with Travis, so far, he hadn't been able to secure any of Travis's blades.

He found it difficult having a conversation about knife safety, while Travis brandished a wickedly sharp sword in his direction amidst his katana practice. One day he vowed he would find a way around the problem, without recourse to using Fulwood, but until then Travis kept all his blades locked in his cabin.

It wasn't long before Jeff Johnson hailed his oppo' Frank Fulwood to discuss the possible problem of John Redshaw's son Lewis.

"The boy's nineteen," explained Johnson. "Legally, he's free to do whatever the hell he wants, when he wants, where he wants."

"Yes, but he's Redshaw's son," argued Fulwood, both knowing the probable implications of that sentence.

"I know," Johnson conceded the point. For several seconds there was silence as each man contemplated Redshaw, his life, and his progeny.

The world fell apart for John Redshaw when he was unknowingly transformed by a lifeform residing within Earth's seas. It wasn't fair and it wasn't an easy ride for any of them. It ended dramatically, with Redshaw leaving Unit One by diving into the Atlantic Ocean never to be seen again. He left behind his multitude of offspring only one of which—Lewis Blaine—was male.

Johnson knew part of Fulwood's problem was his guilt

over Victoria Blaine. Fulwood had been the lead on that fateful mission. Because of the foul act his teammate had perpetrated while they were supposedly rescuing the woman, he refused to view Redshaw as a human being. Fulwood and Johnson both felt beholden to Victoria, knowing that U1 had let her down badly.

Victoria Blaine had contacted Johnson, via the phone number Redshaw had given her all those years ago. It had alerted and linked into their system. Johnson found it hard to refuse her a second time, because John had been his friend, and to his way of thinking; you do things for friends, no matter where they are, or when you last saw them. Maybe it was different in Civvy Street, but in the forces, your family were your brothers-in-arms.

Fulwood didn't think he could be so forgiving, not when he remembered his daughter was only a few years younger at that time. He'd felt like killing Redshaw, but you didn't kill a comrade who's saved your life on countless occasions. No matter how much you disagreed with their actions. You had their back because there would be a time when they had yours.

"You could tell her that he is safe, that he is well," Fulwood eventually suggested.

"She'll want to know more."

"Of course, she will. I would too, but it's that or tell her nothing. What do you think she would want? To be told something no matter how small or nothing at all?" Johnson thought about how Vivienne his wife would feel.

"You're right, and we've got the boy tagged now, so we'll be able to keep an eye on him." Fulwood nodded his agreement.

"What about the Redshaw girls? How are they all doing? You haven't mentioned them in a while."

"Vivienne says they're doing fine," replied Johnson, speaking about his wife, who was also the physiologist who worked on Redshaw's case originally and who, after several false starts, he got around to marrying. "We've lost contact with five of them and as you know six died in childhood."

"Yes, that was sad. What about the missing ones?"

"We don't know. Their trackers went off-line at various points in the last few years. T-cut checked all the data at their last known locations, but nothing turned up. Vivienne reckons they could be dead too, car accidents, surgery, things like that."

There wasn't much to discuss after this. Johnson had already relocated Xiaodan, the Chinese girl they'd rescued from slavery, and the rest of U2 were assisting the police in Ireland mopping up the criminals responsible for the trafficking ring. They ended the conference call agreeing to re-contact seven days hence at the same G.M.T. time.

Fleur Colton had joined U2 three years ago. She stood leaning against the railing, watching the blue-grey water moving from left to right as it flowed past her, out into Dublin Bay and onto the Irish sea. It'd been a long while since she had stood in this exact place, here on this spot east of the O'Connell Monument. She remembered it well. A boyfriend holding her hand, asking her to marry him and her—declining. He was married now with three boys and happy. She was pleased for him. She knew on that day that she'd broken his tender heart. It had taken him several years to find a new life mate.

She didn't regret her decision, then or now. Her ambition to serve in the RAF fulfilled, with a successful career as one of the rare breed of female pilots. The women who served as pilots in the Second World War were long forgotten by today's serving military.

Fleur had passed the exam on the second, and final attempt—one mistake was all they would allow. The RAF career had been prestigious and exciting but serving as part of

U2 was so much more. She got to fly a wide range of aircraft from DeSilva's baby to powerful fast jets.

U1 think they are the bad boys, but they don't have a clue. U2 might be land-based, but we've seen as much action as those lazy men on their Bucket. Fleur had been on the Bucket several times and didn't think it was anything special. *Yes, it has a spa, gym and pool. Yes, they have their own physiotherapist, doctor and nurse on board. Yes, they have gourmet food twenty-four-seven and travel the world.* She could do all that on land except for the travel part and that could be easily arranged, providing Johnson let her play with his personal jet.

Fleur didn't like the thought of being trapped at sea. She'd never planned to be a fish and she didn't miss it. Johnson's idiotic and out-of-date 'no women' rule still existed to this day, with Fulwood backing up his senior commander's regime. There was one exception to that rule—U2 team members. Fleur guessed trying to stop operatives from having personal lives on shore was nigh on impossible. Plus, it would be hypocritical seeing Johnson had a wife and children. *Okay, he is sort of semi-retired,* she admitted begrudgingly.

Fleur ran her fingers through her shoulder-length blonde hair. It had been three years since she had been allowed to grow it long, but she still couldn't get used to not having her military number two cut. At thirty-two, she knew men found her attractive, with her slender waist and long legs which had enabled her to fit well into aircraft designed for men, particularly the Tornado.

I should really get going. Atrax is expecting to meet me by the Spire, or the Stiffy on the Liffey as the tourists call it. Fleur moved away from O'Connell's monument, turning her back on her past, like she had before, and moving forwards up O'Connell Street.

Later that same night, Fleur and Atrax—on mission—were tracking an individual down College Street. Atrax had received a tipoff from a friend that the person they wanted was in a certain bar on the street. Fortunately, the man was easy to recognize with several gold teeth where his originals should have been. *Probably knocked out in a brawl,* Fleur correctly surmised. As they headed towards the bar, Fleur thought about the man Atrax, walking alongside her.

Atrax had been based on the Bucket for a couple of years before deciding to join Johnson in U2. Atrax wasn't his real name, it was a name given to him by those idiots in U1 because of his Greek descent. According to Baptiste—his real name—Atrax was a God in Greek mythology. He confided to Fleur, that Atrax was also the name of one of the most venomous spiders in Australia, and he quite liked the name for that reason. He supposed he could ask to be called by his given name, but it wasn't what teammates did. Almost everybody had a force's nickname either made from their name, what they did, or how they looked.

Fleur had a nickname in the RAF, she hated it and didn't tell anybody this side of civvy-land what it was. Everyone in U2 had called her Fleur from her first day as if they sensed she wouldn't be happy given a nickname, and though she derided those childish boys on the Bucket, she loved them too—as comrades.

They stopped walking, on the pretence of hugging, so as not to give the mark a clue that he was being followed. Atrax watched the man duck into a doorway.

"Did you see that? Did you see what he did before he went inside?"

Fleur had to admit she hadn't seen anything unusual before their target went through the door of the house, wrapped up as she was in Atrax's arms. The property was three doors down from where they were standing.

"He knocked on the window twice as he went towards the door."

"I didn't see or hear that," she replied, speaking in a low

tone so as not to cause attention. "When did he do that? He didn't stop walking."

"No, he did it as he walked. He swung his arm up, tapped the panes twice, then put his hand in his pocket. Obviously, a manoeuvre he has done many times before."

"I saw that. I saw him put his hand in his pocket," she said, glad that she noticed something about his behaviour.

"Yes, that was it. We'll make a spy out of you yet Fleur." Fleur was pleased. Atrax didn't say it in a patronizing way. It felt more like he was mentoring her, for which she was grateful. "Did you notice he lifted his hand higher than he needed to, to put it in his pocket?" Now she thought about it, he did look a bit odd lifting his arm high and then putting it in his pocket. She hadn't noticed the tap on the window though, which annoyed her.

"I'm guessing, if we go to the door without knocking on the window first, there will be gunfire." Fleur checked her firearm for what felt like the seventy-fourth time. She was used to handling guns. She was used to firing guns too, but she felt vulnerable wearing one on mission, in a street surrounded by so many civilians. Much of her military life had been spent either inside a plane or on an air force base. Johnson was taking a risk hiring someone like her without much combat experience. She would much rather carry a blade, like Travis St John, or Swoop as he was known in U1. Without the others knowing, she'd gone and purchased several Karambits similar to the ones used by Travis. She currently deployed two on her person—just in case.

All team members joining Johnson's employment had an induction period, part of which was spent with U1 as backup members on missions. Fleur had seen first-hand, Travis's devastating skill with a blade, and to be honest she was a little in awe of him. Him, and his muscles, and his black hair, his height and those James Bond diamond blue eyes. She sighed longingly. She couldn't remember the last time she got laid.

This won't help, daydreaming about a team member while I'm on mission, she chastised herself. Fleur was starting to appreciate how her jilted ex-boyfriend must have felt after she told him U1 was more important to her than their on-again, off-again relationship.

Atrax and Fleur approached the property quietly using their recognised non-verbal hand signals. Fleur edged around the near side of the building, whilst Atrax strolled towards the front door, tapping twice on the glass beforehand to ensure he wouldn't be shot on sight.

The door opened and Atrax stepped through into the dim pool of light within. Relieved Atrax hadn't been shot, Fleur hurriedly moved to the back of the building, opening and closing the low garden gate as softly as it would allow. She moved up the overgrown path towards the kitchen door, moving shrubs aside where they hampered her progress.

With a hand on the door, she paused, listening to the sounds inside. There were no loud voices. No alarm raised. She couldn't understand why. Surely, there should be shouting, screaming even, and then gun shots, but nothing.

Moving her hand down to the doorknob, she turned it in a painfully slow arc, pulling the door towards her until a whisper of light fell on the back path, revealing the weeds suffocating what was once a pretty cottage garden. Nothing. Gingerly, she pulled the door further.

It was a bit of an anti-climax finding no one in the kitchen, she stepped up into the room, closing the door gently behind her. Thinking she could hear voices coming from the next room, she approached, keeping her knees flexed and her body low as she'd been taught. Removing her gun from its holster under her shoulder, she checked the safety was off and continued to the door on the left, inviting her to open it.

At the door she froze. Now she heard raised voices. She heard swearing. Someone was having a go at someone else in the room beyond the door, and the other person was not saying a word.

Could they be yelling at Atrax? If they were, he was in a whole heap of trouble. She hoped it wasn't him. She hoped it was the bad guys having a go at the man they'd seen entering the building a few minutes before them. And then the other person spoke, and Fleur breathed a sigh of relief. It wasn't Atrax, Baptiste, whatever. *He must be somewhere else in the house.* If so, then Fleur needed to move, because any moment one of those men could come bursting into the kitchen and find her holding a gun. They wouldn't think twice about shooting her, regardless of gender, that much was sure, based on their current criminal activity.

Fleur spied a door to the right and moved towards it, shutting it behind her just as someone opened the opposite door. She'd walked straight into a cupboard. She had nowhere to go, all she could do was wait it out. She listened as the heated conversation continued in the kitchen beyond her temporary confinement.

"I told yer. Don't come around here. There's been people snooping. Asking questions. I don't want anyone coming back here. Finding us. Ruining everything." To emphasise his point, the annoyed man must have shoved the focus of his attention. Fleur heard something strike the kitchen table. There was a man's groan.

"Here! You watch who ye're shoving," retaliated the other man. Fleur didn't need to see the conversation to know, just from the words, how angry these men were getting.

"I'll shove who I damn well want when they jeopardise our activities." Fleur heard the click of a pistol as the safety was taken off. "How do'yer feel now? Yer cocky sod!"

Fleur could imagine the man holding the gun to the other

man's head. "You bring trouble to my door and it's the last trouble you bring anyone. Understand?" He stated, brooking no argument. The man under threat swallowed loudly and Fleur swallowed too, her anxiety at the escalating situation trying to get the better of her.

Where the hell is Atrax? She knew he wouldn't enter the room with an armed assailant and a gun held in readiness. He would wait till the man calmed down, or his subordinate took him out first. She wondered where Atrax had gone.

Did he go straight upstairs? Is he searching the house as we agreed? Is he outside the other door? Without knowing the answer to any of her questions, she waited, thankful that she'd learnt that particular strategy from Davidson aka Texas.

"Fleur? Fleur? You there?" Came a tinny voice in her right ear. *Atrax, thank goodness,* Fleur sagged with relief. She'd been so caught up in the moment, in the struggle going on in the kitchen, on the other side of the cupboard door. She'd forgotten all about the comms device plugged into her right ear, so used to wearing earbuds twenty-four-seven listening to iTunes.

"If you can't speak, tap the device like in training," Atrax reminded her. It was basic one-oh-one procedure when caught in a situation where you might be overheard. Fleur tapped her comms bud. "Roger that," came the reply followed by his debrief. "I've searched the house upstairs. There are four bedrooms. Three of them are locked, but from the sound of it, there are people inside two of the rooms. Judging by the noises I heard, at least two of them are engaged in some type of sexual act."

Seems like everyone is getting it on but me, she groused, then shivered as the implications of what Atrax had said sank in. The thought of slavery in this day and age appalled her. *Slavery ended hundreds of years ago, didn't it? It didn't happen nowadays and certainly not in downtown Dublin.* Yet here it was almost staring her in the face, and she couldn't avoid it. *When had criminals decided dealing in people was better, more profitable, than dealing in drugs?*

"I'm coming downstairs now," Atrax advised.

Please don't ask where I am. Please don't ask where I am. Please don't ask where I am, Fleur recited. She was never going to live this down, getting trapped in a kitchen cupboard of all places.

"Are you inside the house? One tap for yes, two for no." Fleur tapped once. "Inside, fine. Are you near the kitchen?" She tapped once.

"Good. How many people are in the kitchen?" Atrax asked. Fleur tapped once. "Two, confirm two," Fleur repeated her reply.

"How many guns?" He asked next. *How many guns?* She didn't know the precise amount. She knew there was one gun, and obviously, the man being threatened didn't have a gun or they would have started shooting, but whether the aggressor had more than one gun, she couldn't tell. Her hesitation told Atrax she wasn't sure, so he rephrased his question.

"Are there guns in the kitchen?" She tapped once for yes. "Is it on one of the men?" One tap. "Is it on both of the men?" Two taps. Atrax confirmed. "One of the men is holding a gun or guns." One tap.

Fleur felt helpless in the kitchen cupboard. She felt so stupid. With hindsight, she should have stepped out of the house, maybe re-entered through the front door like her colleague. She wondered why Atrax hadn't been accosted when he entered the premises. She supposed she would find out the reason later, if there was a later, and she hadn't been shot. For now, she had to wait for an opportunity to act.

Atrax crept towards the kitchen through what was once the parlour. He stopped on the other side of the door, placing his ear to it to listen to the men inside. One of them was angry. He was haranguing the other, for being stupid and inferior. The other man just took the verbal beating. Atrax wouldn't take that from any man. He'd kill the person who told him he was stupid. Maybe not kill, he amended, but injure them enough so they wouldn't say it again. He smiled, a wicked mischievous smile and decided it was Showtime.

Grasping the door handle, ensuring his Beretta was ready to go, Atrax opened the door and shot the man holding the gun in one smooth motion in the leg. The man fell, grabbing his bleeding leg with one hand and yelling. Still holding his pistol in his other hand, he fired. Luckily, the angle of the bullet's trajectory was off, it went straight through the kitchen window—narrowly missing the other man's head—out into the garden beyond. The second man fainted.

The man with the gun injury didn't notice. He was busy screaming his head off and jumping around the kitchen holding his leg.

"Yer bastard you shot me!" He yelled in total disbelief. This, from the same man who moments earlier, had no qualms about shooting his colleague in the head.

Several loud thumps came from upstairs. People unlocked doors. They fled down the stairs, disappearing out into the street. Sensibly, not one came to investigate the disturbance.

Fleur came out of hiding like a jack-in-the-box. Gun held in both hands, arms pointing at the man who'd been shot and who was now bleeding on the floor. The second man, coming around from his initial shock and knowing the game was up, sat up, raised his hands, and put them on top of his head.

"Fleur," said Atrax, smiling over at her. "Call the Garda Síochána, would you?" Fleur reached into her inside jacket pocket, and pulling out her mobile, dialled the emergency number of the Irish Police. All their mobile phones were untraceable to the authorities, thanks to an app courtesy of T-cut, though he had included back door access for emergencies.

Fleur provided the information requested by the response call centre until they asked for her name, then she ended the call saying, "a well-meaning friend." All the while, the man

Atrax had shot, was still screaming, "You bastard, you bastard," in the background. She was pretty sure the Garda would take her call seriously and still attend, given the man's shouted profanities and obvious pain.

Atrax held himself in check. He could see Fleur's adrenaline levels were high in the wake of the action, despite it being brief. She had a tremor in her voice and her movements were edgy, not fluid, and relaxed. He'd almost said, "Good Girl" to reassure her, but thought that might sound patronising, even if he did mean it. Fleur wasn't a natural in these missions, her strengths were in combat flying and Intel, but they made a good team regardless.

Fleur caught Atrax checking out the door she'd come through.

"A cleaning cupboard heh?" She nodded, as she bent to tie-wrap the second man to the kitchen taps. The first man wasn't going anywhere. He'd slumped to the ground groaning, a puddle of blood growing on the floor.

"Good hiding place," Atrax enthused, making her feel slightly less embarrassed about her choice of hiding places.

They watched from a discreet distance as the Garda arrived, blue sirens wailing as they surrounded the slavers' house. The uninjured man was arrested and taken away in an unmarked van. There was a short wait, then two ambulances arrived at once. The man Atrax had shot, was taken to hospital under armed guard in one of them.

Fleur watched in dismay as a female police officer led five young women out of the house into the second waiting ambulance. Atrax glanced at the beautiful woman standing next to him, to see how she was coping with the situation. He wasn't unduly worried. Fleur was a seasoned U2 professional, but she was still a woman and could still feel strong emotions at such injustice. He, on the other hand, had long since left his emotions firmly behind a closed iron door in his mind. He didn't plan to unlock it any time soon.

85

"Good work both of you," concluded Johnson, as the two of them debriefed the mission in Dublin. "The Garda found enough clues in the house, together with the girls' evidence, to track the importation route back to Albania this time."

"What about the girls they found?" Fleur asked.

Johnson paused for a moment to collect his thoughts. "Four of the girls are being repatriated back to Albania and their families. They were fourteen and had been missing for over two years."

Fleur gasped involuntarily hearing this news. She brought her hand up to her mouth to cover her slip. It didn't look good to be so affected in her line of work. She was supposed to be tough and able to take stressful things in her stride. Regardless, Atrax and Johnson caught Fleur's reaction.

Johnson was concerned. How would Fleur take the information regarding the fifth girl? He stalled, not wanting to cause her more distress. He realised he had no right to withhold such information from his team members who'd risked their lives to secure the girl's freedom.

"What about the fifth girl? Where was she from? Was she Albanian too? Is she going back home?"

"No, she wasn't Albanian," he replied, dreading his next words. "She was from the Middle East. Yemen to be exact." Johnson waited to let that information, and all that it signified, sink in before imparting the final piece. "There is no easy way to say this, but she committed suicide while she was free." Johnson paused again. "She left a note. She decided her parents, her family, would never accept her home again, now she had, in her own words, been soiled by an infidel. Suicide was her only way of keeping her honour and her family's respect."

Fleur stifled a shudder at the tragic news. They'd rescued the girl, only for her to end her life—it was heartbreaking. She hung her head and looked at the floor, there was nothing really to say. Tears fell from her cheeks onto her trousers.

Atrax put an arm out and placed it on her shoulder in a comforting gesture.

That night Fleur thought about the girl from Yemen. She could relate to her feeling sullied and unclean, given her own experience with her stepfather. That her family, would feel dishonoured and shamed by a life forced upon her was troubling. That feeling was unknown to Fleur, who regardless of her past troubles, now lived a good life. She knew her mother loved her, she just didn't believe her or want to believe what had occurred. Whereas the girl's parents believed her but couldn't bring themselves to forgive what had happened. It was a hard lesson to learn, and her heart ached for the girl's lost life.

Atrax meanwhile, had found the nearest bar and started drinking. For all his hard edge and unemotional detachment, he still had a heart. He endeavoured to fight for the right side and God help those who stood against him.

Johnson knew both operatives would need time to assimilate the information he'd given them before they could move on emotionally. He'd let them have a few days R & R and then give them an easier mission to handle. Perhaps, some bodyguard detail or shadowing position, he had plenty of those on his books.

CHAPTER SIX – SALZBURG

Lewis Blaine was getting fed up with Stuttgart. It wasn't the city. The city and its surroundings were fine. He liked walking around the streets, through the park, to the zoo, and even up the hill overlooking the city to sit in the café on the top of T.V. tower. He positively loved and drooled over the Porsche and Mercedes museums.

No, it was his boss, Hannah. Lewis was finding her behaviour overwhelming. She was becoming too possessive. She hung around him full-time, both at work and during most of his leisure hours. Frankly, she wasn't that exciting as a person or a love interest. He thought back to Madeleine. She'd been exciting, and adventurous, but he'd reached the sad conclusion that he'd just been work to her. Finding that out had dented his heart.

It was time to move on. He'd had space and time to think these last few months working in Stuttgart—in between Hannah—and realised that he was searching for something. He didn't know what, but there was something, or someone, messing with his thoughts and he was determined to find answers. Because he had a conscience, he gave a week's notice at the bar, despite not needing to, and said goodbye to Hannah and several of the waitresses who had come on strong to him over his time there.

He had numerous regular customers too, mostly female. Several would have been upset, probably cried if he told them he was leaving, so he didn't. Hannah was distraught, she tried to get Lewis to stay. She offered a tempting wage increase. When that didn't work, she begged him to move in with her. He declined, and because he didn't want anyone to know when he left, he worked the whole shift on Friday night, leaving early Saturday morning before the sun was up.

He'd saved enough money to get the S-Bahn train from Hauptbahnhof station. He smiled up at the iconic twelve-story tower, a symbol of the city's success, a rotating illuminated Mercedes star sign lighting his way. Stepping through the entrance, located inside one of the huge archways, Lewis was surprised by the size of the main hall and the height of the ceiling. He was aware there was a massive building project underway in the station, from information gleaned listening to customers who patronized Hannah's bar. Evidence of the huge reconstruction work was everywhere. He located the services counter, to the right of the entrance. Between the automatic ticket dispensers, a huge map of Germany and the countries which bordered it were displayed.

Up till now, Lewis didn't know where he was heading. He knew it was East, but he hadn't thought much further than that. His eyes moved over the wall map and settled on Austria, and in particular, Salzburg, which lay just inside its country's border. Running his finger down the map, the route by train seemed to be straightforward and direct.

He left the map and walked to the counter with a plan in his head to buy a ticket first to Munich, and then maybe, Austria later. As he moved away from the wall, he felt a bizarre yearning when he thought of the town of Salzburg. It was odd because he'd never been there, didn't even know what the place looked like. *So, why am I standing in the middle of this hall feeling homesick?* Lewis couldn't understand it. In the past, he'd always followed his instincts. They had always served him right, so he took notice of them now and spoke to the counter attendant regarding travel to Austria.

The journey wasn't as straightforward as the simplified map suggested. To get to Austria, he'd need to change trains at Munich, a trip of two hours twenty, and it would cost him a lot more. Lewis knew Munich was famous for its annual

Oktoberfest celebration and its beer halls. Lewis had reckoned finding bar work there would be easy. Despite his original intention, he didn't stop at Munich. Instead he boarded a second train to Salzburg.

Stepping down onto the platform, felt like coming home to Lewis as he arrived in Salzburg—the right place at the right time. He just didn't know why. Easing his backpack onto his shoulders he headed out of the station and followed his nose to the nearest source of food. He was famished. He'd been travelling seven hours, and apart from a drink and a packet of crisps on the train, he'd had nothing in the way of a meal since the day before.

He settled into the window seat of a cafe opposite a shopping precinct and did a spot of people-watching. He needed to find an employer and a bed for the night. He had just enough euros left to purchase a meal and pay for a room for a couple of nights. The two train tickets had cost a lot more than he budgeted for, leaving him short on options.

The sound of heated conversation rose behind him, and he turned to see two members of staff arguing. The tension rose further, as did the voices. All customers' eyes were riveted on the drama unfolding in the room. Then with a tearing sound, the waitress ripped her apron off, gave her boss the middle finger and stormed out. Lewis smiled. *Finding employment here might not be so difficult after all.* He rose from his chair and approached the teary-eyed manager.

That was a week ago, now Lewis was employed in the cafe in the waitress's place and although he couldn't speak much German or any Austrian, he managed quite well. He liked the city, its claim to fame being Mozart. He loved riding the funicular up the side of the hill to the cemetery. Here folk were buried vertically to save space and allow more relatives to be buried alongside each other. He thought that was neat and cost-effective too.

Like Stuttgart, the women here were comfortable around

him. He'd already had to dissuade a couple whose flirting got out of hand on the premises. And then she appeared.

He was in the process of clearing the table in the window, where he had sat not seven days earlier, when a young woman, roughly his age came in. Lewis didn't notice her at first, nor she him. She sat right at the back of the room, almost hidden. Someone else took her order because the tables at the back were not his patch.

His new employer was wise and knew a good thing when she saw it. She made sure that her customers saw it too. She gave Lewis tables to work which were highly visible from the outside. As a result, this attracted more clientele to her establishment. Soon the place was bustling. There was hardly anywhere to sit on most days and people started filling the high stalls and counters that ran along one wall.

Lewis's customers were settled and enjoying a relaxing meal this lunchtime. Meanwhile, the people at the back of the café appeared to be running their waitress ragged. Lewis stepped in, offering to give Giselle a hand, reassuring her that he would hand over any tips. That was when he saw the most amazing girl.

Their eyes made contact. Neither seemed able to tear their gaze away. Lewis imagined this was what love, at first sight, must feel like. As he was working, he couldn't do much about his soaring feelings. He kept glancing over to where the girl sat in the dim lighting looking back at him. He knew her. He was sure he knew her, but where from? Had she been at a school where he studied? Had she lived somewhere he'd lived? He had to know. He was about to speak to her when another person entered the cafe, a man. He sat down without asking at her table. Lewis's opportunity to speak vanished and his own tables became busy with new people and new orders.

He couldn't believe he missed her exit. He wanted to run out into the street and call for her, but he couldn't, he didn't know her name. He didn't know where she went or where she lived. And then panic hit him. She might not even live in Salzburg or Austria for that matter. He might never see her again. Then, he remembered the feeling in his chest. The feeling that told him this was the right place. He now recognized what it was telling him. She was here. She lived here. And knowing that, Lewis knew, she would be back.

He worked through the rest of the day in a blur, taking orders, forgetting orders, apologizing for not doing orders, and providing orders people hadn't actually requested. His customers, mainly women, took it all in their stride. They smiled sweetly at Lewis and told him it didn't matter.

Jeff Johnson sat pondering the situation regarding Lewis Blaine. *What is the lad up too? Where is he going? Is he trying to find his father? Well, good luck with that one.* Jeff hadn't seen Redshaw since that fateful day nineteen years ago. When, taking permission from his Commander and friend, John Redshaw leapt over the railing of the Bucket, and like a salmon cast himself into the sea.

Johnson could have sworn he'd seen a fishtail appear just before Redshaw dived for the last time, but over the years he convinced himself it was fanciful thinking. *Yes, the man had gills and webbed digits, but fins and a tail? That's science fiction.* He'd tried locating Redshaw in the early years, investigating odd news items about unusual sightings at sea. More a hobby than a mission and none of the reports amounted to a hill of beans.

What about the boy? He reflected, his thoughts never straying far from Lewis. He'd observed him growing up over the years—from a distance naturally. He hadn't needed money. His rich senator grandfather saw to that. Anything the boy wanted, he got. Yet despite all the trappings he never became a spoilt brat. *He'll make a fine man. Make Redshaw proud—if he knew*. The thought made Johnson smile and think of his children.

He had hoped his son Joel would follow him into the army, but it didn't seem likely given his tech obsession. Having them both at the same school made it easier for Johnson to keep an eye on things. If Joel wondered why his busy father suddenly found time to visit him face-to-face, rather than online, as he had in past years, he never commented on it.

Johnson's second child was a daughter his wife had named Odette, she was eight years old. Despite his preference for boarding school, Odette still lived at home with them. Vivienne felt that boarding children out from home under the age of eleven wasn't a good idea. She had only acquiesced to Joel leaving because he asked to go. Joel had gone to his father's old school in Edgbaston, and Johnson planned to send Odette there too, with Joel supporting her.

Thoughts of his family brought his thinking round to Frank Fulwood and his daughter, Mya. Originally, one of Johnson's golden rules for Unit One members was 'no family ties.' That all changed after Fulwood got kidnapped and U1 discovered Frank had a daughter hidden away. Then there were Redshaw's numerous offspring and finally, his relationship with Vivienne Oakwood, the expert brought in to salvage Redshaw's mess. Little by little Johnson's rules sank into the waves, never to re-surface—much like Redshaw. He'd tried to discourage relationships in the active Units, but some team members and crew had land-based families nowadays.

Johnson asked Fulwood if he wanted his job running U1 when he decided to step down as commander and start a family fourteen years ago. He informed Frank that he planned to innovate a second unit, imaginatively entitled Unit Two. Fulwood didn't accept immediately. He told Johnson he needed time to consider the proposition. He had responsibilities and wanted to discuss them with Mya who was then only twelve.

Mya knew, even at that young age, that her father's heart lay with U1. He loved her too, of that she had no doubt, but it wasn't enough for her daddy, her 'Action Man daddy' as she called him. He deserved a promotion, needed it to validate his worth and demonstrate the faith Johnson had in him to do the job well.

Mya, now twenty-six, married and divorced, still wasn't privy to the specifics of her father's job. He flew around the world, worked unusual hours, and got paid obscene amounts of money. She knew he rescued people. When she discovered it wasn't anything *too illegal*—he wouldn't tell her more—she supported him wholeheartedly.

The two men agreed the mission requests would come to Johnson, for him to assess and decide whether their input was warranted. In front of him on his desk at the moment were a pile of requests, waiting for him to re-arrange them into date order.

"I could do with a personal assistant to keep this paperwork in check," he grumbled.

Johnson understood every team member's skills and abilities. He accepted those jobs which would benefit everyone. Currently, he was considering a mission in Hawaii. A case of a missing person, the man had been AWOL for years. It was an unusual case of heir-hunting, which could have been achieved using cheaper people, except this person didn't want to be found—much like Redshaw. With a career in the US military as a D'boy, or Delta Force, the Army equivalent of the Navy Seals, and specialising in undercover work, Johnson knew he'd be a hard one to locate, let alone encourage to come home.

Johnson contemplated each Unit and each operative in his mind. Either Unit had the ability to complete the task competently. U1 was more gung-ho, more shoot-first, ask-later. This mission was going to require subtlety, and though he'd been slow to admit it, a woman could sometimes do what a man could not. His wife had taught him early on that he'd been wrong in that respect.

Regardless of this admission—his admiration for Fleur and his wife's haranguing—Johnson wouldn't be budged on his insistence of, 'No Women living on board the Bucket.' He felt he'd relaxed this rule enough by allowing Vivienne, and later Fleur, on board during daylight hours. In addition to those serving onboard having family on land.

Then there was the case of Sebastian Verde's missing sister, who was discovered working in the ship's engineering department, masquerading as a man, all those years ago. She'd convinced everybody that she, was a he.

Nowadays, Johnson insisted all employees undertook a full medical before the commencement of duties, whatever their role on board. Michael Tobin, the Irish-born registered nurse, and paramedic based on the Bucket, took that role very seriously, insisting that he couldn't face another situation like last time. Apart from those incidences, no women lived on board the Bucket. Frank Fulwood never questioned his superior's decision.

Turning his mind back to the pending mission in Hawaii, Johnson decided Fleur and Atrax could handle it. He contacted them, then arranged airport flights, transfers and accommodation. He let the client know that U2 had accepted the task.

"I still think it's pretty vague," sulked Fleur, as their first-class flight landed at Honolulu airport eighteen hours later.

Johnson had booked them rooms at the Sheraton Hotel in Waikiki. The hotel sat at an angle to the famous beach with an infinity pool on the first floor making it look like it was nestled in the bay. As usual, it was first class for U2. Fleur found it hard to remain sulky for long given the sumptuous luxury her boss had bestowed upon them. His reasoning behind choosing Waikiki as their base, he informed them, was because it was the major destination for any individual escaping from America.

These were mainly male, men with warrants out for their arrest, or people needing to get away from their commitments, as in the case of Austin Novak. Despite being a seasoned veteran of special ops, Austin had run away like a teenager from an over-bearing tyrannical father, and because he was an adult the Police weren't interested. The best private detectives had been hired to find him without any luck. However, this year, things were about to change. Novak Senior had passed away seven years ago, and the legal authorities were about to declare Austin Novak officially dead, as the seven-year statute was about to be realised.

When Austin, out of the blue, contacted his home five months ago, the call was traced and found to have originated from the island of Oahu, part of the Hawaiian chain. Waikiki beach was where most human flotsam ended up. The weather hardly ever turned cold, even in January the coldest month, it was a balmy twenty-three degrees.

That first evening found Fleur and Atrax strolling along the pavements in the guise of taking a romantic walk. In reality, they were doing a sweep of the area. They'd discussed possible avenues for study, memorising Austin Novak's face so they could identify him. The last picture taken of Novak showed him clean-shaven in military uniform. He was wearing a Delta Force shoulder insignia on one sleeve. It depicted the famous Fair-bairn-Sykes fighting knife inside an arrowhead outline on a red background. How Johnson had secured the photo was a mystery to Atrax since special forces never appeared in uniform.

These days, it was more likely the man in question sported a full beard and wore clothing that probably wouldn't be amiss outside a thrift shop, rather than the ivy-league heritage he came from.

As night fell so the tourists on the pavements dwindled,

moving into the safer bars, restaurants, and clubs up and down the main drag. Curious individuals emerged from places where they'd been holed up during the day, away from the prying eyes of the law. They began setting up blankets and sleeping bags, some pushing trolleys, others with backpacks, a few resorting to begging from passers-by, while the majority attempted to get their heads down for the night in the safer lit areas.

Fleur had thought about saving up to take a holiday in the Hawaiian islands. She never expected to be there so soon on a mission. They each studied the resigned faces of the homeless before them, who'd travelled on a one-way ticket to paradise, and apart from the climate, found it no different to home. Hawaii was one of the most expensive places to live in the United States. Many of the native population were unable to afford homes on the islands due to the influx of wealthy ex-pats, who built extravagant homes on their prized but limited land.

Fleur could see why. As the evening drew on, the lights from the many hotels and bars across the bay made the water sparkle. It looked magical and inviting. The pale beach sloped gently down into the azure blue making it a safe place to relax, play or swim.

While Fleur contemplated the local economics of the state, Atrax took in the differing stages of homelessness. From the newly arrived, unkempt individuals who'd probably been here mere weeks and were still trying to shave and wash every few days, to the hardened characters with years of despondency on their worn-out beard-infested faces. Their target tonight was one of those. The faceless nameless legion with a professional edge to their state of vagrancy.

These individuals knew where handouts came from. Who would give them a bite to eat, or a place to crash. A number of them, already performing criminal activities, before they left their homeland for warmer climes, had honed their pick-pocket and shop-lifting skills, till they resembled nothing less than

Fagin. Needles and haystacks sprang to mind, as Atrax surveyed more and more empty faces in the growing darkness.

They'd travelled along the entire beach-side of the pavement, or side-walk as it was called in America, acknowledged Fleur. Then promenaded back on the opposite urban side, doing the expected touristy thing, when Atrax, on a spontaneous impulse glanced down a side alley. Folk weren't just setting up their mobile overnight 'homes' on the main street, but also down the darkened passageways which led to it too. It was most likely that their target was ensconced in the dark, rather than out on the brightly lit roads if he didn't want to be found. They couldn't very well saunter down the alleys. The places fairly screamed 'tourist beware.'

Atrax squeezed Fleur's hand in their guise of a romantic couple. She glanced down at their joined hands, then up at her tall partner, and caught the motion as he flicked his eyes to the left. She followed his gaze, catching sight of movement beyond in the gloom. Her head nodded imperceptibly as she agreed they needed to investigate the alleys. They continued their casual stroll. Unless a person was security trained they wouldn't have spotted their non-verbal communication.

Atrax was surprised when moments later, Fleur squeezed his hand in turn. *She can't have spotted the target already,* he thought in disbelief, and he was right. This time, he followed her gaze and nodded his understanding. *How the hell did I miss that?* Atrax wondered, indirectly taking in the tableau behind them through a shop reflection. They headed straight back to the hotel, their tail in hot pursuit.

"A tail?" Johnson repeated, over the secure video link.

"That's right and we only landed this afternoon," confirmed Atrax. They both came to the same conclusion.

"Then there must be a leak. The most likely place is the solicitor's company asking for U1's assistance." Nobody knew U2 existed. Clients didn't need to know.

"What do you plan to do?"

"Don't worry, it won't affect the mission," Atrax answered smoothly, his demeanour close-lipped and calm as he and Johnson finished their call.

Atrax was irritated that he hadn't noticed the man shadowing them. The man, who even now stood outside their hotel, thinking he'd got away with his deception, leant against a lamppost pretending to read a newspaper.

"Atrax, I know what you're thinking," said Fleur, entering his room through their open adjoining door.

"Just a little bit? He wheedled, not needing to deny her assessment of his aggressive thoughts.

"No!"

"Just a tiny, weeny bit?" He held his thumb and index finger an inch apart to emphasize his point.

"No," Fleur repeated with mock sternness. "You know what happened last time. Besides, we can easily give him the slip now we know he's there." Atrax's face fell.

"You're no fun," he grumbled, sulking.

"I know. Come on, I'll buy you a drink to make it up to you before we start our alley search tonight." Atrax begrudgingly accepted Fleur's offer.

Their first foray into the back alleys of Waikiki provided no clues to Austin Novak's whereabouts, but they were not deterred. They knew homeless folk led transient lives moving from place to place. Here folk were restricted to remaining on the island unless they had money or contacts. Novak had neither—or so they thought.

After three nights of searching, out-witting their slow-minded watchdog, Fleur decided they needed a different tack. They'd been speaking directly to people, giving them money in exchange for information, in the forlorn hope word might spread to Novak. These people were wary of strangers. They often took to telling stories and could make up lies until the cows came home and went to bed. There was no proof anyone told them the truth.

"Okay, you can take out Pluto," Fleur agreed, flopping onto Atrax's sofa later that night.

"Pluto?"

"Our watchdog," grumped Fleur, crossing her arms. "I'm pretty sure Pluto is putting folk off, even though we've managed to give him the slip every time. It's clear he's scaring the locals just by hanging around."

"Ah, You named him?" There was a pause. "How much?" He asked, eager to cause the irritating bug some damage. The man, Pluto, was an affront to Atrax's professional sensibilities. Being stalked like a punter got under his skin.

Noticing Atrax was quiet, and probably busy considering his various temporary maiming methods, Fleur added.

"Just enough so he stops following us."

"I can do that," grinned Atrax wickedly.

The following night, Pluto was missing from his usual haunt by the street light across from the hotel. When Fleur knocked and entered through their connecting door, Atrax almost fell off his bed. He didn't know whether what he was seeing was shocking or hilarious.

"One word, just one word," Fleur cautioned, "and you'll take my place." Atrax slammed his hand over his mouth to stop any further sound escaping.

In his doorway, stood a creature who Atrax almost didn't recognise. In flat dirty pumps, wearing shabby loose clothes, without make-up, her hair messed up deliberately, and a thin blanket under her arm, his teammate stood, an absolute picture of rejection and loneliness. She'd even gone as far as smearing her mascara to stain her pale cheeks. She looked more like a nineteen-year-old run-away than her real age of thirty-two—which was her intent.

"Are you sure you want to do this?" He asked when he'd sobered up enough to speak. Fleur nodded, not trusting herself to say yes, when she wanted to shout, "No."

Fleur Colton was no stranger to this state of being, she'd

been here before many years ago. She knew the risks and hazards of being an unattached girl alone in the under-class world. Her team members never knew that she spent nearly two years sleeping rough in the city, after she ran away from her abusive step-father at the age of fourteen. Her mother—despite loving her daughter—never believed her. When she told her of the times he came into her room, her mother said Fleur was jealous, making it up, but Fleur knew the truth. Knowing the truth, didn't save her from the nightmares that still haunted her dreams.

Her mother's relationship ended within weeks of Fleur's return home. Escalating rows, and finally extreme domestic violence when Fleur refused to be coerced, resulted in the Police and Social Services becoming involved.

As if sensing her negative memories, Atrax rose from the sofa and came over to her.

"I'll be there, even if you can't see me. I'll be there," he reassured her, touching her lightly on her arm. She looked down at his hand, then up into his sincere brown eyes and nodded. She trusted Atrax with her life.

Fleur had picked out an unused sleeping spot the previous evening. She settled down in the doorway of the closed down nail-bar, one street back from the beach-side road. She huddled under her blanket with the two cushions she'd smuggled out of her room. The first she sat on, to stop her bottom getting cold and going numb on the concrete step beneath her. The second she rested at the side of her head on the wall and leant against it—she wasn't ready to lie down and sleep yet. It wasn't until her third night sleeping rough, their sixth on the island, that someone approached her.

"You ok girl?" Whispered a scratchy voice. It belonged to a skinny thirty-something man crouching down in front of her. Fleur opened her eyes and froze. He reminded her slightly of her bastard step-father, though the word father should never have been added to his title. The man didn't look underfed, despite his slender build. He had a shop-bought cigarette hanging loosely from his stained fingers. She shuffled upright, hoping Atrax was somewhere nearby, being frosty, as he always put it.

CHAPTER SEVEN – WAIKIKI

"G IRLY," he whispered again, adding a Y to the end of the word. The tone of his voice gave her the shivers. She remembered other nights where the same letter was added to the same word. Staying in role—it wasn't difficult—she answered, pretending to be half asleep.

"Who are you?" Her voice naturally vulnerable and tremulous. "What do you want?" She looked up into the gimlet eyes from the edge of her blanket, noting his English accent.

"Me?" He pointed to himself with both thumbs. "I don't want nuffin. I was just checking you were okay. Seen you here a couple of nights now. Been wondering to myself, what's a sweet thing like you doing sleeping in a doorway?"

Fleur felt contaminated. The man wasn't on the face of it saying anything odd or impolite, but the words which crept in like 'sweet thing' wasn't something someone said, unless they had already considered the idea. She had to answer, or he'd think it strange.

"Ran away," she announced as if it was the most natural thing in the world to do. Then, to prevent further questioning, she burst into tears. It wasn't difficult, she dredged up an episode from her past and the tears came. It put paid to any more questions from the man, like how did she run away in Hawaii when she too clearly had a British accent?

"There, there, sweet thing," he crooned, inching closer to pat her on the shoulder in a brotherly type of way. Her sobs subsided to gulps of air as she appeared to get her emotions under control. At this point, the man began his tried and tested grooming strategy.

"What you need," he stated in a confiding tone and looking

around as if neither of them was safe. "Is someone to watch out for you. Someone to take care of things. To be there for you when things get rough, or rather rougher." He used these last three words deliberately, knowing from experience that they increased his victim's anxiety. He was pleased when she answered exactly as expected.

"Get rougher?" She repeated, adding an edge to her voice that she knew he was waiting for.

"Why yes," he asserted, breaking into his long-practised spiel. "There are lots of dangers lurking in the dark." He stopped talking, glancing left and right again as if checking for demons, or the like. Fleur almost laughed and gave the game away, but she held the blanket up over her mouth, so he missed her smile. The man continued—unaware the player was being played.

"All manner of strange people fill this island, from drug dealers to sex fiends and mad men." Fleur's eyes widened in horror, at least to him they did. In reality, Atrax had stepped into view behind her supposed rescuer. He stood, a menacing silhouette in the darkness. Oblivious, and deep into his patter the man gave her his offer. "I could look after you. I could keep you safe." Fleur sincerely doubted it. She knew exactly what he had in mind, and it didn't include keeping her safe, it involved making money out of her.

The man almost shot two feet into the air from his crouching position, and that was impressive, as Atrax announced his arrival.

"She is safe," Atrax boomed. The man clutched his chest in terror as he rallied from his physical shock. For a moment, Fleur thought the man might be having a heart attack. He recovered well, and grovelling, moved to one side to get a better look at his new adversary. He had undoubtedly been at the receiving end of this type of treatment before, for he knew how to react to a superior.

"Sorry, sorry," he whined, bobbing his head like some kind

of duck. "I didn't mean to step on your patch, Sir," he mumbled, mistakenly thinking the sweet thing he was interested in already had her own pimp. "Of course, she's yours," he conceded like he knew such was the case.

When Atrax failed to speak further but continued glaring at him like he was about to slice and dice, the man retreated into the dark alley as fast as his skinny legs could carry him. Atrax marched over to Fleur, towering over her like some missing apocalyptic horseman. *He is magnificent.*

"This stops now!" Atrax declared, staring down at Fleur who shook her head in negation.

"We can't stop, we've only just started." Fleur's voice was low and quiet, as she checked out that no other people were listening nearby.

"I am not comfortable with you putting yourself at risk like this every night."

"What else can we do? You can't do it, look at you. No one in their right mind is going to approach you in a dark alley." Atrax fumed, she had a point.

"Then we find somewhere else, somewhere others hang out, rather than this shady hellhole." Fleur was surprised to find Atrax so ruffled. Normally, he coped quite well with her putting herself in danger. She didn't know what was different in this situation. There was something he wasn't telling her.

"Okay, we'll do it your way. I'll go somewhere brighter. I'll do a bit of begging. Who knows maybe I'll earn some money?" That remark earned her a scowl. They didn't need money and Fleur knew that. Atrax wasn't sure why she was taunting him. Not trusting himself to say more, he nodded and backed away into the dark. Fleur stood, gathered her possessions, and moved on to the road facing the beach.

It was much brighter here, louder, with more people. Fleur found an empty spot to set down her blanket. She took out a Chinese takeaway food tray from her bag and laid it on the ground in front of her. *If only I'd brought my guitar,* she reflected. *I could have played and felt more at ease with begging. It feels uncomfortable pretending to be poor when I'm not.*

Atrax however, was much happier with Fleur's new position. He settled himself across the road in one of the many tourist bars which littered the streets. Ordering himself a large beer, he relaxed and took on the appearance of a contented tourist.

Two days later, Fleur saw him. Austin Novak looked awful. He had lost every ounce of weight that made him look healthy. His gaunt skin hung off his bones and his head looked like a skull. This was a young man, aged by homelessness. In addition, he sported a long unkempt beard, and hair the same length which hung in rat-tail strands down his back. He wore typical army boots minus the shoelaces, and a long trench coat with standard trousers and T-shirt beneath.

Under one arm, was a rolled up grey sleeping bag, which had probably once been white and belonged to a young girl, judging by the faded My Little Pony theme across it. This came complete with a matching pillow. This man wasn't bothered by the pictures on his bedclothes, he needed to be warm at night and that was his only criteria. Fleur doubted he fit well inside the bedding. The one ray of brightness in Novak's ensemble was the guitar slung across his back.

Novak walked down the pavement on the beach side of Waikiki. He treated Fleur to fleeting eye contact as he passed her place, acknowledging her existence then continuing to pace down the bay. She couldn't move. She couldn't get up and follow him, it would be too obvious. She stared over at Atrax across the road. He was gone.

Searching the reams of tourists on both sides of the road, Fleur found him two blocks down, before he disappeared again in Novak's wake. Once she was sure Novak was out of sight, Fleur rose from her spot, collected her things and disappeared too.

Atrax joined her back in the hotel three hours later. He'd

watched Novak set up, put out his bowl and play his guitar for two hours while tourists, including himself, dropped dollars in his bowl. When Novak finished his set, Atrax tailed him to a warehouse two blocks away. Inside, he set up his sleeping bag and went to sleep. Atrax returned to the hotel at that point to plan their next move.

The following night, Fleur arrived at the beachside location at the same time. She had a guitar slung across her back. After setting up her space, she swung the guitar around and began to play.

Learning to play the guitar at school, had been a way for Fleur to escape all the problems at home. She'd shown an affinity with the instrument early on, advancing rapidly through the stages with her teacher, until she was as proficient as he. She could have easily gone on to music college, as she also played the piano, but it was never her choice of career.

Plucking a haunting melody from her past, she concentrated, letting the music take her spirit on a journey, forgetting for a short while why they were here. Atrax listened as the notes floated across the road in between the passing cars. The traffic didn't hinder the sweet sounds, if anything it added to it, becoming the supporting orchestra to Fleur's tune. When she began to sing, tourists stopped strolling to listen.

After playing for about twenty minutes, Fleur lifted her head from her guitar and saw two legs directly in front of her. Her eyes rose upwards. There stood Austin Novak.

"That was good," he commented, in a gravelly voice that appeared unused to speaking.

"Thanks," she responded. The plan had worked better than they imagined. Fleur had thought it would take a week or more to strike up a conversation with their elusive target. Her idea to use the guitar as a way to start that talk had been brilliant. Atrax watched from the other side of the road. Fleur wasn't quite sure what to say next. Should she ask him to join her? That might seem too forward, especially as he seemed skittish.

She didn't want to scare him away. Instead, she commented on her own playing.

"I wasn't sure the second passage would work in that key," she reflected honestly.

"No, it worked quite well. I'll have to try it changing to that key myself," he said, encouraging her. She wanted to say, maybe we could play together, but it seemed too fast, too forward. She settled for a less threatening sentence.

"See you around?"

"Mmmm, yes, I'd like that."

Fleur watched as Novak moved along her side of the pavement until he was out of sight. He obviously didn't want to clash with the sounds they were each making, and she appreciated that. Two days later, Novak stopped in front of her again. This time he didn't move on. He put his things down and made his own space next to hers.

"I thought we might play together for a while," he said shyly. Fleur smiled and inclined her head. The two played a variety of acoustic arrangements for several hours. Both their begging bowls were full by the end of their set.

"Where did you learn to play so well?" Novak asked, setting up his bedroll in the same space for the night.

"I had an inspiring school tutor when I was young," replied Fleur, realising that she would have to stay the night too, to keep up her role as a homeless person. She set about preparing her blanket and cushions for the night. Novak glanced over at her frugal sleeping arrangements.

"Is that all you have? Here, I have plenty, have one of mine." He handed her another blanket. Fleur was starting to feel uncomfortable at the deception she was playing. Novak seemed to be genuine, and she and Atrax were pulling him into their baited trap. She accepted the blanket reluctantly.

"Thanks," she muttered, trying to console herself that what she was doing was for the man's greater good. Across the road, Atrax, realising she was settling in for the night, finished his beer and left the bar. She watched him stroll towards the hotel, assuming that he'd be gone till the morning. She envied his comfy mattress.

The sound of somebody struggling and breathing heavily woke her in the early hours. A scuffle had broken out next to her, a couple of minutes earlier. It was clear Novak was involved and fighting hard. Rising to her feet, she tried to assess the situation. Novak was trying to hold off two other men, both strong by the look of it. When she identified a syringe raised in the air, Fleur didn't stop to think. Her guitar smashed over the hand holding the syringe. With a loud yell and lots of cursing the syringe fell to the ground, where Fleur stamped it to pieces beneath her feet. Without a means to subdue their victim, the two men ran off. Moving over to a breathless Novak she helped him stand up.

"Does that happen here often?" Fleur asked, knowing full well these were likely accomplices of the man Atrax had incapacitated.

"No, not very often," answered Novak, breathing heavily. "But now and again. Every few years someone tries to take me home."

"Don't you want to go home?"

"No, do you?" He had her there. What could she say that wouldn't give her away? She thought back to her own childhood home.

"No. I don't, ever." He nodded with complete understanding.

"Look at your guitar!" He exclaimed, turning around to check on his belongings. "It's ruined! How will you ever get enough money together to buy another one?"

Guitars were the last thing on Fleur's mind. She was thinking hard about the assault. If people came regularly to try and kidnap Novak, then his family must've always known where he was. Unit One were being strung along, but why? She decided to test out her theory.

"Do your family know where you are?" She asked, expecting him to say no. Novak looked up from where he was inspecting her damaged instrument.

"Oh yes, they've always known. If I need any money I just have to ask, but I don't. I'm happy here." When Novak caught Fleur eyeing his clothing, he added. "If I dressed well and looked fed, tourists wouldn't leave any money. I love my life and wouldn't want it any different."

That sentence changed everything for Fleur. They were being paid to find him, recover him and return him to America where he would take over the family business. If she felt bad about begging, she felt even worse about kidnapping, because that is what they had intended to do if all else failed. Just like the men he fought off. She needed to talk to Atrax, and Johnson back at base, urgently. Feigning distress and needing the toilet, she bid Novak good-night and hurried off.

"That's right," Fleur advised Johnson over the secure comms link. Atrax sat in the background shaking his head. They'd been ordered to carry out a mission and here was Fleur, a subordinate in rank, arguing the toss with her commander. *It wouldn't have happened in my day,* he reflected. *I would have gone in and done the job, no problem.* He didn't have a sense of right and wrong like she did. He replayed that last thought because it didn't sound correct. He did have a sense of right and wrong, it's just that orders from your commander-in-chief overrode your principles. You had to trust the line of command, or you had nothing, you had no command. Yet he could see she was right; something was off.

"You two sit tight," Johnson ordered tersely.

Atrax smiled. That's how it should be.

"I'm not happy with this situation either," Johnson continued. "Something doesn't add up from what you say. In fact, it stinks. I want you to both be bodyguards to Austin Novak until I say otherwise. Is that clear?" That order woke Atrax up from his smug pose. Fleur smirked over at him.

"Bodyguards, Sir?" Atrax queried, not sure he heard Johnson right.

"Yes, bodyguards. Keep him safe. Is that going to be a problem for you, Estefan?" Only Johnson ever called Atrax by his real last name.

Fleur correctly surmised Johnson had noted Atrax's tense non-verbal body language.

"No Sir, I know what a bodyguard is sir, I've been one plenty of times. We will keep him safe don't you fear." It wasn't a thought, it was a statement of fact in Atrax's mind.

"Good man." Johnson ended the call.

"You do know that you'll have to stay undercover?" Atrax taunted. "While I lounge about playing the rich boy around town." It was Fleur's turn to scowl.

"Shit, I forgot that." She turned to look in a nearby mirror. A pale-faced bedraggled young woman with black rings under her eyes stared back at her. "At least I'll save Unit Two money, not having fancy facials and massages this time, unlike you," she teased back. Atrax threw a cushion at his teammate as she flounced out of the room and back to her night job.

The following night Fleur arrived at her spot, unpacked her two blankets, and prepared to settle down. Without a guitar, there was no reason to stay awake. With her eyes closed, she heard footsteps approach along the pavement. Assuming it was yet another tourist she didn't move. She had nothing to sell and nothing to beg with.

"I thought this might be helpful," said a quiet unassuming voice.

Fleur opened her eyes. Crouched low in front of her was Austin Novak holding out a guitar. Her stomach did a flip. *Could this man make me feel any worse than I do?* She wanted to run away and hide. As if he could read her thoughts he said;

"Don't go. Play with me."

The pair drew a bigger crowd than the night before, and the bar manager from across the road—where coincidently

111

Atrax was sitting—requested that they come and play inside.

"Well?" Novak asked. "Are you up for it?"

"I'm not that good," replied Fleur, feeling a little intimidated. "I'm not as good as you."

"It's not about who is as good as who," insisted Novak. "They've asked us to play, and you could do with the money. It's about time you went home." Fleur was a bit surprised at that statement. She wondered whether Novak had seen through their charade, but he appeared to be collecting his things and she paid it no more attention.

When the bar owner offered them both a permanent spot playing, Fleur felt a thrill of excitement. It was quickly drowned when Novak rejected the offer out of turn.

"Don't you want somewhere to live and a place to work?" asked the manager, stymied by his reply.

"No," Novak answered simply. "I don't need either. The weather here is great. The people are fantastic, and I never want for anything. What more is there?" Novak asked. This was the opportunity Fleur had been waiting for. She asked the manager if they could have time to think and led Novak down to the beach.

"What about family? Don't you ever think of them? Don't you ever want to go home?"

"What for? I don't have any family of my own and my father died leaving me everything. This is what I want in life. Waikiki is where I want to be." Fleur sort of understood. It appeared that he did have access to money if he wanted it. He did have a place to live on the island of Oahu, and he was happy here. Who am I to take this away?

"Let's play this evening and tomorrow say goodbye," Novak suggested, then as an afterthought, he added, "And tell your friend he can come too."

✤ ✤ ✤ ✤ ✤ ✤ ✤

Back in England Fleur and Atrax debriefed to Johnson. The mission hadn't been a complete success. Johnson was beginning to realise that nowadays Unit One was unlikely to maintain its hundred per cent success record.

"Seamark investigated the background to the company, and it appears there was a takeover bid in the offing. Guess who was behind it?"

"Austin Novak," remarked Fleur smugly. Johnson's eyebrows rose. Fleur Colton was proving to be smarter than he realised.

"Yes, Austin Novak. He left the family company several years ago and set up his own consortium which he oversees from a distance. He never wanted his father's firm. It was rife with corruption and cruelty to its employees. He'd never been able to change that from the inside and with the current executive board and greedy shareholders, things weren't about to change if he accepted the chair. So, using money from his father's estate and assets, he put in a takeover bid buying the whole company out from underneath them. The shareholders have gone. The board is gone. He alone has control again."

"With today's global internet structure, he can probably run the whole company from a tablet or smartphone," reflected Fleur. Johnson nodded. "Clever man."

Atrax had enough debriefing. He hoisted his tall frame out of the chair that Johnson liked to use for guests and walked towards his commander's desk.

"Have you got another mission? One that doesn't involve not doing anything in the dark." Fleur sniggered behind him.

"Oh, about that. I heard you put one of Novak's security guards in the hospital—for a week." Atrax shrugged his shoulders. They weren't to know the man watching the hotel was one of Novak's men, and with him out of action, as his competitors hoped, the man was easy prey.

"Mission lead's decision," he intoned.

"Really?" Johnson replied. He turned to face Fleur. "Mr

Novak has kindly wavered the hospital bill regarding his employee. He requests that the next time you desire to seek him out, you take your guitar with you." Fleur rose from her chair as regally as possible and turned to go.

"I might consider it," she deigned to say, as she passed through the doors into the hall. Atrax gave his boss a one-sided lean of the head as if to say 'women!' And Johnson couldn't help but agree.

Like his father before him, luck was on Lewis Blaine's side when the girl he thought he could fall in love with, reappeared outside the cafe one week later. She made no attempt to enter the building but stood staring in through the picture window like a frozen angel. Lewis was wiping down the tables of the large busy room when he sensed her presence. It felt like someone tickling the back of his neck with a feather. Without needing to look, he knew she was behind him. Knew she was outside the cafe and knew she was looking directly at him. He turned around, and despite being far back inside the room he stared straight at her. She didn't flinch or turn away. She didn't run or hide. She stood her ground as if to say, *Here I am*.

It had taken her a week to come to that decision. A week when her heart was in turmoil. She'd broken off her relationship with her partner of eighteen months. He couldn't understand it. Had no answer for her bizarre behaviour over the last seven days. He was devastated and told her so repeatedly. Regardless, she left him and walked out of their apartment carrying all her belongings with her. She'd been born on Saint Lucia but always known her heart was waiting in Salzburg. Her name was Joannie Redshaw Neem.

CHAPTER EIGHT - RELATIONS

T-CUT hummed to himself in the comms room as he cared for his babies. From the computer he'd built by hand, to the satellite tracking system, T-cut worshipped all things IT. He glanced over at the empty chair next to him. He still missed his partner in crime. Despite his oppo being dead these last five years, Johnson hadn't found anyone good enough to replace T-cut's teammate and friend.

"You would have loved this, Sureswift man," he confided to the empty space to his left. Since Gavin Sureswift's tragic death, on a mission to rescue five families trapped in a war zone, Johnson had secured an agreement with the space programme to have U1 equipment installed, when the next satellite was repaired or modified. That was four years ago.

Now they were invincible, according to T-cut. He could track anything, almost anywhere, globally. Providing there was a digital phone nearby, he could locate whatever they were after, listen in on conversations, even if an individual's phone was on standby.

In addition to supporting their field missions, T-Cut could also directly monitor the trackers implanted in individuals around the world. Nor did he need to do it manually, that is he didn't need to sit there with mouse in hand and physically move the cursor to get things done. He'd invented a software programme which did all that for him, scanning each person every day and flagging up changes in their location and health status as required.

Sadly, for T-cut, with so much tech to oversee, he rarely got to go on missions anymore. He missed that. The recent one in Saudi had been his first active mission in two years.

After checking everything was, 'in the pipe five-by-five' his favourite film phrase, he left the comms room to attend the daily briefing in the Ready Room. If he had stayed put, he might have noticed a certain young lady had boarded a flight bound for Austria.

Fulwood was waiting to start. T-cut noticed that every U1 member was present. This only happened when there was big news. He scanned the room. Doc Williams was in the corner resting in his favourite armchair, his perennial cup of tea in hand. *Will that old bloke never retire?* T-cut wondered, though he had to admit the Doc was an excellent surgeon. All of them bore the marks of their trade and Doc always improved the result.

Travis St John sat honing his latest blade, another karambit by the look of it. Tobin waited expectantly, notepad in front of him on the table. He liked taking notes. Yin appeared to be asleep, his short thin legs stretched out in front of him like some exotic Siamese cat. De Silva was reading a flight magazine, and Davidson was eating as usual. *Hold on.* T-cut's head swivelled. *Who's that new guy behind Fulwood?* T-cut marvelled. *Can't be more than twelve.*

"Morning," Fulwood began, never one to put a 'good' in where it wasn't needed. "As you know we have been a man down…" he caught T-cut's eye. "…for a while now. Meanwhile, our missions involving high-tech specs have increased dramatically." Everyone nodded, including Doc. *Why's Doc nodding? What high-tech spec has he ever used?* T-cut thought. *The most I've ever seen him use is that gadget for opening wine bottles.* He smirked, remembering the Christmas present Doc got last year from Fulwood. *Took him two days to open the box.* T-cut's grin widened.

"Something funny T-cut?" Fulwood asked, not privy to T-cut's internal meanderings.

"No Sir," he responded, trying to stay straight-faced for the sake of the briefing.

The others were looking at him with mild curiosity. Despite being second in command of the Bucket, their home, Terrance Mason or T-cut to his friends, remained the Unit's joker, always finding humour in the most unlikely places and never one to resist a practical joke. Yin couldn't understand how he made it to second in the Unit.

"As I was saying, because of all the high-powered stuff." Fulwood wasn't a techy man. "Jeff Johnson and I have decided we need a new Unit One member. Meet our newest recruit, Pav Riviera."

Pav? What sort of name is Pav? T-cut wondered. *The others don't seem too bothered, but then they won't have to work with him day in, day out.* T-cut grumbled in his head. The boy barely looked eighteen.

"Pav, this is Mason or T-cut," Fulwood amended hastily, as T-cut glared at him. Only his mother or Johnson ever called him Mason. No one ever called him Terrance—which is what the capital T stood for—and walked away on their own feet afterwards.

"Nice to meet you, Sir," responded Pav respectfully, putting his hand out to shake. T-cut stared down at it. No one ever called him, Sir. He liked it. *Maybe the lad will grow on me.* He reached out and shook hands.

"Thought you might show him around," continued Fulwood. "Show him the ropes." Then remembering T-cut's personality, Fulwood added, "the correct ropes T-cut." He inclined his head meaningfully in the slim hope that T-cut understood. T-cut deliberately chose to misunderstand. The others in the room sniggered knowing precisely what was going to come out of T-cut's mouth.

"Where shall we start Pav old boy?" T-cut began, putting his arm around the boy in a token fatherly gesture.

Pav looked at T-cut's arm intruding on his personal space but didn't remove it, his good manners deciding for him.

"The hookers in L.A. or maybe the excellent brothel I

frequent in St Lucia?" T-cut remarked, seemingly oblivious to Pav's discomfort.

The boy's face was a picture torn between horror, excitement, and something else. T-cut winked back at Fulwood over his shoulder and Fulwood retreated, shaking his head. Wondering whether Johnson was insane when he suggested T-cut as a mentor for the boy. He was going to be eaten alive.

"Thank goodness," interrupted Yin. "I'm no longer the newbie." The others cheered and grinned wickedly at Pav. Their enthusiastic responses left Pav wondering what on Earth he'd got himself into.

As Johnson suspected, Pav and T-cut hit it off from the start because of their love of all things computer-orientated. They played the same online games, and once set up, battled each other regularly in their downtime. It was what T-cut needed, a new diversion to move his mind and activity forward after his friend's death.

There was nothing any of them could have done. Sureswift had stepped on a landmine during a mission, as they re-crossed the land with the families they'd freed from the traffickers' camp. How they avoided the other mines was a miracle. Maybe they weren't activated or were so old they failed to detonate. The mine, a homemade step-plate contraption had been built with a huge amount of explosives. It was overkill—literally.

One moment Sureswift was there. The next, pieces of him were spread everywhere, across most of his teammates too. Ironically, Sureswift had been the mission paramedic, but no amount of morphine could fix T-cut's buddy.

Johnson was glad T-cut had been the backup team member on the Bucket, their usual SOP. He suffered greatly, knowing his brother-in-arms was dead, and what's more he had nothing and nobody to mourn, which made it harder to grieve. They held a memorial service on the Bucket, but it wasn't the same as saying goodbye to him in person. T-cut had needed space and time. Johnson had given him that, but now he felt that time was over. He was certain Sureswift would have agreed.

Fulwood was surprised when a timid knock came on the door of his Ready Room. Anyone else on the Bucket would have either knocked the door down or bowled right in. He suspected Pav and said so.

"Come in Pav," he called out, observing Pav as he moved into the room. He didn't barge or stomp, he moved without moving if that were possible. Fulwood found the boy a little unearthly and much too young. He couldn't believe he was twenty-four. *Was I ever that young? Still, it's Johnson's call and T-cut seems to be taken with him.* He'd overheard them planning some high-jinx but hadn't figured out what dastardly scheme T-cut was up to. He wasn't sure how much Pav had told the other U1 members about his abilities either.

In addition to being smart with tech—Pav had hacked into several prominent organisations in his teens—he was also proficient in jujutsu with a third Dan belt which he attained at the age of twenty. Fulwood was looking forward to seeing how he fared against Yin and the others. Pav's quiet voice interrupted Fulwood's musings.

"It's about the people we're tracking."

"Yes?"

"T-cut wanted me to tell you that a Miss Joannie Redshaw Neem has arrived in Salzburg." That information made Fulwood's mouth drop open, exactly as T-cut had told Pav it would. Pav held back his smile not wanting his boss to think him disrespectful.

"That's very interesting," answered Fulwood when he'd recovered from the news. He couldn't wait to tell Johnson. "Anything else Pav?"

"No Sir."

"Okay, tell T-cut thank you."

"Yes Sir," repeated Pav.

For one bizarre moment, Fulwood thought he was going

to bow backwards out of the room like somebody born into slavery, but at the last-minute Pav turned around and fled. That single behaviour made Fulwood pause.

Pavit Rivera was born to a Filipino mother and an older English father. His father died aged seventy-eight from emphysema, leaving Pav, then eight years old, and his mother to fend for themselves. Pav's father had been in receipt of a private pension which was sufficient for the family's needs. When he died, because he never married Pav's mother, so did the money. They had no recourse to fight. His father had refused to put his name on Pav's birth certificate, hence his Filipino last name, so his mother had no claim to his estate or pension, and no funds to fight probate. The paternal relatives— who'd disowned Pav's father when he set up home with Pav's mother—swooped in and took everything. Without any income, they lost their home and were forced out of their community too.

In a new town, Pav's mother took on two jobs. She spent her days cleaning posh people's houses and at night worked in a local bar. She told her son it was so they could make ends meet and afford the rent on their tiny one-bedroom flat. Pav naturally believed his god-fearing mother's words.

After spending several contented years at the nearby primary school Pav transferred, aged twelve, to the larger lower secondary, high school. His problems began with his move to the new school. Some of the older students started saying horrible things about his mother, calling her awful names. Pav stood up for his mother's reputation and fought for his beliefs. He couldn't let people get away with it. He joined a local jujutsu club, paying for the lessons by running errands at his mother's place of work.

Pretty soon Pav figured out what trade the bar did in addition to selling alcohol, but she was his mother and what she did, she did so they could survive. He worked hard at school to make her proud and always had her back because she had his heart. At fourteen, his mother died of AIDs. He had no family, no home, and was placed into care.

Fortunately, he was settled into a good foster home. For the first time in a long while he didn't have to guess where the next meal was coming from, and he got more than one a day. Time was not on Pav's side though as puberty finished its ascent, along with his mother's genetics it meant he'd never be tall. Those genetics, combined with many years spent malnourished resulted in a very short thin teenager, by seventeen he looked almost twelve.

Now at twenty-four he looked seventeen and was destined to stay that way permanently. It had its drawbacks but also its benefits too. If people thought he was a kid they underestimated his abilities, especially in situations where he needed to fight. A seventeen-year-old wouldn't have three black belts. In a fight, despite his light weight, Pav won hands down with his lightning-fast reflexes and speed.

Back in the comms room, Pav settled into the chair that his predecessor once occupied. He'd received information on Sureswift's death and T-cut had made it clear, pretty quickly, that he could never replace his life friend. Nor would he want to, he told T-cut. He'd lost both his parents. Nobody could replace them either. Though to be honest, he only remembered his father vaguely as someone who trotted out adages like they were going out of fashion.

As a small child, Pav thought his father had invented these pearls of wisdom. When he heard others uttering his father's words, he decided they'd learnt them from his dad. It wasn't until much later that Pav learnt these were traditional sayings and not the products of his father's clever brain. Despite this, he revered many of the sayings his father spoke.

"How'd Fulwood take the news Pav?" T-cut asked a large grin slapped across his face.

"A picture is worth a thousand words," Pav replied thoughtfully, causing T-cut to pause a moment before replying.

"It certainly is Pav, it certainly is," he said, understanding Pav's response. "Wish I'd been there though," he added, returning to his current project. Pav smiled. He liked T-cut. T-cut got him.

She ordered a coffee, and waited at a table near the window until Lewis had a break, then he came over and sat in the chair facing her.

"Hi."

"Hi," she replied, her voice both soft and exotic. She felt empowered by her assertiveness, and also terrified.

Lewis drank in her appearance, from her liquid brown eyes to her full pouting lips. In moments, he became drunk with passion on her beauty, and something else. Something indefinable. He *knew* her. Not in the way people know their neighbours and friends, but in a deeper more profound, stronger way. Like she was a rock, and his lifeline was tethered to it. He couldn't pull himself away. He took a long breath in through his nose and inhaled the scent of her, a sweet perfume of jasmine and vanilla. *Is it perfume?* He wondered. *I don't think so, I think it's her.* He stumbled for the right word to describe her pheromone essence. *It's intoxicating,* he marvelled.

Neither had spoken a word since their initial brief greeting, each tied up in the other's feelings and aura. Lewis felt a dig in his side which made him inhale sharply.

"Wake up, sleepy head." It was his opposite number in the café. "I've been covering your tables these last ten minutes," grumbled Klaude, grinning despite his grumble. "I've taken your tips as well, while you've been moping here like a moonstruck sheep," he continued, getting his adjectives muddled in his attempt to use English. "Get a room already," he huffed, irritated when Lewis failed to rise to the bait about his tips.

Lewis rose from his seat. *Wait for me,* he mouthed. She nodded and watched him return to his other tables. Several minutes later, another Americano coffee that she hadn't ordered, arrived, together with a piece of apple strudel and cream, her favourite.

"Compliments of lover boy." Klaude smiled, and placed a plate on her table, flicking his head in Lewis's direction.

Joannie felt her cheeks burn at the comment. Despite this, she ate the food with relish, remembering she hadn't eaten since yesterday. She hadn't let her mother, Nyla, know she was safe either as she had promised last night during her call home. Her mother had taken the news of her break-up well and was expecting Joannie to return home to St Lucia on the first plane.

She used the waiting time to text home, reassuring her mum she was fine and going to stay with her friends in Salzburg, Austria. She wasn't, but she didn't want her mum to worry. Joannie didn't have anywhere to stay—yet.

"God help us," muttered Frank Fulwood, as he received further intel from T-cut and Pav informing him that Lewis Blaine and Joannie Neem had made contact in Salzburg. Judging by the proximity of their trackers, one of which sat over the other, they were apparently in the same room.

Fulwood wondered how Johnson was getting on asking his wife for advice on the possible scenarios, and whether U1 should, or could do anything. He had visions of a hundred-plus girls, sisters to the boy, making their way to Salzburg, descending on Lewis Blaine.

Joannie Neem could be the first of many, Fulwood theorised. He shook his head as he sat down in his chair. *Who am I kidding? This chair will always be Jeff Johnson's chair. It's just on temporary loan to me.* He smiled, and just as he did so Doc Williams walked in. *Did the man ever knock?*

"Morning, good to see you smiling Frank. Got good news for us?" Doc asked as he moved over to the drinks shelf setting the kettle to boil. He prepared a teapot for two without asking.

"Sorry Doc, more bad news I'm afraid." Doc's eyes widened, but he didn't say anything. "It would appear Lewis Blaine and Joannie Neem have connected."

"Oh," Doc paused a moment, spoon in hand, before replying. "It could be worse. You could have a hundred-plus girls descending on Salzburg." Fulwood groaned and put his head in his hands. *Why did Doc have to say it out loud? It sounds so much worse!*

"What can we do?" Johnson asked Fulwood, over their conference link a few hours later. Doc was present listening to the conversation.

"I don't know, but I don't like it. First Lewis Blaine goes globe-trotting. Now Joannie Neem does the same, and they— he used inverted air quotes—'co-incidentally' both end up in the same city. Travis reports they have met up with each other. They're brother and sister for god's sake, Jeff!"

"I know, and I don't know what to do about it," he admitted, leaning forward on his desk as if that would reduce the distance, and make talking to Fulwood easier.

"Speak to Vivienne at least," pleaded Fulwood. He had hoped Johnson had done that already, but it appeared not.

"She's not here," he confessed, his voice tight with emotion.

"Oh."

"No, we… we argued. She's gone to South America for a break."

"Really?"

"Yes."

"Sorry to hear that Jeff." Fulwood felt like a real shit, for pushing his boss at a time when things were not good at home.

"Maybe you could contact her. Or I could," he added as an afterthought.

"No, no. I'll do it. I haven't spoken to her for a while is all."

That doesn't sound promising, thought Fulwood, glancing towards Doc, who appeared to be taking in every word. That in itself was unusual. Doc nodded to Frank encouragingly.

"If you're sure?"

"No, I mean, yes. It'll be fine, trust me," concluded Johnson. He ended the call shortly after.

"That didn't sound good," said Doc Williams, rising from his chair and heading for the whisky decanter instead of the teapot this time. "No, not good at all."

"I feel like a prat. The man's obviously having a tough time and I'm hassling him."

"It needed doing," insisted Doc, trying to make Frank feel better. "Have one of these. I prescribe it."

Fulwood looked down at the tumbler of whisky Doc had placed in front of him. It was almost a third full. He grinned. Doc knew him so well. *A single malt too,* his favourite tipple, Fulwood sighed. It was Johnson's too he seemed to remember, and Redshaw's. *Bloody Redshaw! Where is he now? He's dropped all this shit in our lap; then scarpered, leaving us literally holding the baby, or babies in this case.*

Johnson's phone call to his estranged wife Vivienne, who was supposed to be staying with friends in Peru had to wait till he organised U2's next mission. Seamark and his wife Lolita, formerly De Silva, were both out taking some well-earned R & R. They'd recently finished an undercover mission in Istanbul and from there flown to the Caribbean for their downtime. Johnson was loathe to recall anyone on leave.

Lolita, or Lola, as she preferred to be called, had told José her second cousin, to apply for the role of pilot for U1, telling him he'd never regret it if he got selected. Johnson reflected, what with José, and now one of their aunts, Camilla, working for him as housekeeper in his home, U1 was fast becoming their family business too.

"Lola would have been perfect for this job," Johnson mused. Lola used to be a legitimate diamond courier. It was how Thomas Seamark from U1 met her. Lola was one of U1's past missions. She'd recruited them to escort her due to threats on her life. Later, Seamark married her, beating T-cut to the finishing line. Johnson offered her a position when U2 was set up, bringing her into their fold.

"That means, either sending Fleur and Atrax in, who have only just come back from Hawaii, or borrowing someone from U1." Johnson could use U1 members, but he was reluctant to do so. This mission was on a cruise ship with a casino. He had a feeling if the U1 team went in, he'd never hear from any of them again. They'd get pissed, gamble and sleep with any number of women throwing themselves bodily at these A-type predator men. Probably get thrown off the ship at the next port before the mission even got underway. That wasn't true, his operatives were professional through and through, but he could imagine it happening.

No, U1 were his hard-core boys for dangerous death-defying missions where strength, skill and badass attitude ruled the day. The cruise ship mission required finesse and discretion, in order to trip up the illegal diamond smuggling ring coming out of South Africa. Word had it, someone was stealing diamonds and using the cruise as a cover, transporting the loot to a fence stationed on board.

Joannie Neem and Lewis Blaine had been living together for a month in Lewis's tiny one-room apartment. They were in love. Nothing mattered outside their relationship. The world could detonate. As long as they were in each other's arms, it would be fine. They admitted it was bizarre that they both had the same middle name, Redshaw, but Lewis had never been so happy, and Joannie positively glowed, so they didn't dwell on that fact. They were born in different countries to different parents, though neither had shared any specific details about their fathers so far.

Being in love with love was amazing—and then they felt it—something more. Another had arrived in Salzburg.

CHAPTER NINE - PERU

JEFF Johnson down in Kent, wasn't in a good place when he received more news that another tracked individual had landed in Salzburg. He hadn't been able to contact Vivienne his wife either, since she'd landed at Jorge Chávez International Airport, Lima. It was stressing him out.

It seemed Vivienne didn't make it to her friend's home as planned, which had him concerned. Jeff still loved his wife very much and was feeling more than a little guilty about their senseless argument, over which school their youngest child, Odette, attended when she reached eleven.

He'd thought they'd both agreed, that Odette would follow Joel to Edgbaston. Vivienne had apparently changed her mind since sending Joel away to board. She now wanted their daughter to stay at home and continue attending the local private school as a day pupil. Johnson, on the other hand, didn't think his daughter should receive any less of an education than their son. He wanted her to receive the same benefits, as Joel did, by boarding at the same exclusive school.

Johnson didn't realise that Vivienne's feelings had changed as a direct result of sending Joel to another part of the country. She would have laughed, BC—Before Children—at a mother who couldn't bear to be parted from her offspring. She used to think them weak-minded ninnies and couldn't see their point of view. Then Joel left her side. She felt bereft. She mourned the loss of their time together. She was missing him growing up. She wasn't there for him, to share his fears and his joys.

Vivienne decided she could never face that again. She needed and wanted her children close. These days, Joel seemed distant when he came home on the holidays. He didn't want his mother, her time, or apparently her love, and that hurt. If she could have turned back time and brought Joel home, she would have, but Jeff was adamant he should stay where he was, explaining he was settled and happy. Vivienne wasn't so sure. Especially when, according to his head of house, their son was experiencing a few *difficulties*. Difficulties Joel hadn't thought to mention to his parents the last time he was home. She wasn't going to let her daughter go down the same route.

After their argument, Vivienne had taken Odette with her to Peru.

"For a last period of mother-daughter time," she advised Jeff. She hoped her absence would give her husband time to, "come to his senses," as she put it.

Johnson was regretting everything about their argument. He could see Vivienne's point of view—belatedly. She needed her children, as much as he did, if not more so. He recognized with her departure, that she wasn't putting her needs first. She truly believed both their children would benefit more by being at home, than by whatever a private boarded education could give them. And now, he had the headmaster advising him that Joel was likely to get a temporary exclusion for cheating in an exam. Except, the Head admitted, they couldn't figure out how he'd succeeded, and that was the only reason why he hadn't been seriously sanctioned—yet.

Fortunately, it had been a mock exam, otherwise, Joel would probably have been slung out of school. Johnson didn't see it as any different otherwise, cheating was cheating in his book. A man with principles, he couldn't abide lying, cheating, or stealing. He needed to have a serious discussion with his son soon, but first, he needed to make contact with his wife.

Vivienne and Odette Johnson landed at Lima's Jorge Chavez airport, at nine-forty-five in the morning, after a long eighteen-hour flight from Heathrow, with one stopover in Amsterdam. Vivienne hailed a taxi from the rank out front and gave directions to her friend's home situated in Miraflores to the south of the airport.

Her friend from Uni, Sally, had moved to Miraflores because it was close to her husband's workplace at the new Hilton Lima hotel. Although travel was perennially bad in Lima, it wasn't a busy time, and Vivienne roughly knew the route to get there, having visited Sally once before.

The taxi travelled south along the Expressway, then continued along the beach road before dog-legging back inland. It was a journey of roughly six and a half miles and should have taken forty minutes on a good day.

Vivienne and Odette were settled in the back of the car. They were enjoying each other's company during the trip, and Odette was occupied reading her favourite book out loud— again—to her mother.

When the driver failed to change direction off the coast road, Vivienne didn't notice immediately. Then she lifted her eyes from her daughter's story and looked outside. The sea still ran along the road to their right. *I thought we'd have been there by now. Must be busier on the roads today than last time I visited.* Not unduly concerned, she turned her attention back to her beautiful daughter, who as always captivated her heart, by smiling and telling her mummy how much she loved her. They returned to reading the book.

Several minutes went by, and Vivienne discovered they were still travelling south with the sea on their right. *We definitely should have turned by now. I don't recognize any of these landmarks.* It was difficult because she didn't want to alarm Odette unnecessarily.

"We don't seem to be going the usual way," she stated to the taxi driver.

"No miss, mending road."

That makes sense, reflected Vivienne, sitting back with

her daughter who hadn't noticed anything amiss. Several more minutes passed. She glanced at her watch. They had been travelling for an hour and fifteen minutes and still were following the coast road. Then the taxi finally turned off. Vivienne saw the road sign, 'Chroillos.'

"Excuse me," she called, moving forwards to the edge of her seat. There was no response. She said it louder and knocked on the partition glass, causing her daughter to glance up.

"What is it, mummy?" Odette asked.

The driver didn't acknowledge Vivienne's insistent knocking. He didn't turn around. He just kept driving, face forward. Fear trickled down Vivienne's spine. She checked the doors and tried the handles. Centrally locked by the driver from the front. Her daughter wasn't stupid, with her mother's voice rising, and her trying to open a moving car door, Odette guessed something was amiss.

"Nothing child," replied Vivienne, trying hard to maintain the illusion that all was as it should be. "Go back to reading your book sweetheart."

Then, in that second, she saw her daughter from a new perspective.

She saw a beautiful girl with long blonde hair like her mother, piercing diamond blue eyes like her father, an angel, a treasure worth stealing. She shivered, and it went down to the ends of her fingers. No one was going to hurt her little girl. She'd die keeping her safe first.

Jeff Johnson had taught his wife several lessons in safety and self-defence over the years. The most important one he instilled into her was not to panic. People who panicked didn't think properly, did silly things and usually died because of it. Vivienne didn't want either of them to die, so she needed to stay calm. She saw the driver watching her in his rear-view mirror. His glance kept moving to her precious daughter and he grinned widely. *You Bastard,* she thought angrily, not risking the words out loud with Odette present. *Think, think,* she forced herself to consider her situation rationally. *Handbag!* She drew Odette into her arms on the pretence of hugging her daughter. At the same time, she reached for her handbag dropping it down to the floor beside her, out of sight of the driver's view.

"I love you, baby," she whispered into her daughter's ear.

"And I love you too mummy," answered Odette, hugging her back. Vivienne almost sobbed.

Inside the bag was her phone and kindle among her usual stuff. Holding the phone down low so the driver couldn't see she was using it, Vivienne pressed speed dial for Jeff. It advised her to leave a message. *Oh, why did we bloody argue?* She groaned. *I love the man. I'm a stupid, stupid woman.* The last remark had more to do with getting into a car without checking it was a bonafide taxi than anything about their relationship. *How on earth am I going to tell him we're in trouble?* She thought a moment, then pressed voice mail message.

"Where are you taking us?" She asked the driver. "This is the road to Chorillos, not Miraflores. Please let us out."

"Mummy, why are you using the phone?" Odette asked innocently. Vivienne's heart sank.

The sliding partition flew open. It had been locked from the driver's side. An arm grabbed Vivienne's phone off her. She screamed and pulled back, not releasing her hold on the one item that could save them. She attempted to yank the man's arm and shoulder towards her. She reasoned, he couldn't do two things at once, drive and fight her in the back seat.

The taxi careered back and forth across the road travelling at fifty miles an hour. It was only a matter of seconds before they hit something.

"Mummy, mummy stop," screamed Odette. Vivienne glanced at her frightened daughter and released the phone. The partition slammed shut. She watched her phone fly out of the driver's window to be crushed under the wheels of a tanker going the other way.

⁂

The Bucket was cruising off the west coast of Costa Rica, after passing through the Panama canal a few days earlier, when the emergency call came in. Fulwood took the intel. He couldn't believe it until Johnson played back the voice mail from his wife. He swallowed hard not knowing how to comfort his friend and colleague.

"We will get her back," he stated firmly. "Her and Odette." Johnson nodded on the video link struggling to speak, his heart full of torn emotions, most of which would result in him falling apart in front of one of his best friends.

"I know." The only words he managed to utter.

"Got to go, Jeff," Fulwood added, needing to end the call, but worried about doing so for Johnson's sake. "Got to get things moving." Johnson nodded again and ended the call his end.

Instead of the usual daily briefing, the ship-wide tannoy sounded, announcing emergency conditions. It mobilised all departments on board, each knowing and proceeding to battle station readiness at once. The Conference room was utilized when an emergency was announced, not just because of its size, but because it contained interactive whiteboards and other IT paraphernalia.

By the time Fulwood reached the room, everyone in U1 was present, except for Owen Spencer their sniper, he was on a deep undercover assignment. Fulwood had ordered the Captain to alter the Bucket's course to Lima, Peru. T-cut already knew the score, thanks to his hot-wired spyware in the Ready Room—and anywhere else he had a mind to eavesdrop. Johnson and Fulwood had given up trying to stop him years ago—it never worked. He nodded to Fulwood as he entered, his nod telling Fulwood that he already knew the intel from Johnson.

"De Silva, I need you to prep the Spade for immediate evac stat."

"Yes, Boss, where we going?" De Silva queried, needing the information for refuelling and landing permissions.

"Lima, Peru. You can go now." De Silva left to work out routes over air space and check the tiltrotor's preparedness.

"T-Cut you're coming with us this time."

T-Cut punched the air.

"Yes!" He high-fived Pav.

"Travis, you too, and Davidson, and Yin. Pav you have back-up and comms." Pav's eyes widened in alarm.

"Me? On my own?"

Recognising Pav needed encouragement and reassurance Fulwood added.

"I've watched over you these last few weeks with T-Cut. He's been giving me good feedback on your progress. We think you're ready."

T-Cut smiled and ruffled Pav's hair, forgetting the man was twenty-four. Pav blushed at the unexpected praise. The hair tousling was irritating, he was sure T-cut thought him a pet.

"I'll do my best, Sir."

"I know you will."

Travis St John, not slow to catch on, asked a question.

"You said us, Sir?"

"Yes, that's right I will be joining you on this mission." That was a first. Fulwood hadn't been on any missions in years.

"Errr, Sir," interrupted T-Cut. He was the only one who could say the next sentence. "Do you think you're up to it?" Fulwood glared at Mason.

"It doesn't matter if I'm not. I'm coming. It's Jeff Johnson's wife and child that's been kidnapped. If you think I'm going to sit here on my backside while they are out there, you've got another thing coming Terence T-cut Mason." A gasp sounded at the back of the room. Fulwood had used T-cut's full name.

"Do we have a problem?" Frank Fulwood addressed the room.

"Sir, No sir," bellowed every U1 member.

"Fifteen minutes to evac. Load up and head out," announced Fulwood, and to prevent any further discussion on the subject he left. Doc raised his eyebrows.

"Well, that went well," mumbled Tobin, the Bucket's nurse and counsellor. He rose and followed Fulwood out.

"Don't you try and talk me out of it either," snarled Fulwood, hearing Tobin step up behind him.

"I wouldn't dream of trying, Boss," he answered respectfully.

"That's ok then," replied Fulwood, his proverbial feathers settling down. He began walking briskly back to his Ready Room.

"I just want you to remember, you are not that young hot-shot lad anymore. Do us all a favour and leave the hand-to-hand combat to the others. Use your mind to do the planning and organising instead."

"What are you saying?" Fulwood glared, turning to face the registered nurse. "Stay out of the action?"

"That's not what I'm saying. I'm saying play to your strengths, not your weaknesses. The boys can handle the warfare. They're going to need someone with a cool head, which until this moment, is usually you."

"It's Vivienne and Odette! Jeff Johnson's wife and child for God's sake Tobin!"

"I know, but we need someone in U1 to stay in control and frosty. That has to be you."

Fulwood was about to give Tobin an earful when he finally recognised that Johnson's anxiety had infected him. He gave a heavy sigh and halted his headlong march through the corridors.

"You're right."

"Good. Then go, get U1 to beat the crap out of them for me too, but be the boss, the voice of reason, and you'll bring them home safe. I know it." Tobin turned to go.

"Michael."

Tobin turned back.

"Thank you."

Michael Tobin smiled, gave a salute, about-turned and left Fulwood to his thoughts.

Unit members never used first names unless under a great deal of stress. Fulwood's use of T-cut's real name in the briefing had alerted Tobin to the stress the man was under, that and his non-verbal body language. He only hoped Fulwood would heed his advice. He was far too old to take part physically in the shit that was about to go down. When U1 rescued Vivienne and Odette Johnson, their hero's family, Tobin didn't want to be arranging body bags home for anyone from Unit One.

T-cut was already on it, as the Spade—the Unit's preferred method of transport a Bell tiltrotor aircraft—lifted off. He hacked into the airport's software system to access the closed-circuit cameras using his hand-built laptop. It took some time, due to the security firewalls established in every airport after nine-eleven. Fulwood heard T-cut muttering and swearing several times as he attempted to review the twenty-four-hour logs in the public areas, working from Vivienne and Odette's expected time of arrival.

"Anything yet?" Fulwood asked, stretching his neck to look over T-cut's shoulder at the laptop to the right of him. T-cut shook his head without lifting his eyes from the screen. He couldn't afford to miss any detail or movement no matter how small. Their flight was three hours, fifty minutes to Lima from Costa Rica, though De Silva managed to shave a few minutes off that.

Halfway there.

"Got 'em!" T-cut bellowed, hunching low over the screen to reduce the outside glare. Fulwood's heart jumped at T-cut's yell. His body moved a minuscule amount as outwardly he tried to maintain his composure as Tobin had suggested.

"Where? Where?" He demanded, his voice betraying his emotions.

"Hold on, There!" T-cut leaned back triumphantly. He moved his laptop across so he and Fulwood were sharing the computer.

"There they are." He pointed top left of the screen as two indistinct people vanished through the door.

"Are you sure?" Fulwood squinted at the images.

"I'd know those legs anywhere and I can't miss my Odette, cute as a kitten," he confirmed.

"Where did they go?"

"Hang on, I need to bring up the camera in the area where they were heading." His fingers moved rapidly over the small keyboard, and before he'd finished talking a second view appeared. Vivienne and Odette centre-stage. "There! They're heading towards customs. I'll pick them up on the other side." True to his word, another camera angle caught them coming out of the customs hall, heading across the busy concourse to the waiting taxi rank outside. T-cut was on it again, as Travis moved over to sit next to him, in order to view the screen from the right side.

Vivienne selected a taxi. Their luggage was stowed by the driver in the boot. He then performed a shifty manoeuvre, scanning the area around him, before getting back in the car. T-cut paused the screen.

"Dodgy," Travis murmured, saying out loud what Fulwood and T-cut were thinking.

"Close up on that driver."

"On it." T-cut had a photo of the man streaming through police security checks in seconds.

"Nothing on the driver so far. Unknown to security agencies locally," he advised Fulwood.

"Check out the taxi company." Lima Limo's proved to be legit, but there was no record of an employee matching the driver's description.

"Stolen I'll bet," stated Travis. T-cut searched the company's database and emails. He identified that a car with the same description and number plate was reported stolen to the police by the company yesterday. Dead end.

T-cut took his hand off the keyboard and ran his fingers through his short number two cut. Fulwood, remembering Tobin's words about staying calm and using his brains—used his brains.

"Can you jump to highway cameras?"

"Of course! Sorry, wasn't thinking."

"No need Mason, we're all under pressure on this one—it's personal." T-cut sighed his agreement and patched himself into Lima's highway patrol network.

"A damn sight easier than the airport security system that's for sure."

"There!" Travis exclaimed, pointing to a speeding car on the screen.

"It's heading towards Miraflores."

"That's where Vivienne's friend Sally lives," offered Fulwood.

"Here… it's gone past the turnoff." T-cut groaned. "Cameras are going to run out in a minute." No sooner had the words left his mouth, than the screen went blank. He tried moving to another camera, but it hadn't been set up properly.

"Shit!" He hollered. "What now?"

He turned to Fulwood, who thought for a moment.

"Bring up a road map of the area."

"Done."

Fulwood studied the map.

"They'll either continue on south here or head inland to Chorrillos," Fulwood concluded pointing at the screen. Taking a huge leap of faith, his next word potentially dooming the females to their fate if he got it wrong, he recalled in his mind the voice message Johnson played to him. "Bring up Chorrillos."

T-cut patched into the Chorrillos highway logs at the relevant date entries, such as they were. The black and white cameras were few and not always operational.

"There, there!" Travis screamed. The high-pitched noise sounded bizarre coming from the mouth of the normally uber-calm man. Travis it seemed, had got caught up in the race against time too. Davidson and Yin glanced at each other; eyebrows raised; eyes wide. They looked over at Travis from their bench on the other side of the craft.

"You definitely did not hear me just say that." Travis glared menacingly at his comrades, his voice a tone lower than normal. T-cut smirked, then concentrated on his hacking so they could follow the taxi Travis identified, from camera to camera.

They very nearly all screamed, when it stopped outside a shabby bar, sporting the name El Loco. Vivienne and Odette were being hustled out of the taxi, at obvious gunpoint.

T-cut ground his teeth and clenched his fists tight to stop himself from shaking with anger. His colleagues were all more or less struggling in a similar way. Each person present would have died for Jeff Johnson, he meant so much to them. They were more than family, they were brothers-in-arms.

"Thank fuck for that," sighed Fulwood, switching on his head mike.

"De Silva, change of course. Chorrillos south of Lima. I'll give further details when we're in the area. Check for a nearby heliport for landing the Spade."

"Roger that," De Silva answered.

Fulwood changed headphones and put a call into Johnson, rather than send an impersonal text.

"Yes...Picked up by a taxi...No not legit. Stolen," he confirmed, rattling off answers to Jeff Johnson's questions. "Should have them both in a jiffy," he reassured his friend, hoping his voice sounded more confident than he felt.

Following this, Fulwood got on organising ground transport to meet them, depending on where De Silva touched down. They had over an hour's flight to go, plenty of time to arrange vehicles to be delivered at an area he'd later designate. Fulwood learnt early on, that if you had enough money, you could get anything done, even if time was tight.

"Boss?" De Silva spoke into Fulwood's earpiece.

"Go ahead, De Silva."

"I found the nearest airport. Las Palmas is an airbase for the Peruvian military."

"Is that a problem?"

"Could be, we'd need to get the necessary clearances to land there."

"Roger on that. How far away is it from Chorrillos?"

"Two-point-three miles, Sir."

"Too far. Anything nearer?"

"A golf club, country club, or a sports complex. I'd still need clearance to land." He paused. "It might cost a bit," he added, meaning they'd need to offer some more bribes to get the job done.

"Do it and check whether we can land on one of the main roads nearby."

Fulwood listened in, as José hailed the local aviation authorities in fluent Spanish, which the majority of Peruvians spoke. Not for the first time, he was thankful De Silva, along with most of the team, spoke several languages and dialects. Disappointingly, they couldn't get permission to land on the main drag, no matter how much Fulwood wanted to. He thought for a moment about vetoing their refusal but recognised that could start an inferno he couldn't put out, with them being so close to a military establishment.

They were prepped and ready to go when De Silva landed the Tiltrotor, as smooth as a swan landing on water, inside the sports complex. The complex was three blocks west of Tupac Avenue, where El Loco was situated. Their vehicles were outside the grounds. A member of staff from the hiring company handed Fulwood the keys and left in his own car, his drivers in the back seat. No words were needed. Two four-by-four BMWs stood waiting, Fulwood's favourite ride—naturally.

T-cut smirked. *What I wouldn't give for a go in an Audi or Jeep occasionally. I wonder whether Fulwood has shares in the company?*

"What?" Fulwood asked, his voice rising slightly in irritation. He knew why T-cut smirked, but he wasn't in the mood to admit how predictable he was.

They bundled into the cars, Travis driving one and Fulwood the other, sending word to Johnson that they were going in, this time via text to prevent chat. De Silva stayed with the aircraft; it was bound to result in some attention.

T-cut had his laptop open before they'd pulled away from the kerb. During the flight, he'd secured plans of the block from the Ministry of Housing database after an Environmental Certificate was granted for change of use several years ago.

They pulled the cars over a short distance down the avenue staying inside to discuss the upcoming plan. They could eyeball the bar without being detected in this location. The members in the second car listened via their earpieces.

"Cameras?" Fulwood asked, going into classic military one-word speak.

"Two," replied T cut. "One on each door, front and back. Picking up more security inside, inconsistent for business registered at single storey premises address." T-cut had the specific stats up on the El Loco bar, including details of the owner and licensee. "Door sensors, pressure sensors and something else can't identify. Want a drone sent in?"

"Any point?"

"Not really. Drone likely to be spotted a mile away if felons inside." T-cut had altered his communication to condensed sentences in preparation for action.

"We go in," Fulwood decided.

141

"Roger that," his team replied in unison.

"Park round the back. Don't need the whole world to know," Fulwood instructed, as he manoeuvred his vehicle into the alleyway running behind the buildings.

T cut glanced at the drunk asleep in a doorway three doors down, the hooker on the corner, and the dealer sitting in his car with his hand hanging out ready for payment.

"Judging by the area we won't be something they haven't seen before," T-cut concluded, noticing the businesses to the right of El Loco were boarded up.

Travis navigated his vehicle round the block following his Boss. They stationed the four-by-fours with their tail lights facing the building's rear door. It was locked. A camera monitored the entrance. T-cut disabled the camera before they left the vehicles. Travis overcame the door lock in seconds.

"Piece of cake," he grunted, wiping his hands now covered in filth.

"Good work." Fulwood acknowledged Travis's efforts, then held up his hand before they entered. "Stay frosty. This is Jeff Johnson's family."

T-cut put his free hand on Fulwood's shoulder, the other holding his precious laptop.

"We know it, brother." Travis, Davidson and Yin nodded; the sincerity clear in all their eyes. .

The back corridor was quiet, no sounds. They didn't know how many perps were on the premises but based on experience, any prisoners would be held in the basement.

They could see the bar area from their limited visual through the glass panel in the fire door beyond. No bar staff were evident moving about which was odd. The place was deserted despite the open sign on the door.

Using military hand signals, they proceeded along the corridor which ran behind the bar. At the far end was a set of steps. They started down the flight of stairs, Davidson staying on the ground floor to cover their backs. The stairs turned a hundred and eighty degrees, and carried on down for a further flight, ending in a storeroom containing boxes of stock and beer kegs. Nothing else was evident.

"Bring up the building specs again," Fulwood whispered into T-cut's ear. He nodded and moved off to one side, while Travis began checking the walls. He'd seen plenty of false walls during his years in the military. Strange to spend money on walls and not good security. No guards. Either they were overconfident or had nothing left to steal, which was more worrying.

T-cut raised his head and stared at the wall to his right which should be the next property. He pointed.

"There." They moved over to the wall indicated.

"Next door?"

"Yup."

They searched the wall, found a seam, but no opening or handle. Fulwood had had enough.

"Blow it."

The four-foot jagged hole, the result of the detonation, showered plaster dust over everything, and more importantly, into a huge room beyond. It ran the length of the entire block and explained why the bars to the right of El Loco were closed.

Inside the room, on the left were rows of cells, and in front of them were guards, most of whom were reeling from the shock of the explosion. More came running down the stairs at the far end, located about four shop lengths away.

The people in the cells, all women, dived under their makeshift beds as bullets flew—as if a piece of wood and blankets would protect them. Vivian Johnson covered her daughter Odette with her own body. They lay flat on the ground at the back of their cell, Vivienne never realising that Jeff sharing tips about his action days would prove so useful. She could hear his wise words as the battle outside their cell raged.

"Get as far away as possible from the guns or lie flat on

143

the floor. People who get injured are usually standing up. Always run away if the option presents."

She'd looked it up on Google. A bullet shot out of a medium-sized handgun will travel roughly one and a half miles before it falls to the ground. However, a bullet rarely travels that far without hitting something first. It got complicated after that with terms such as spin, yaw, and drag. When angles of guns and shapes of bullets appeared, Vivienne felt she'd read enough. Now she was thankful for her husband's advice.

The air filled with gunfire. Women screamed. Odette screamed, and T-cut's mind went into overdrive. That was the sound she'd made as a five-year-old. She'd dashed down the front steps of her home to greet him. She fell, her arm had broken. T-cut would carry the guilt with him always.

Usually, the geeky one in U1, content to stay in the background, T-cut's goddaughter's wail of terror, sent painful shards straight through his heart. He stormed through the gaping hole with his teammates, laying waste to any bastard that dared to imprison his family, whether blood-related or not.

The death count was high when they'd finished. Between the four of them, they'd terminated over thirty men in the basement of the hidden jail, while Davidson upstairs had picked off the fleeing stragglers one by one. U1 had no compulsion about killing evil people.

Travis worked his magic on the cell doors as he had on the rear door of the premises. The women mobbed him. Sobbing, in various languages, at how grateful they were, but also wailing the loss of their missing children. All of them, like Vivian and Odette, were blonde-haired. All of them had been kidnapped from the airport.

"We need to go. We can't take these women with us," advised Fulwood to his team. T-cut was carrying Odette, with Vivienne Johnson holding on to his arm like her life depended on it. "I've contacted the local police to attend. I'm guessing they'll arrive any minute, sooner if someone has reported our gunfire." Bullet casings littered the floor and it stank of gunpowder. "T-cut take the girls. Travis cover the rear. I'll speak to the women and bring them through to the car park. Go."

They left.

Odette ran into her father's open arms at Heathrow airport, and Jeff Johnson, a man of countless active war zones and mercenary missions, sobbed like a child. He held on to Odette, his head buried in her hair. He breathed in the scent of her, his daughter, one of his reasons for living, grasping her tightly until she squealed.

"Daddy! You're squashing me!" Ignoring her protestations, Jeff rose with Odette in his arms, to greet his wife Vivienne, crushing her to him much as he had his child. She didn't complain but held him firm in return.

"I'm so sorry," he whispered in her ear.

"No need," she murmured, unwilling to let him go just yet.

Tobin, who had joined them for the journey home, stood some way back to let the family reunite. He'd give the full debrief later. Johnson looked over at him, tears brimming his eyes, and mouthed, 'thank you.' Tobin waved his hand dismissively. He'd done very little, in comparison to the team that rescued over sixty women, shutting down the trafficking ring permanently.

Tobin had accompanied them from Costa Rica, where the rescue party had re-joined the Bucket. Knowing Jeff Johnson needed his family home, he'd organised first class priority seating on the next direct flight to London. Johnson, unable to wait, met his family at the airport.

"Mrs Johnson and Odette had fallen foul of a made-to-measure trafficking ring," reported Tobin, as he sat in the

145

comfort of Johnson's office later that evening. With a brandy in one hand, he felt slightly ill-at-ease, as he usually stood to give his reports. "Someone is in the market for young blonde girls. Odette fitted the bill."

Johnson shuddered, he needed to hear this, but he didn't want to. The thought of his daughter…

Tobin paused. Johnson was struggling to keep his emotions in check. His eyes were closed, and his fingers gripped the arms of his office chair until his knuckles were white. Jeff Johnson understood his wife's point of view now, but it was a shitty way to learn it.

"The other women found on the premises had already had their girls taken from them to God knows where. Sadly, T-cut didn't leave anyone alive to question." Johnson nodded. He totally understood T-cut's actions. He would have killed everyone in the place too.

Logically, however, it was going to be much harder to locate the girls that were taken previously. Any criminals—now in hiding—would disappear off the radar. Their only hope was the unknown driver of the taxi, and the fingerprints found at the scene, though Johnson reckoned the majority belonged to the dead. Fulwood had alerted Interpol, so they could check, and monitor in case the driver surfaced elsewhere. *Then God help him.*

One good thing came out of the horrific episode. Jeff Johnson agreed wholeheartedly with his wife about Odette going to school locally. He seriously considered putting a tracker in her too, but when he mentioned it to Vivienne she scowled and said no. He also thought about reversing his decision to have Joel board away from home, especially given his Headmaster's pending decision over exclusion. It would be easier to monitor his son's antics closer to home, but again Vivienne disagreed, and Jeff acquiesced too afraid to lose her, literally again.

Fulwood was relieved the rescue of Vivienne and Odette

146

was over. Tobin was right. He was much better at making decisions than actions these days. When T-cut went berserker on him, he froze. Travis was almost as close to T-cut in the headcount. Fulwood probably only got off a couple of shots, he guessed and doubted whether either of them did much damage in the general melee.

He sat at his desk alone, stirring his tea absentmindedly, whilst reliving the mission. *Next time, heaven forbid there'll be a next time, I'm not going to let my heart rule my head. I shouldn't have gone in with the unit. What was I thinking? It was a mistake and could have been very costly. If I'd stayed on the Bucket, I might have been able to control things better. Stopped T-cut before he went on the rampage. Given orders not to kill everybody, so we had people to interrogate. I didn't. I was caught up in the moment as much as T-cut. I wanted all those men dead too. My bad.*

Doc chose this moment to barge into the Ready Room in his, I-don't-care-what-you're-doing manner, ignoring Fulwood's annoyed glare.

"Don't you ever knock?" Fulwood grumped. "I could have been naked or something." Not that Doc seeing any of them naked was an issue. He'd seen more of their bodies than most women, considering the number of times he'd stitched them up or removed bullets and glass after missions.

Doc Williams was taken aback. He *never* knocked. It was like an unwritten rule. A privilege afforded him, giving him a bit of status. He didn't need to be a psychiatrist to know something was up. Disregarding Fulwood's outburst, he walked over and poured himself a cup of tea—it was that kind of day—then sat back in his chair and waited.

Doc spent decades assessing mental health and anxiety states. He knew every U1 member's personality traits and behaviours as intimately as their physical health. This was not Fulwood's normal operating mode. The silence between them filled the air becoming a noise in its own right.

"I shouldn't have gone," came the sentence a few minutes later. Doc said nothing. "I was a hindrance. I could have got Vivienne and Odette, or any of those women killed."

"But you didn't," came the calm voice of reason, from the corner of the Ready Room.

"But I could have," Fulwood responded.

"But you didn't," came Doc's refrain. Frank Fulwood sighed.

"No, I didn't," he admitted, dropping his head in his hands, and taking a few breaths to steady himself before asking the next question out loud. "Do you think I'm too old for this Doc?"

"Do you feel too old?" Doc asked, before risking a sip of tea.

"Today? Yes. No, maybe. Hell! I don't know…I did in Peru, afterwards. I almost phoned Johnson to tell him I was chucking it all in."

Doc thought about it. He knew why, but he needed to see if Frank Fulwood knew why this mission had been different.

"T-cut went berserk."

"I know," Doc replied.

"He told you?"

"Travis did. He needed to talk."

"I'm surprised. He seemed to hold his own. It was me that was the liability," Frank muttered, seeing in his head the scene playing out yet again. Men dropping to the floor from both of his teammates' pistols and later, Travis's blade as he dealt out mercy punishment to speed those dying on their way. "There was blood everywhere…I froze."

"I know."

"How?"

"Travis."

"Shit! That's it then," he said, rising from his chair.

"Is it?"

"Yes, and you bloody well know it, David." The use of

Doc William's first name provided proof that Fulwood was feeling under immense pressure.

Disregarding his tea, Fulwood walked over to the cabinet helping himself to a huge whiskey, large enough to make Doc's eyebrows raise almost into his white hairline.

"If I've lost the respect of the men in U1, I'll have no choice but to tell Johnson and offer my resignation." Doc thought Fulwood was overreacting, a product of the anxiety he was feeling.

"Who said you'd lost their respect?" Fulwood turned on Doc.

"It's obvious, isn't it? Travis told you," he snarled, not sounding like someone ready to give up.

"Travis came to me, concerned about T-cut, not you." Doc let that sink in before he continued. "T-cut is in his cabin, totally stressed out because he thinks he failed you." That surprised Fulwood.

"Really?"

"Yes, really. Can you imagine how he is feeling? He shot the only lead to finding those mothers' children. He is heartbroken. What he needs is his commanding officer telling him he didn't do anything wrong. That it'll all work out. Can you do that?...Because if you can't, I suggest you go and hand in your resignation and I'll support it," Doc finished bluntly.

Frank Fulwood was out of the room before Doc Williams had completed the second half of his last sentence. Terrance Mason was more than his Unit One team member; he was his comrade. It was unthinkable not to offer support to his brother-in-arms.

CHAPTER TEN – SOUTH AFRICA

Fᴌᴇᴜʀ and Atrax had boarded the 'Queen of the Seas' at Southampton, along with the usual tourist cargo. Johnson had identified that the person smuggling diamonds illegally out of South Africa wasn't travelling in third class, or steerage as it used to be called. He'd been provided with a list of twelve names as possible suspects by the South African mine owners.

"Superior class," Fleur crooned, throwing herself diagonally across the huge bed which dominated their suite of rooms.

"Remember we're sharing. Johnson's not going to fork out for two suites at these exorbitant prices.

"Well, this bed is…" she sighed, stretching her fingers out to stroke the amazingly soft fur coverlet, worth at least four hundred pounds per metre, "…divine and I'm sure the mine owners will be footing the bill."

Watching Fleur spread out on the bed like a meal for the eating, Atrax almost jumped her. Struggling to maintain his professional distance he turned away on the pretence of inspecting the bathroom to hide the tightness in his trousers and his hard erection. Thankfully when he came back out, Fleur was over by the balcony admiring the sea view.

"I could get used to this," she murmured, her behaviour not the usual teammate banter Atrax expected from the forces brat and RAF pilot. Here was the woman he never saw, in an unguarded moment of girly innocence. Teasing her, Atrax asked the question that tackled the elephant in the room.

"What side of the bed do you want? Left or right?"

For a split second, Fleur flushed at the image this conjured up in her mind. Unsettled, she turned her face away to recover her composure, but not before Atrax caught sight of the endearing blush on her cheeks. *Has Johnson put us together like this deliberately?*

"I am not sharing *my* bed with anyone, even someone as tall, dark and handsome as you." *Shit! Did I just say that?*

Atrax smiled confidently. So, he wasn't the only one with a heightened awareness of their predicament. That made him feel better. He relaxed slightly.

"You can have the pull-out bed," she advised haughtily, still ruffled at her previous words.

"To be fair, I am six-four, and you are…what five-six?"

"I'm five foot ten as you damn well know, Atrax." Fleur fumed in mock indignation. His smile widened, knowing she was touchy about her height.

"You can't keep calling me Atrax either if we're supposed to be a couple." *Is she trying to remember my real name?* He wondered, feeling a little deflated.

"Fine, you can have the bed, Baptiste." She did know it. His heart did a weird flutter, his spirits lifting. It would have lifted more if Fleur had agreed to share the bed with him in it. He grinned at the image in his mind.

They sat together at breakfast the following morning re-considering their plan. It had been suggested by Johnson, that they split up and tail six suspects each, but it was proving impractical. Three hadn't emerged from their cabins since arriving onboard ship.

Instead, as Fleur sipped her orange juice, Atrax suggested, as the ship was at sea for the next two days, they narrow down the suspects by breaking into their rooms.

"Really!" Fleur exclaimed. "What are we? Common criminals just like them?"

"If you like. I still think we should whittle the list down before the ship docks in the first port of call, Tenerife."

Fleur was still cranky after spending the night on the convertible sofa, while Atrax lazed like a gorgeous lion on the

151

Emperor-sized bed. He'd watched her toss and turn, trying to get comfortable, and considered doing some tossing of his own. He smiled.

"What have you got to smile about?" Fleur groused, throwing a bread roll at him across the table. He caught it deftly in one hand without so much as a blink.

"Nothing," he replied, placing the roll gently on his side plate, and reaching for the butter. Atrax had done a bit of reconnaissance earlier that morning, while Fleur caught up on her sleep. He'd identified each target's room location while the person had gone for breakfast, and before the daily housekeeping service arrival.

"Let's start reviewing the information we have," he suggested. Fleur nodded between mouthfuls of fruit salad. "We don't have long to find our culprit. I don't think Johnson will be happy if we arrive home empty-handed with nothing to show for it but a healthy tan. Though it looks good on you," Atrax commented.

He was rewarded with Fleur blushing once more. I wouldn't mind making more of her blush like that, he decided, then regretted the direction of his thoughts as he tried to re-adjust himself discreetly under the small table.

They began with Philip Moss's cabin. All the suspects either lived permanently in South Africa or travelled there regularly from England, using the cruise line as a kind of slow ferry service. Philip Moss resided in South Africa. He always booked an inside room.

Clean, Fleur signalled, reappearing after a few minutes, and holding up her hand to form a capital C. Atrax nodded from his position further along the lobby. They left going separate ways. They had considered one of them standing guard outside the cabin door, but Fleur reasoned that it would look more suspicious and Atrax was inclined to agree. He'd waited a short way down the corridor in the guise of reading his newspaper.

The next three cabins were the same. No clues, such as secondary identity cards, hidden items, or dual passports that Fleur could find.

Atrax had checked their current passport details using the Purser's override security pass code, courtesy of Pav on the Bucket. He'd hacked into the ship's security system with ease.

"That's four wiped off in one day," Fleur grumbled. "At this rate, we'll be finished in two days and Johnson will want us off at Tenerife."

"Don't give up yet. We still have eight more to investigate and I have a feeling things are going to get interesting."

"You were right," Fleur admitted, as she left cabin number five the following morning. "Who'd have thought he, was a she?"

"Told you."

"Yes, you did. Thank goodness there isn't a law against being a different gender than you look."

"Oh? Did you have something you wished to tell me?" Fleur blushed. Atrax grinned. He'd never get tired of making her blush. It was adorable.

"Come on, we've time to do one more today," she insisted, paying no attention to Atrax's teasing. "It's eight days at sea after this," she reminded him.

Number six, Anita Crossfield was definitely up to no good, but was she the smuggler? They found a second passport, identifying her as Anita Morley, locked away in her room safe. Atrax had obtained the management access code for the guest safes on the pretence of getting locked out of theirs. They surmised that Anita was probably keeping her current passport on her. It wasn't in the cabin.

"That's one likely suspect," remarked Fleur, flopping onto their communal bed. It was a given, that if Atrax wasn't sleeping in it, she was free to flounce across it whenever she liked.

Atrax was beginning to feel guilty about taking the bed,

but he wasn't sure how to bring up the subject without losing face. On the other hand, it was a delight watching her roll around the bed, and several interesting ideas floated across his mind.

"Tomorrow, we'll check out more," Fleur continued, oblivious to Atrax's inner turmoil.

The next four passengers were dull and non-descript. One of them was so dull there was nothing in his room to indicate he existed. Atrax's instincts flared, something was off. He could feel it. This was their perp, but they had to finish the last two suspects tomorrow before they could concentrate on Anita and this one.

"Okay, so that's all of them checked. My money is on Anita," announced Fleur at lunchtime, as they sat on the balcony outside the Italian restaurant in what would otherwise have been a romantic setting.

"I'll take that bet. My money's on Mr Gray."

"Mr Gray?" Fleur was surprised Atrax had picked the least interesting of their twelve suspects. She blushed, remembering the name's sexual association. Atrax looked blankly at her. He clearly wasn't clued up on the literary uproar that the name caused globally. *He obviously isn't a book person.*

"Why Mr Gray?" She asked again, intrigued despite herself.

"Because that's what I feel. There's no sense of a real person. Mr Gray is a shadow with no life. Maybe, he doesn't exist."

"That's silly, of course, he exists. He had to get on the boat, didn't he? He had to pass through customs. Set up his room account. Use the restaurant after he collected his ID card."

"But did he? We haven't actually seen him yet. We've taken great efforts to search their rooms when they're not there. Maybe, he's never there," offered Atrax mysteriously.

"Now I know you're talking daft. I intend to eat my lunch and forget your comments."

"Now who's being silly?"

"Okay, game on. I'll tail Anita and you shadow Mr Gray." She smiled at her choice of words, turning Atrax's words back to him. Atrax was game.

"And, if his first name turns out to be Christian, you lose double."

Not having any idea what Fleur was talking about Atrax held out his hand.

"You're on."

Tailing Anita Crossfield proved to be as boring as watching mud dry. Anita was in her mid-fifties with dyed peroxide blonde hair—or a blonde wig—false eyelashes, red pouty lipstick, and clothes better suited to a seventeen-year-old. She teetered around the deck from bar to bar fluttering her eyes at anything vaguely resembling a man. Fleur wasn't quite sure what Anita's goal was. Was she after a good time, someone with money, or was she just lonely? *Of course, she could be all three*, decided Fleur watching Anita as she leant over yet another man on the pretence of asking the time. Her assets not just on show, but about to roll out of the box. Fleur covered her mouth to hide her grin at the image she evoked.

"If I have to follow that woman in and out of the ten bars on this ship any longer, I think I might just push her overboard and save us a lot of bother," sighed Fleur dramatically. Atrax smiled. They'd met up to review their progress in one of the smaller coffee lounges on the front deck. "How did you get on?"

"It doesn't sound like I had as much fun as you," he replied earnestly. "I think Mr Gray doesn't exist. I've searched the ship. I watched his cabin. I managed to sneak a peek at his daily account records too."

"How the hell did you manage that?"

"A certain lady was very generous and kind."

"And she let you view the ship's records?"

"Of course not. I had to create a little diversion."

155

"I'm all ears," said Fleur intrigued. Atrax went on to explain how he arrived in the accounting office 'by mistake' whilst trying to locate the ship's gymnasium. He'd taken the precaution of wearing the appropriate clothing, a.k.a. tightfitting Lycra T-shirt and shorts. The woman couldn't keep her eyes off him. "Let alone her hands," he advised Fleur, and along with the chocolate he'd procured, which was supposed to be for a friend, she was putty in his hands.

"Oh, come on," muttered Fleur. "No woman is going to let you look at confidential records just because you look amazing in Lycra and had chocolate on you." Atrax wasn't slow in catching on. His ploy had been deliberate to see Fleur's response.

"You think I'm amazing in Lycra?"

Realising she might have said more than she should have, Fleur back-peddled trying to sound nonchalant and uninterested.

"I said, just because, not that you were." Her explanation sounded weak even to her ears. She could only imagine what Atrax was thinking and an image of him in Lycra popped into her head unbidden.

There was an uncomfortable pause while the two of them digested their conversation as they sipped their coffees.

"So, the upshot is, you haven't found Mr Gray yet." Atrax nodded. "And my fifty-something lonely-hearts-club hooker is as likely to be a diamond smuggler as the Pope is Queen of England." Atrax nodded again. "It's Mr Gray isn't it?" A third nod and Fleur leaned back in her chair in defeat.

Atrax explained his theory that nobody stayed onboard ship.

"Well, not one person, maybe several." Fleur looked confused. He continued. "By my reckoning, at least two came on board. They also possibly left again. Which is why there is nothing in the cabin. The cabin was booked and paid for ahead of the journey. One person must have come on board at South

Africa. Secreted the diamonds somewhere in the cabin, not the safe, then left. Either, a second person arrives whilst the ship is still in port, or another person comes on board in another port, using the same name. They only had to know where the diamonds were hidden, remove them and leave.

"So, it's more like an expensive locker in a train station?"

"Precisely."

"Okay, we monitor the cabin when it's next in port."

"Yes, but we can't assume people are getting on and off at each port. They may have a different cabin on board, we can't search every cabin. Lord knows how much contraband we'd find. Besides, the next port is Walvis Bay and that's a week away. My guess is that a member of staff is on the take and somehow involved in the supply chain. How else are they managing to get the person off the ship once they'd been counted on unless staff are involved?"

"It's always an inside job," bemoaned Fleur. "Why couldn't it be my lady? She's up to something with two passports and two names. I know it."

"I think you're right, but I don't think she is our mission." He watched Fleur's face fall. "We could run both her names through T-cut's special programme though, just to be on the safe side," he suggested, taking in Fleur's defeated expression.

Atrax was talking about another one of T-cuts' ingenious piggyback schemes. This one, hacked into Interpol, apparently following an episode where T-cut got bored one night playing GTA alone. Fleur's face lifted.

"For that, I'll take you out to dinner."

"But all the meals are paid for on the cruise ship," Atrax reminded her.

"I didn't say I'd pay for it, just that I'd take you out for it," Fleur grinned mischievously. Atrax rolled his eyes to the ceiling and held back his impulse to take her over his knee and swat her delicious backside.

U2 missions always included a bag of tech gear, and this

mission was no different. Seamark had thoughtfully packed a variety of remote control visual and sound devices developed by T-cut. Each of these were linked to their central control mobile phone, meaning Fleur and Atrax could monitor spyware from anywhere aboard the ship.

They'd done a second search of the suspected cabin and still found nothing. It was difficult because everything they moved they had to replace in exactly the same position. They couldn't tear, break, or in any way change the layout of the room, or else their perp would be aware. Fleur took the toilet apart and didn't find anything. Atrax removed all the lights and the fittings and didn't find anything either. They both rebuilt everything they dismantled.

"It's no good, we're going to have to bug it," Atrax declared, demoralised that he couldn't find the contraband. He scanned the room trying to decide where best to set their equipment in an invisible yet viable position. Fortunately, the sound bug was simply micro dots which, with a bit of luck, would be missed as he incorporated them into the design on the bedside lampshade. The camera was harder to place because they'd searched the room and knew the other person, whoever it was, was likely to do the same search and find their stuff.

Instead, Atrax placed a camera outside the cabin on the balcony, sticking it under the railing looking back into the room. With the cabin having floor-to-ceiling glass on the balcony doors, the camera should be able to pick up any person within. He worried that the adhesive wouldn't hold with all the seawater. He thought about a second camera and decided to put it outside in the corridor, facing the cabin door. Without any cameras in the room, hopefully, the person they were trying to catch out, would not catch them.

Fleur spent the next couple of days lounging in the sun on the top deck, in the guise of getting a good tan. On and off through the day, she picked up her mobile phone to all intents and purposes to look at messages and various items of interest, much as the majority of people on board.

Atrax sometimes joined Fleur on the next lounger. Other times, he was swimming lengths in the pool or working out in the gym lifting all the stack of weights on each machine. Regular users of the gym were somewhat in awe of him. The number of women attending during his sessions rose dramatically after the first couple of days—including Anita Crossfield. He ignored them all. He remained focused on mission regardless of what activity he was doing.

He'd just finished another rigorous circuit of the gym when Fleur pinged him.

"Bingo." That one word was sufficient. Atrax grabbed his towel, threw it across his shoulder and left the gym without a backward glance. The seven women in the room at the time were crestfallen. He'd only been there thirty minutes, and they were expecting to gaze longingly for at least another hour, in the hope he might notice them. At least that's what the word around the Jacuzzi pool said.

Noticing their distress, the gym staff came over to ask if they would like some assistance using the equipment. One by one, the women shook their heads and trailed out of the room. Their disappointed faces left the staff amused. They knew precisely why more women were visiting the gym in the last few days.

Atrax met Fleur as she reached the lift on their floor. They entered together and travelled down to the floor containing the suspect's cabin. In the lift, Fleur showed Atrax what the camera had picked up. He was as amazed as she. Something black split the camera view on the balcony in half. One moment it was a normal view of the cabin's interior, the next it was split in half. Fleur paused the feed.

"If you like that. You're going to love this," she said cryptically. Atrax watched astonished as the video feed resumed. A pair of feet appeared at the top of the screen. The legs belonging to the feet gradually lowered into the camera's visual field followed by the rest of the man wearing cruise ship livery. His back was towards them, so they weren't able to identify him. But more importantly, he missed spotting their camera.

"Sneaky bastard!" Atrax exclaimed, in an uncharacteristic outburst.

"It's brilliant, isn't it? Imagine renting not one but two cabins, one above the other and lowering yourself down and presumably up again."

"What do you mean presumably?"

"Well, the camera hasn't shown him going back up yet." They both realised what the implications were. If the man was still in the cabin they could apprehend him, or they could wait in the cabin above, and apprehend him there.

However, both of these approaches had flaws. If the man had not secured the diamonds yet, they'd have no proof, and he was a member of the ship's crew. They needed evidence.

"Where is he now?"

"Still in the lower cabin."

They decided to take a two-pronged approach. First, they worked out where the upper cabin was located. Knowing their perp was in the cabin below, they entered using Atrax's lock picking kit, and hastened to the balcony to pull up the dangling rope. Fleur kept her fingers crossed hoping he wouldn't notice it being hoisted back up. He hadn't identified the camera secured beneath the railing either because it continued sending images. With it in place, Fleur was able to monitor and record his movements within the cabin. She waited until he disappeared into the tiny bathroom. They still hadn't seen his face.

"Now," she whispered urgently. Atrax raised the offending item. Without a vertical means of escape, the only way out for their smuggler was through the lower cabin door. It was only going to be a matter of minutes before the man noticed that his exit route was missing, and then he'd panic. At that point, he'd be liable to stash the diamonds back in their hidey-hole, leaving U2 empty-handed in front of a security detail. It wouldn't be difficult for him to argue his way out of the situation, turning the tables on them, citing them as felons breaking into cabins. Johnson would bail them out, but by then the diamonds, their evidence, would be long gone.

They made their way back down and positioned themselves outside the lower cabin door. Fleur stayed glued to her phone.

"What on earth is he doing in there?" She whispered to Atrax.

"I'm guessing the bathroom is where the diamonds are hidden," answered Atrax, leaning over her shoulder to survey the cabin interior. "When he comes out of the bathroom, he'll have the diamonds on him. When he sees the rope missing, he'll return to the bathroom to dispose of the evidence, either secreting them back in their place or flushing them down the toilet, if he thinks the game is up."

"Shit, he could throw them off the balcony." Atrax thought for a moment.

"Yes, he could do that too and we'd be in the wrong."

"The moment he comes out that bathroom, we pounce."

At that exact moment, the only one doing the pouncing was the ship's security officer.

"Do we have a problem, Sir?" He asked, addressing Atrax, as he walked up the corridor towards them with two deck hands strolling behind him.

"No, we don't," replied Atrax coolly, "but you might." Atrax proceeded to advise the security officer of the issue of smuggling on board without mentioning the item concerned. He informed the man that they had the authority to investigate the matter on behalf of the owners of the merchandise, and the cruise line owners were aware of their presence on board.

The officer seemed reasonable and appeared to believe their story, nodding in the right places, and not expressing the expected disbelief, which Atrax should have realised was odd.

"We don't want any diamond smuggling on this ship, Sir. Thank you for bringing it to our attention. If you would like to follow these gentlemen, I'm sure we can accommodate you while I sort out the issue."

Both Atrax and Fleur picked up on the security officer's error. They gave each other the eye and a barely perceptible nod in agreement. The three men didn't know what hit them. All three were unconscious in minutes. Fleur was worried the noise of their take-downs would bring people to investigate. Atrax looked at Fleur.

"If we get the diamonds now and are caught holding on to them, we'll be the ones in trouble." She nodded. "We don't know how many of the crew are in on this apart from the security officer." He glanced down at the three unconscious men lying at their feet with barely concealed disgust. "For the amount of money involved it could go all the way up to the captain. This changes things."

"Can you hide us?" She asked, their plans to capture the smuggler forgotten temporarily. Atrax smiled and grabbing Fleur's hand they fled as the men on the floor began groaning. Fleur punched the U2 emergency beacon on her mobile as they high-tailed it out of the area.

CHAPTER ELEVEN – STUTTGART

"THERE's a call coming in from Fleur's mobile, Sir," Seamark informed Johnson discreetly, as he sat taking tea with his wife in their lounge.

"Excuse me a moment, darling," uttered Johnson, rising to step into place beside Seamark who was leaving the room.

"What happened?" He asked once he was sure they were out of earshot of his wife. Vivienne and Fleur got on well and he didn't want her to worry about his operative.

"Don't know. Emergency beacon's gone off, which means they can't make verbal contact or get away."

"Where's the Bucket?"

Fleur had set off the emergency tracker three hours ago. Currently, both were holed up behind the vast row of dryers at the back of the ship's laundry below the waterline. Atrax had piled bags of laundry in front of the access area to delay their discovery, but they couldn't stay there indefinitely as the service ran twenty-four-seven. Sooner or later, they'd be spotted, and the ship's security officer knew their faces. He'd most likely worked out their cover details, and had their cabin turned over in the search for clues—Atrax would have. He'd know wherever they came from, they were tracking the smugglers.

The mission had gone what the technical people called 'tits-up'. Although they'd identified the method of smuggling and some of those involved, they were no closer to finding the diamonds or catching the culprit behind the scheme. The diamonds must have been placed in the ship prior to its journey from South Africa to Southampton, where Fleur and Atrax boarded. They figured out that the crewmember descending the rope was retrieving the diamonds and stowing the cash in the bathroom, ready for collection by the South African contact. The cash was put in place there in readiness to be sent back in exchange for a new deposit of diamonds.

It was close to midnight when an unknown voice called out to them from across the large laundry room.

"Come out, come out, where ever you are," a female voice sang across the empty dark space. Both of them froze. "Okay only joking. You can come out now, the laundry staff have gone for a fag break." They didn't move. "You're safe for a moment, they're concentrating their search at the other end of the boat," continued the voice trying to make them believe that she'd do them no harm.

Atrax trusted his instincts. His head poked up over the top of a dryer. Anita Crossfield was silhouetted in the doorway.

"Come on," she urged. "I haven't got all night. Do you want a better safe place or not?"

They were out of the laundry room and stowed away in Anita's cabin quicker than a seagull diving on a bag of chips. "There you go," she said, handing each a glass of wine after they'd stuffed their faces. "Next time you decide to search my room please have the decency to ask first," Anita requested.

"You knew?" Fleur asked.

"Of course, I knew. You were very careful though, not the usual rough handling of my clothes."

Atrax glanced at Fleur. She'd checked Anita's room.

"Sorry," she apologised to Anita, and also her colleague, not missing Atrax's glance.

"It's all right," replied Anita. "If you hadn't. I wouldn't have known you were in trouble after I decided to track you."

"You tracked us?"

"Him actually," she said, pointing to Atrax. "Simple to

fool. He never noticed a thing when I talked to him in the bar earlier today. The tracker was easy to place when I mussed up his hair in the pretence of trying to get him to buy me a drink."

It was Fleur's turn to stare at Atrax. There was she feeling guilty because the woman had known she had searched her cabin, and now it appeared Atrax was the one that led her to them.

"Sorry," he mouthed with a lopsided grin, as he absent-mindedly checked his hair. Anita laughed watching his discomfort.

"Insurance investigator," Anita informed them bluntly, holding out her hand to shake as if that title explained everything. Seeing their blank expressions she added, "The mine owners put in a claim for the stolen diamonds. A big claim." She stressed the word big. "The company wasn't prepared to hand out such a large amount without doing their own homework. They initiated an investigation of their own into the smuggling ring. I work for the insurance company. Did the mine owners employ you?" She asked, directing her question at Fleur.

"Yes, but I'm not at liberty to say much more than that," replied Fleur.

"You are good. I mean generally when you don't have to resort to hiding in laundries. I had a devil of a time figuring you both out."

"Thank you," Atrax replied, deliberately keeping his reply brief, so as not to disclose their own agenda.

"Good, good." Again, confusion appeared on their faces. Realising another explanation was required, Anita advised. "It shows us that the mine owners were serious about getting their stuff back, and it's not an inside job on their part, like this set-up." She spread her arms to indicate the cruise ship. "Except, of course, it is an inside job, or they wouldn't have been able to steal the diamonds in the first place."

Without warning, Fleur gave a huge yawn.

165

"Oh, I'm so sorry, please forgive me," she murmured, embarrassed about her body's need to sleep.

"No problem. It's been a long day and we all need to get some shut-eye."

Anita took charge sorting out the sleeping arrangements. Fleur agreed to share her king-size bed, and Atrax was offered the pull-out bed in a role reversal of their previous cabin. Atrax didn't comment but lay down and appeared to go to sleep.

It felt a bit bizarre to Fleur as she settled down with the strangest woman she'd ever met. Anita had lent her a sleeping outfit, so she'd feel comfortable, and found her a spare new toothbrush. *Who carries a spare new toothbrush?* Fleur wondered before her eyelids grew heavy and she drifted off.

They'd contacted Johnson shortly after arriving in Anita's room, advising him that for the moment they were both safe, though they weren't sure how they were going to get off the ship alive. They assumed all of their luggage had been confiscated by the security officer who was in on the smuggling ring. Johnson told them not to worry, the Bucket was on its way and a customs vessel was going to join the party shortly. Johnson had advised its captain, an old friend of his, of the situation and been assured that they would be collected safely. He advised them to stay put with Anita, then Johnson contacted Anita's employers, just to check she was, who she said she was.

The Bucket and the U1 Team, had coincidentally, been travelling towards South Africa from the other side of the continent. The liner had been anchored for a while at Port de Tomasina, Madagascar, the only port deep enough to take its hull, whilst Doc Williams carried out several pioneering operations on the other side of the island. The local hospitals were only too happy to see such an esteemed surgeon offering his services free of charge. Doc's work continued to be a great cover story for U1—wealthy philanthropic semi-retired surgeon doing his bit for humanity.

Afterwards, the Bucket spent eight days travelling down the coast of Madagascar, around the southern tip of the island, and across to the coast of Africa. Passing Durban, East London, and stopping at Port Elizabeth, where Doc Williams had several more plastic surgery reconstructions for burn victims planned. After he finished his work and was happy that his patients were recovering, the Bucket's route took it round the Cape of Good Hope and up the west side of the huge continent. Its next planned port of call was the Canary Islands.

Fulwood got the call to take the Bucket on an intercept course to the Queen of the Seas cruise ship. He'd already been advised by Johnson this might be a possibility when U2 headed off on their mission several days earlier. Frank Fulwood was accustomed to Johnson setting the Bucket's scheduled route, based on Doc's planned surgical interventions. He recognised the mission was probably the reason why Johnson chose the African continent this time around.

Doc had just finished his latest operation in one of the nearby townships. It was forty-five minutes to the nearest airport where Hutch had dropped Doc off. Fulwood contacted Hutch who was waiting at the airport to be Doc's transport back. He advised Hutch to, "pack the Doc up and get their backsides to the Bucket ASAP."

Doc wasn't happy as he heard the Tiltrotor's approach from inside the small rural medical centre. He knew it meant that he'd have to leave. He'd walked out of the operating room, after over three hours of delicate surgery, only moments before. His patient's eyes had been horribly damaged in an acid attack when she was a child. The grafting to the eyelids had been a tricky procedure. He wanted to stay and see his patient come around, at least until he was sure she was out of the recovery phase. Grumbling about how everything stopped for U1, he gave post-operative instructions to the assisting medics, grabbed his belongings, and followed Hutch out to the aircraft. Flying at a respectable pace, they landed on the Bucket, one hour and ten minutes later.

As the Queen of the Seas travelled south, the Bucket and its accompanying custom boat headed north. Fulwood had considered transferring the U1 team members, Yin, Davidson, and Travis, over to the custom boat. They couldn't utilize the Spade for the transfer because the custom boat wasn't big enough to handle an aircraft landing. A zip-wire line was a possibility. He could see Davidson, yelling, "Yee-Hah" all the way over. He'd be in heaven.

While the rescue vessels headed their way, and the corrupt staff continued their search of the cruise ship, Fleur, Atrax and Anita, tried to come up with an idea to find evidence of the smuggling ring.

"We could go back to the cabin and locate the cash," Fleur suggested.

"It is the last place they would look for you on the ship," agreed Anita.

"It's far too risky," admonished Atrax. "If I was looking for you that would be the first place I'd look."

"What?" He said when he noticed both women staring at him.

"Really? Is it that obvious?" Fleur asked. Atrax gave his usual nod. Anita had another idea.

"What about the cabin above? We could stay there." Fleur wasn't slow to catch on.

"What do you mean we? You aren't the one they're hunting. You've got your perfect cover, drunken lonely woman looking for love." Anita giggled.

"Yes, I have got that down pat, haven't I?" She paused in contemplation. "Been thinking about changing my persona for my next task. Getting a bit bored with the over-the-top lonely-woman-seeking-love routine. Maybe slightly too close to home," she suggested demurely.

"Well, for what it's worth, I think you're brilliant. You had us both fooled. Didn't she Atrax?" Atrax said nothing.

"Don't tell me you weren't fooled by my acting, because you offered to take me out later." Fleur turned to Atrax. Her eyebrows raised in surprise.

"Is this true Baptiste?"

Atrax thought he detected a tiny hint of jealousy in her tone, and the sudden use of his first name was interesting. At least he hoped that was what he heard. He decided to tease her just a little bit more.

"Might have said something along those lines," he admitted. Fleur huffed and sat down with her arms folded. Anita winked discreetly at Atrax.

On the Bucket, the team were getting ready for the rescue mission. Michael Davidson, a.k.a Texas, a veteran of seventeen years with U1 was going to be the mission lead this time, in parallel with the customs staff. Yin and Travis St John were included in the team, with Pav as the backup team member at base. T-cut was going to sit back and observe Pav in action in the comms room. Unlike T-cut, Pav would never be going out on missions. This was due to his lack of experience; he'd never worked in an active security role or in the armed forces.

Pav was destined to become U1's permanent onboard comms officer, and he seemed to be loving every minute of his hands-on training. Who would have thought a child with his background, from his poor beginnings, would end up being part of such a huge undertaking. It was a little bit terrifying to Pav, being the one in charge instead of T-cut, but the man had great faith in him, and he wasn't about to let him down at this point.

"New message coming in from U2 operatives aboard the cruise ship, Sir," Pav announced to Fulwood over the intercom in his Ready Room.

"Thank you, Pav, I'll take it in here."

"Yes, Sir." Pav put the call through, but before he could hang up his end, T-cut intervened.

"This is a little piece of equipment I set up some years ago." Pav watched with interest as T-cut removed the headphones from Pav and placed them onto the dummy head that sat in the corner behind the monitors. Pav had wondered what it was for, he assumed it was part prank, part mascot, and in a way he was right. T-cut flicked a switch on the side of his computer tower and suddenly they were spliced into Fulwood's call.

"How on earth did you do that?" Pav asked intrigued. T-cut grinned.

"I learnt a long time ago to stay one step ahead of my boss, and because of that, I have always been someone he can count on. By boss, I mean Jeff Johnson. Frank Fulwood still doesn't know the equipment is in his room, and I'd like it to stay that way."

It felt a bit disloyal to Pav's way of thinking, but T-cut was his immediate boss, and he didn't feel the need to say anything. They sat back and listened to the conversation between Fleur and Atrax, who had decided to enter the cabin above the targeted one.

Moving to the chosen cabin was a lot easier with Anita helping them. She stood on guard, checked for surveillance cameras, and knew the route around the different decks. Soon they were outside the correct door and Atrax performed his magic, allowing them speedy access into the room. The inside was no different to any of the other cabins on this floor. The same soft furnishings in claret and gold, the same light pine veneer and the endless mirror running along one wall. The difference in this cabin was the long piece of rope now coiled up and laying on the bed.

"So, do we go down the same way as he did?" Fleur asked as she began tying her hair back.

"There's no we. I go down. You two stay here, and make

sure you cover my back," Atrax added quickly, so they didn't feel left out. "I don't want anyone pulling the rope back up and leaving me stranded. Anita has already confirmed they've placed a man outside the target cabin." Anita nodded. "Besides, I've got the best chance of climbing back up the rope afterwards." Thankfully nobody argued with him.

"Let's get on with it then," said Fleur, not wanting to be in the cabin any longer than they needed to be. They picked up the rope and Atrax secured it to the railings. Once he was happy it would take his weight, he climbed over to the outside. Holding the rope, he lent out over the ocean facing them.

Fleur's heart was in her mouth. It was a long way down if he fell, and she'd never forgive herself if he got injured, or worse, died. She watched, trying to resist the temptation of raising her fingers to her mouth to bite her nails, whilst Atrax was still in view.

Within minutes, Atrax was on the balcony below. He gave them the thumbs-up and signalled for them to lift the rope so it wouldn't be noticed. He had his mobile phone with him on vibrate in case they needed to communicate. They'd already decided the bathroom was where the stash and money were located. Atrax would search until he discovered the place of concealment. None of them knew whether it would contain anything valuable, it was a case of search-and-see.

"He's been gone ages," remarked Anita, after several fretful minutes. "You think we should go down after him?"

"No, he knows what he's doing," replied Fleur calmly, assured of Atrax's abilities, knowing he would contact if necessary. Anita's next question surprised her.

"Is he seeing anyone?" She asked, her voice turning softer with the emotions she was expressing.

Really, at a time like this? Get a grip woman, thought Fleur, horrified at the idea of Anita with her Atrax. *My Baptiste,* she amended. The phrase intrigued her. She'd not really thought of him that way before, but now she thought about it, it didn't disgust her. In fact, it appealed.

To Anita, she replied, "No, I don't think he's seeing anyone, but I know there is someone he likes." She added the last few words hoping that would put the lecherous woman off. Watching a fifty-year-old woman pout in answer to her comment, wasn't an attractive look to Fleur's mind.

Fifteen minutes later, there was a ping on Fleur's phone. She looked down to read the text from Atrax. It read, 'Found It.' She grinned. They swung the rope back over the railing and within moments the rope tensed. Atrax's hands, and then his head appeared. He climbed back over the railing effortlessly once more.

"You found it?" Despite her words, she knew Atrax would not have returned without finding something.

"No problem."

"So where was it? I'm dying to know," Fleur begged. "Put me out of my misery."

"Me too," joined in Anita belatedly, her voice sounding strangely devoid of emotion. Ignoring Anita's lack of enthusiasm, he answered Fleur's question.

"Behind the fourth tile from the bottom, in the shower." Atrax pulled a brown envelope out of his inside jacket pocket, and when they peeked inside, Fleur gave a little squeal of excitement at the wad of notes. Anita and Atrax grinned.

"Gotcha!"

"It was a good hiding place," Atrax told them. "Remind me to tap all the tiles next time we search somewhere." Fleur grinned even wider.

"I already do that when I search a bathroom," she teased. "It's number one on my list every time." Atrax knew she was lying, and amazingly when he stuck his tongue out at her, she giggled adoringly.

Anita was happy because she reckoned her company would be able to lift several sets of fingerprints from the money and the envelope.

"If that security officer or any of the ship's crew have matching fingerprints on it, we've got them," she stated.

Atrax and Fleur were busy relaying their find to Johnson, so they missed Anita leaving the cabin.

"Where's Anita gone?" Atrax queried a few minutes later looking around.

"Checking the coast is clear I guess. I think she's a bit taken with you," smirked Fleur. Atrax's face blanched.

"She's not my type. I prefer them younger with not so much make-up, and a pulse." He noticed Fleur's wide eyes and raised eyebrows. Atrax had his back to the door and a sinking feeling in his stomach. "She's behind me, isn't she?"

"Yes, she is," answered Anita, her tone bristling with anger. "Do you want this dead person's help or not?" She growled, before storming back out through the door.

Fleur was trying hard not to laugh. Atrax didn't know what to do. He'd just upset the woman who saved them, she fancied him too. Nothing compared to a woman scorned. *God help him,* chuckled Fleur.

Atrax couldn't believe this was happening. First, the mission went down the pan, and they were forced to call for back-up—the most humiliating thing a U2 operative could ever do. *Heaven knows when that will arrive.* They'd been hiding out for nearly two days. The ship's crew continued searching for them, probably knowing that once they hit port, they'd vanish. Fortunately, the crew weren't aware help was on the way. Atrax wondered what the crooked security officer had told his captain, and whether he was in it up to his neck too. Otherwise, why would they still be searching?

To cap it all, he'd just upset the one person on the whole ship able to help them, and whom they trusted. He hoped it wouldn't jeopardise their safety. *Perhaps if I slept with the woman,* he wondered briefly. *No, really bad idea. His stomach roiled at the thought.*

They trooped back to Anita's cabin in silence, where she

173

disappeared into the bathroom and didn't come out again for ages. Atrax had hurt her feelings. *Probably the comment about not having a pulse* decided Fleur. Though the other words weren't much better. Eventually, the bathroom door opened, and a red-eyed Anita shuffled out. She'd removed most of her make-up and it was surprising to see that the hair had been a wig. What they saw now was a younger woman in her mid-forties rather than her late fifties. Atrax swallowed uncomfortably. She looked a whole lot better without make-up, and with her own hair which was pale blonde.

"Wow!" Fleur exclaimed. "You look amazing! Gosh, you had me fooled. I thought you were at least ten years older."

Anita smiled, but it didn't reach her eyes. Atrax couldn't take back his comments, but he could apologise, he was man enough for that.

"I'm sorry for what I said. It wasn't nice and it wasn't necessary. You're a beautiful woman and I should have realised that, regardless of the make-up and wig. I hope you'll forgive me."

Anita, looking a lot more vulnerable without her fifties armour, gave a slight shrug of her shoulders, one side of her mouth lifting in a genuine smile this time. Atrax acknowledged they had to get on together otherwise the next few days were going to be intolerable. Neither of them could leave the cabin, and with the search still on, Anita was finding it difficult to secure extra food without anyone noticing.

"It's okay. I put a lot into my role-playing, in order to appear as something that I'm not. I suppose I should be pleased that I'm good enough to fool you. Besides, Fleur already told me you were interested in someone else." Atrax turned to face Fleur, his own eyes wide this time.

"Did she indeed?" He commented, looking Fleur clear in the face until her eyes dropped and she blushed enchantingly. "I can see the next few days are going to be very interesting."

They still weren't free. There was no way Fleur or Atrax could move around the ship. To leave Anita's cabin might very well lead to their deaths, and possibly the death of anyone assisting them. They had to wait, as Fulwood had ordered until the custom personnel boarded. Then they needed to make their presence known, otherwise, the entire cruise ship could be impounded whilst customs searched it. All the passengers would be made to disembark at the next port of call—their holiday at an end. It could mean ruination for the cruise line company, not just because of claims from discontented passengers, but because their reputation could be damaged if the press caught wind of it. That was without the damning news of a diamond smuggling ring on board.

In Salzburg, Lewis was becoming increasingly restless. He'd found Joannie, but now he felt a new urge calling him. He couldn't ignore it. It interrupted his thoughts during the day and filled his dreams at night. Despite his yearning to travel further east, for some inexplicable reason something was telling him he had unfinished business back in Stuttgart. He shared his feelings with Joannie. She seemed to understand, encouraging him to follow his heart. After all, they'd found each other by following theirs.

"Will you come with me?" He pleaded. It was a lot to ask of her, after all, they were both settled in full-time employment, and happy in Salzburg—up till this point. Joannie answered without hesitation. She had noticed the change in Lewis's behaviour. There were moments when he didn't seem present, and those moments were getting more noticeable— longer. An unusual sensation filled her chest.

"I will go, wherever you are." To some, her reply might seem concerning, obsessive even. All Lewis felt was relief. He couldn't imagine leaving Joannie behind, she was his world. If she'd said no, despite the growing ache inside his body, he would have stayed.

"I have a confession," she added, grabbing hold of Lewis's hand. "I've been feeling a strange pain here." She indicated her chest and placed his hand over her heart. He looked into her eyes and smiled.

"Ditto," he replied.

They terminated their employment in Salzburg and handed back the keys of the small rental flat to their landlady, advising her of their decision to leave the area. She'd observed a couple in love, looking to settle down, their sudden change of heart took her completely by surprise.

The intensity inside their chests increased as Lewis and Joannie arrived at the outskirts of Stuttgart. They scoured the city for the first couple of days after their arrival. Neither of them knew whether the person was male or female, but they knew there was someone, someone they needed to meet. Lewis had a hunch it was a girl. He didn't tell Joannie for fear of upsetting her.

When they couldn't locate her, they reverted back to their normal habits which involved working in the local bars, visiting touristy places, eating in quiet cafes, and making love.

Lewis had learnt a lot from Madeline Marnier about how to please a woman. How, by putting her needs first, he ensured his own were met also. The couple enjoyed each other's company immensely. Lewis was worried that a third person might unbalance their fledgling relationship. *What if the person we're sensing is a man and Joannie fancies him more than me?*

They'd decided to visit the Mercedes Museum that afternoon. It was a popular haunt of Lewis's, he was turning into a right petrol-head. On his current wages, he couldn't afford a car, but he could gawp at the latest models and prototypes on the ground floor of the museum, which also incorporated a dealer showroom. He loved the museum. The building was a feat of architectural engineering in itself. The history of the

Mercedes story started on the top floor continuing down to the ground floor, with every possible example of Mercedes transport represented.

Joannie had gone to look at the prototype cars on the ground floor, while Lewis was on the floor containing military and post-Second World War exhibits, which also caught his attention. That's where he saw her.

Joni Miyamoto stood unsure of herself, clutching a small brown suitcase in both hands. She didn't know whether she'd done the right thing travelling halfway across the world, but something called to her. It had done so for as long as she could remember. She'd tried ignoring it, blocking it out. Nothing worked. To the other students at her school, she was always distant and strange.

Joni had grown up in Shinjuku, a suburb of Tokyo city. She was born to an elderly couple. A surprise birth, her mother aged sixty, thought she'd gone through menopause ten years earlier. It made the national papers in Tokyo.

It had been difficult being a child of an elderly couple eighteen years ago. Others in her school, staff, and students alike, looked down on her. Told her she wasn't normal, she didn't look Japanese enough and wasn't good enough to be there. She proved them wrong, excelling in all her subjects and for some reason, instead of making her more likeable, it made things worse.

One evening, finding her daughter crying in her room, Joni's mother broke down and admitted her real father was an English man.

"A very strong, very beautiful man, and an accomplished master Kancho in Kyokushin karate."

With the constant insults, threats, and bullying attacks, when she was old enough Joni joined a Kyokushin club, and

177

not just any club, but the precise one where the Korean-born, Sosai, Masutatsu Oyama had trained.

The dojo was situated down a side street at the rear of a four-story building. Joni surmised that in its day the building must've looked amazing. From the spotless dojos to the pictures of their Sosai, and the large mural of him with one of the bulls he supposedly wrestled, painted on the wall to the left of the front door.

She visited Mas Oyama's grave on occasion, travelling up the wide steps and passing the ornate red-painted temple, where individuals used the space to train in various styles of martial arts and Tai Chi. Joni would bow deeply in front of the dignified vertical piece of black marble, inlaid with gold lettering, his photo, and the Kyokushin kai symbol, feeling very humble. She loved going there to pay her respects. Every time she came, students would have left items in front of the marble slab offering their respects to the master.

Secretly, she had always hoped her father may have visited Mas Oyama's shrine, but she had no way of knowing. In her younger days, she'd left notes addressed to him, notes which always vanished, adding to her fantasy that her father somehow watched over her from afar. She didn't write notes anymore. Instead, she followed her instincts, and they led her to Stuttgart and a man who she'd later discover was Lewis Blaine.

Like Joannie before, she stood staring at Lewis. Straight at him. For a moment, he thought she was looking at someone over his shoulder. He glanced around to check who the lucky man was, but when he turned back she was still staring—straight at him. He felt different. First a racing, or acceleration within his heart, but it wasn't just his heart, which felt on fire, it was his entire being. He had a burning need to hold her, to

178

crush her body to his. It was precisely the same way he'd felt when he met Joannie.

There was no need for words. They walked slowly toward each other. When they were close enough, they wrapped their arms around each other, and then just stood there, ignoring the side-ways glances from passers-by and odd looks from the staff.

They stood until Joannie found them, and when she found them, she didn't say a word either. She wrapped her arms around the two of them. They all stood together—a trio of belonging.

It must have looked decidedly odd to an outsider. The three of them standing together. Not looking at any of the exhibits or listening on their headphones to the story of the Mercedes family. No one moved. No one said anything. It was like they couldn't be seen or didn't exist. Somehow, they'd created an invisible shield around themselves.

"The museum will close in fifteen minutes," came the anonymous announcement over the tannoy. The words were like a key. They unlocked, separating back into three people. This new girl, or more accurately woman, was Asian. Lewis correctly guessed she was Japanese. It was his favourite country, and one he'd vowed one day to visit. He'd studied it extensively, its customs, its countryside, and fortunately for this moment, its language.

"Kon'nichiwa. Watashinonamaeha Ruisudesu," he said effortlessly. "Onamaehanandesuka?"

"My name is Jona," she replied answering his question.

"Oh, you speak English," Lewis responded, disappointed that he wouldn't need his much-practised Japanese.

"Yes, I studied at college. I love English," she stated in turn.

"I love Japanese too," interrupted Joannie, who had been standing next to them whilst they introduced each other. She put her arms out wide and added, "And I love both of you."

179

Jona giggled cutely, covering her mouth with the flat of her hand in that classic Japanese way that Lewis loved. It made her look sweet, feminine, and amazingly sexy to him. None of them spoke further, words seemingly unnecessary. They were connected at some basic instinctual level. Taking one hand of each girl, Lewis led them out of the museum.

CHAPTER TWELVE – TOKYO

T-CUT couldn't believe his eyes. He'd watched one of the trackers, based in Tokyo Japan for eighteen years, board a plane to Germany. *Fulwood, Doc, and Johnson are going to have a stroke*. He grinned in anticipation at sharing the news.

Pav glanced over at his colleague and saw him smirking as he watched the trackers. He didn't understand the programme. He knew that U1 had various people around the world, with trackers implanted at a subcutaneous level. T-cut appeared to monitor their health and movements. Pav wondered whether it was a type of safety programme. He also wondered if it was legal, till he'd learnt from T-cut that was irrelevant since few laws existed in international waters, and those that did were often unenforceable.

T-cut didn't appear to do a lot with the information, except get very excited when the people being tracked met up. It wasn't any of Pav's business, or maybe it was, he wasn't sure. The really interesting thing was that ninety-five per cent of those people with trackers were eighteen years old. He knew all of U1 and U2 personnel had them inserted. He guessed Fulwood might be speaking to him soon about having a tracker too.

"Don't tell me. Not another one!" Frank Fulwood groaned, pulling a dour face as T-cut entered his Ready Room with a smile threatening to cut his face in half. T-cut had come to impart his information, but also to gloat a tiny bit. He could have emailed, messaged, or phoned, but face-to-face was so much more enjoyable.

"I know, it's amazing isn't it?" He replied, his face glowing with glee.

"You think there'll be more?"

Doc was sitting in his usual chair in the corner shaking his head.

"Definitely. I bet my next R and R on it," stated T-cut.

"No good will come of this," Doc prophesied.

"God, you sound like my mother," Fulwood moaned at Doc, reaching for his desk phone to speed dial Johnson in Kent.

"What if all of them meet up?" T-cut suggested, playing devil's advocate. He was imagining the outcome of such a reunion. *Or should that be union since they haven't met yet. An orgy union!* His grin widened.

"Don't, don't even go there T-cut. I don't want to think about such a thing. And take that stupid grin off your face. Unless you want to spend tomorrow on dishwasher duty in the galley."

T-cut's grin vanished. The thought of being stuck in a tiny room in the bowels of the Bucket dealing with disgusting food leftovers made him shudder.

"Any news from Vivienne, regarding the prognosis of sibling sexual relations?" Doc asked, moving the conversation on by typically considering the medical angle, choosing to ignore Fulwood's discomfort completely. Doc had always been sweet on the professor. Her marrying his best friend and commander had not lessened his feelings towards her. He called her Vivienne too, which irritated Fulwood no end because he felt obliged to call her Mrs Johnson.

"No word yet," sighed Fulwood, feeling like the situation was getting out of hand. He ran his fingers through his number two haircut before continuing. "I didn't like to hassle them considering what they'd been through recently."

"I know but time is ticking."

"Yes, time is ticking, and it feels like a fucking timebomb is about to explode."

Doc and T-cut rarely heard their boss swear. T-cut, deciding it wasn't in his best interests to rile Fulwood further mumbled, "see you later" and left. Doc decided he would contact Johnson later to discover if he wanted him to do anything, and if so what, rather than add more pressure to Fulwood who was obviously in need of a break.

On the cruise ship, Fleur and Atrax were getting fidgety. It was only a matter of time before the corrupt crew found them. Anita advised that the crew had been ordered to undertake a discreet ship-wide search going from cabin to cabin without informing the passengers. It seemed likely the Captain was also involved in the smuggling ring too.

They needed to find another hidey-hole fast before they were discovered. If found, all three would probably be killed and thrown overboard. Atrax bet his good bottle of whisky, that they wouldn't be the first to end up in the drink on this ship. *That's the trouble with ships,* he bemoaned. *If you don't like a person you can just toss them over the railings. They either drown or the fish eat them. No messy ends.* He quite liked that idea when he thought about it—providing it wasn't him being fed to the fishes.

"Quick," whispered Anita. "You need to leave now." She waved her arm beckoning them out of her cabin. Fleur poked her head out first, checking the coast was clear despite Anita's reassurance—old habits dying hard.

"Where are you taking us?" She asked as they shuffled out of the room.

"Somewhere I'm hoping they won't think to search." That sounded mysterious. They knew the Bucket and customs boat were on their way, the customs vessel nearer, the liner plodding gracefully behind.

"I don't like this cat and mouse game," grumbled Fleur to no one in particular. *Will they get here in time?* She wondered, not wanting to voice her concerns out loud and tempt fate. She seriously hoped so because their lives might depend on it.

Anita drew them down a quiet back corridor on the port side of the ship. It wasn't one Fleur had travelled along before, and then she saw a sign. She hoped it wasn't where Anita was taking them. Unfortunately, her instinct proved correct.

"No way José," muttered Atrax. "I'm not getting in there."

"You have to," encouraged Anita. "It's the last place they'd think of looking."

"You know why that is, don't you?" Fleur murmured.

Anita at least had the grace to look at the floor. She knew what she was asking them to do was difficult. It wasn't an easy option, but it was a darn good one.

"Why does it have to be both of us? Why can't he go in there, and I go somewhere else?"

"Because…"

Anita hadn't told them her whole plan when she'd led them into the ship's chapel. She'd led them past the small altar with its brass cross and regalia, portraying an atmosphere of calm and peace, to the area behind the purple curtain.

In the back room, it was cold for a reason. Along the far wall were three mortuary shelves, just like Fleur had seen on the telly. With those massive chrome levers and pull-out trays that bodies lay on. She shivered. Anita hadn't told them the worst bit yet.

She knew at least one of the three shelves was occupied because that was how she came up with the idea. An elderly lady passenger passed away during dinner yesterday. It happened now and again on ships, oil rigs, and other maritime structures. Relatives didn't want their loved ones anonymously dropped over the side anymore. These days, companies were better prepared. In the recent past, the deceased were stowed in the bottom of food freezers, until Health and Safety became the norm. Nowadays modern vessels had their own refrigerated mortuary spaces. However, Anita knew something about mortuary trays that the general public probably never considered.

Sometimes, when someone died, their deaths were in peaceful repose, like most of us wanted. Other times, they were the result of accidents, falls, and work injuries. People's bodies didn't just lay there like angels asleep, as most folks imagined. On those occasions they bled, or seeped, or oozed, covering the floor of the shelves with all manner of bodily fluids. The shelves were built so they could be cleaned thoroughly. At the far end, there was enough room for a person to stand up at the end of the tray and not be seen from the door, maybe two at a push. It was a traditional mortuary assistant trick, to jump out on an unsuspecting trainee and scare the bejesus out of them.

"Hold on, you don't just want us to get in there and lie down on the tray. You want us to climb to the other end, jump out and stay there?" Atrax clarified. Fleur almost screamed at the thought. Atrax felt her grabbing his forearm in fear.

"Do you want to live or don't you?" Anita stated hand on hip. "You can go in here alive now, or you could end up dead in here later. Your choice." She was starting to get annoyed at these whinging so-called, secret operatives. She'd done far worse things working in a hospital years ago. *Cleaning up after splitting dead bodies isn't fun either,* she recalled.

"The doors open from both sides so you won't be locked in."

"Why would they need to open…?"

Fleur's question was interrupted. Beyond the chapel, a flurry of noise set up. People were arguing. Doors were slamming open and closed. It appeared some of the passengers had discovered the impromptu search and weren't happy.

"Hurry, they're almost here," Anita cajoled, pushing them both forward.

The morgue was in reality a big walk-in fridge when the shelves were removed. Currently, it held two residents.

"Go!" Anita ordered. Luckily for Fleur, the occupants filled the two upper shelves. She was able to crouch down on the floor and crawl along the bottom one. Atrax was close behind. They reached the far end and Anita hurriedly closed the door, leaving them in total darkness.

"Mute your phone," Atrax whispered in Fleur's ear. She

didn't want to but did as he asked, after sending a brief text, the light from the screen blinding her temporarily.

Rushing back out to the chapel space, Anita knelt on one of the raised pads in front of the altar just in time. The door to the chapel sprang open and banged against the wall. She gasped, trying to look surprised, and drew her hankie out to pat her eyes as a man in cruise livery glared down at her.

"Woman, what are you doing in here?" He bellowed. Anita sobbed louder, pretending to try and hold back her tears.

"My friend died," she mumbled, pointing towards the rear area. The crewman rushed over, pulling the curtains aside as a Chaplain ran in, in the process of donning his jacket.

"What in God's name do you think you are doing, man?" The Chaplin demanded. "Can't you see this woman is grieving? How dare you intrude on her communion with the Lord." The man had the decency to look embarrassed, and excusing himself, made the sign of the father, son, and holy ghost, and fled the room.

"Are you okay?" The Chaplin asked Anita. Glancing up, he didn't look like any Chaplin she'd ever seen. He was wearing a traditional Chaplin's jacket with a gold embroidered cross on the upper pocket, but that's where the resemblance ended. He was packed with muscles for a start, his jacket straining to contain his chest and upper arms. She couldn't pull her eyes away from his chest. *How can a man of the cloth have pecs like that? And matching biceps. Should be illegal!* She almost drooled. Realising she could hear someone talking to her, Anita looked up.

"Where are they?"

"Sorry what?" She replied, thinking, I sound like some senile old lady, ready for the care home.

"Fleur and Atrax. Where are they hiding?"

"Who are you?" She asked, blown over, and not just by the fact this gorgeous take-me-to-bed hunk of a man, knew her new friends' names. Then her brain kicked in. *What is the matter with me?*

"I'm Davidson, Michael Davidson," the man offered, realising the religious clothing he'd borrowed appeared to be confusing this gorgeous woman kneeling in front of him, like she was about to worship him, in more ways than one. He smiled down at her, still on her knees and when she smiled in return the room lit up. "From Unit One," he added, hoping that would bring this voluptuous woman out of her stupor. She was built just the way he liked—plenty of curves to hold and hug.

"Oh!" *Pull yourself together woman, you're supposed to be an investigator.* The pep talk did the trick. Anita rose off her knees and assessed the man standing in front of her with a critical eye, rather than that of a bitch on heat.

"Yes, Fleur and Atrax. Do you have any evidence to prove that you are who you say you are?" She enquired, wanting to keep the mountain of lusciousness speaking for as long as possible.

"No, I could always go over to the mortuary and ask them," he replied, his tone slightly sarcastic. Anita tittered like a teenager. She couldn't believe it. *What is wrong with me? Get a grip woman!* Somehow he knew where they both were, so the pretence was over, regardless of what Anita said or did.

"How did you know?" She asked, sauntering over and pulling the curtain aside once more. Davidson was distracted by her delightful backside as it swayed provocatively.

"Er, Fleur texted a couple of minutes ago, saying she had to mute her phone. Said she was in the chapel. The mortuary was the natural conclusion."

"Yes, that would do it. Clever move with the jacket by the way." Davidson smirked.

He'd seen it hanging on a hook outside the door. Hearing the crew member shouting inside, he'd grabbed it. It was far too small and looked silly on him, but the crew member failed to notice. Anita walked to the three doors and bending low, pulled the lever opening the bottom one. Davidson sighed. Fleur and Atrax shuffled out moments later.

Fleur was shivering fit to burst, waving her arms about in an effort to warm herself. Atrax didn't think twice about pulling her to him and hugging her close again—as he had inside the cabinet—knowing their body temperatures together were better than apart. Davidson, walking back to the curtain, ripped it from the ceiling rail and proceeded to wrap Fleur up in it.

"My kind of man," sighed Anita, not realising she'd said it out loud. All heads turned in her direction.

"The customs boat, beat the Bucket to the cruise ship by forty-five minutes," Fulwood reported to Johnson as he gave his account of the rescue. "The noise and banging they all heard were the customs officials and U1 searching the ship, not the smugglers as they imagined, but they were right to hide. I never would have thought of searching a mortuary shelf."

"No," agreed Johnson, "quick thinking on the investigator's part." Fulwood agreed. "We could do with more people like that in Unit One," he suggested, hoping Johnson would take the bait and succumb to women on board U1. He didn't. *Nice try Frank, better luck next time,* thought Jeff, hiding his smile.

"And the diamonds?" He enquired, bringing the debriefing back to the mission parameters.

"Two of the ship's crew, plus the SSO."

"A corrupt Ship Security Officer. Not good for a company's reputation. Did we manage to keep it hush-hush?"

"Yes, the man was taken off by the officials with 'suspected appendicitis.' He was then transferred to the security base at Libreville, in Gabon. The passengers were none the wiser. The noise and banging were explained away by cavitation around the propeller." Living on board for several years, each had first-hand experience of the phenomenon caused when air bubbles imploded under extreme pressure.

"Good work U1."

"Thank you, Sir." Johnson was about to sign off.

"Sir?"

"Yes, Frank?"

"About that other problem, the Blaine boy. You still have Travis on it?"

"Yes, I'm working on it."

"Good to hear. We await your update. U1 out."

"Roger that, U2 over and out." It was only a video call, but Johnson and Fulwood always signed-off military-style.

After three months, Lewis and his girlfriends moved out of their small one-bedroom apartment in the poorer part of Stuttgart. With three of them working full-time they could afford the deposit for a bigger place, despite the fact they all slept together in one king-sized bed. Both girls were petite and didn't take up a lot of room. The other residents in the rundown apartment block thought him a lucky bugger to have secured not one, but two stunning girlfriends. They weren't quite sure how he did it, especially considering how young he was.

Lewis would have agreed with them if he'd known their thoughts. The girls were both so different. Joannie was an experienced sexual partner. She reminded him a lot of Madelaine. Her knowledge made their bedroom antics a lot more fun. *The things she can do with that mouth are obscene.* Lewis felt his cock harden just thinking of her hot wet mouth wrapped around it. He was pleased he'd been able to teach her a couple of new moves, though they hadn't had sex up against the front door letterbox—yet.

Joni was the complete opposite. A virgin when they met. Was it really only seven months ago that he was one too?

Lewis gently schooled her in the art of love-making, helped along by Joannie supporting and reassuring her new friend. Neither of them were interested in each other, their love interest lay with Lewis and him alone. He could hardly believe how much his life had changed, from the sullen schoolboy to a working adult with responsibilities and not one, but two women to care for.

It was a bizarre coincidence that all three of them had never known their birth fathers. That two of their mothers had raised them single-handedly. They accepted these facts and moved on, agreeing they were more interested in getting on with their new lives together than wallowing over their past histories.

Jeff Johnson contacted Lewis Blaine's mother Victoria, to tell her they had found her son. The tracker Travis placed hadn't lasted long on Lewis's skin, as suspected, but long enough for Travis to build up a picture of the boy's daily routine.

Since that first tracker, Travis had managed to apply several permanent trackers on various articles belonging to Lewis. Currently, there was one inside the heel of his left shoe, another inside his wallet and a third sewn inside the lapel of his favourite jacket. The ingenious methods Travis St John employed to apply them included; a despatch rider running Lewis over, a pick-pocket who owed Travis a favour, and a local prostitute.

Victoria Blaine was relieved and furious in equal measure when U1, or more accurately U2, contacted her. Johnson advised her that her son was safe and well and working in Europe. He would not give her any more details, despite her shouting and crying down the phone at him. He told her if she didn't stop creating he would be forced to put the phone down. Her cries reduced to sobs and her sobs to the occasional sniffle as she tried to take in what he had said, and what he wouldn't say.

Johnson reminded Lewis's mother that her boy was over

eighteen. As such, they weren't obliged to advise her of his whereabouts, or indeed the fact he was alive. They did so, as a favour to their past colleague, John Redshaw.

Victoria Blaine realised belatedly, that her son had turned nineteen, soon after he had left England. It broke her heart. She'd planned a big event for him, with the presentation of his first car despite him not having a driving licence, or even taking lessons. It was a Mercedes, his favourite. She felt sure it would give him the incentive to learn to drive and pass his test.

Lewis's mother didn't know her son had already taken his driving test in Stuttgart, at the age of nineteen, with barely a smattering of German. He'd passed, driving a beat-up nineteen-eighty-four Mercedes Benz borrowed from his boss, Hannah.

"Why won't you tell me?"

"I've told you, Mrs Blaine. Your son Lewis is over eighteen and is considered legally to be an adult. I am therefore not required to give details of his whereabouts without his consent."

"But I'm his mother. Surely, I have a right to know."

"I'm afraid your rights ended when your son turned eighteen," Johnson repeated again.

"That's not fair."

"I know, but it's the law."

"Isn't there some way you can tell me, or at least give me a clue of where he might be?" Victoria Blaine could feel her son's life slipping away from her. She used her trump card in her final sentence. "What would his father John Redshaw say to you?"

That sentence stopped Jeff Johnson in his tracks. John Redshaw, his friend and comrade, was often in his thoughts over the intervening years. He could see the moment, as clear as yesterday, the moment replaying over and over in his mind. John receiving permission from Jeff, grabbing the rail on the

Bucket, his home, and vaulting over the side into the water, then swimming away, disappearing forever.

He thought about his children. How he might feel if someone told him he could never see them again. His heart twisted inside his chest. Especially, considering how close he'd come to losing Odette only a few weeks prior.

"There is one way."

"Anything."

"I could send in an operative posing as a private detective. We could say you'd sent him, but I still won't tell you where he is unless he agrees." It was the best offer Victoria Blaine could get and it was better than nothing. She took it.

Fulwood called Travis to the Ready Room to discuss his next mission, or rather the continuation of his current one.

"Let me get this straight. You want me to pose as a Private Eye, pretending to be employed by Lewis Blaine's mother. Have I got that right?"

Fulwood nodded.

Travis St John was getting fed up with babysitting duty. Four times now he had gone to Stuttgart, and placed trackers, on or around this young Casanova shacked up with two girls having the time of his life.

Lucky bugger, thought Travis, who though never short of girly action, couldn't get any while he was on the Bucket. *I suppose at least I'll be able to have some fun on dry land because it's like a sexless desert out here,* he concluded, thinking about Johnson's stupid, 'No Women On Board' rule.

Stuttgart airport was an unusual building. A huge open plan warehouse-style facility with pillars stylized as huge white trees, bare of leaves, holding up the roof like it was Christmas indoors. As before, Travis hired a car from the dealership on the left-hand side of the main doors. His car was driven around to where he waited in the designated space outside the entrance. He stayed in the same hotel as before too, the Maritim on Silk Road. He loved the food there and the pool, though shallow, was enough for him to do his lengths.

Travis decided to come straight out with it and tell Lewis the lie, that his mother had hired him to find her son. It would be the type of thing Lewis would expect, seeing as how his grandfather owned shed loads of money. It wouldn't have been difficult for Victoria to convince her father to hire a detective, and to be honest, if U1 could find him, so could others. True, most may not have had state-of-the-art trackers at their disposal.

Travis climbed the grimy stairs of the five-story apartment, the lift being out of order, according to the notice sellotaped over the call buttons. It wasn't a grand affair, and it wasn't particularly clean in the communal areas. Travis hoped that the inside of Lewis's apartment was in a better state for him and his girls. He knocked on the door and waited.

After a few moments, the door was opened by the petite Japanese girl, Joni. She tipped her head to one side, apparently considering Travis's appearance. Then straightened her head suddenly, so her hair flicked vertically into the air.

"Why are you here? What do you want?" Joni had never seen the man before in her life, and though she felt confident in her karate abilities, this man unnerved her. His presence was intimidating.

"I'm looking for Lewis Blaine," answered Travis, slightly taken back by Joni's unusual style of communication. He put it down to being a cultural thing.

"Oh… He's not here." Joni panicked when she realised the man might think she was alone, so she blurted out another sentence. "He's due back soon though."

Her accent was utterly captivating to Travis. *Too young*, he chided himself. *She looks about twelve, not my thing at all.*

"May I come in and wait for him?"

Joni wasn't sure about that. Lewis hadn't told her to expect anybody looking for him. She wasn't sure whether Lewis knew this man or not.

"How do you know Lewis?" Travis avoided Joni's question.

"His mother sent me. She's worried about him." He'd decided the explanation was as close to the truth as possible, given the circumstances. Seeing this as a plausible reason, Joni opened the door wider and stepping to one side invited him in.

Such a trusting girl. Trusting and naïve. Anyone could walk in here and she wouldn't be able to do a thing about it. Travis didn't know what Joni was capable of, he incorrectly assumed she was vulnerable.

"Can I make you a coffee while you wait?" She didn't give Travis a moment to reply before she repeated her previous question, realising belatedly, he hadn't actually answered it. "How exactly do you know Lewis?"

"I don't," Travis admitted.

Recognising she may have made a terrible mistake, Joni wondered whether she should ask the man to leave their apartment.

"I thought you said you knew him," she accused.

"No, I said his mother sent me. Or more correctly, his father. Or more accurately his surrogate father." Joni wasn't sure what to do with all this information. She was becoming more confused the longer the stranger stayed in their home. Lewis hadn't mentioned a father. Joni was regretting her impulse decision to open the door to a man she didn't know.

"What time are you expecting Lewis home?" Travis queried, changing his tack as he noticed the girl fidgeting.

Joni was starting to worry. She didn't know whether to tell this man the truth or not. She didn't know whether he was sent by Lewis's mother. He could be there to harm them. She wasn't sure why she thought that and she had no proof, but...

"Do you have any proof of identity?" She asked him

abruptly. With hindsight, she should have done that before she let him in. *He could be a madman or an axe murderer.* She'd read about those in her crime novels.

"I do," he replied, calmly reaching into the inside pocket of his jacket. He pulled out a conveniently forged—courtesy of Seamark—business card identifying him as Private Detective John Travis. It was a good play on the words in his name, Travis St John, and one he liked to use when needing a different ID.

Joni turned the card over in her fingers reading his name and business details. There wasn't a lot written there, he could have printed the card himself, so it didn't really prove who he was. She still hadn't answered his question, so he prompted her again.

"When did you say you were expecting Lewis home?"

"I didn't," she replied, feeling more uncomfortable by the second. Sensing her increasing discomfort Travis decided to shorten his stay.

"I don't want to be in your way or make you feel uncomfortable. If you don't mind, I'll go and wait in my car." She nodded, simultaneously relieved and suspicious that he might have sensed her feelings and decided to go before she asked him to leave.

Travis missed Lewis entering the building. Instead of arriving through the main entrance, he'd parked his car at the back of the apartment block and gone in through a maintenance door.

The first time Travis caught sight of Lewis, was when he exited the front doors with both girls in tow, some twenty minutes later. He concluded Joni had told Lewis about his visit and his comment about waiting outside in the car. He watched as Joni expertly pointed out where he sat five cars down on the left-hand side.

Lewis, together with his entourage, strode across the road at a determined pace. They were almost halfway to him when the first shot rang out. Travis knew what it was instantly. A bullet from a high-powered sniper rifle, the shot probably taken from… He turned, tracing by line of sight, the bullet's probable trajectory in reverse.

Lewis ducked. His reflexes super-humanly fast, automatically shielding the girls with his body. Having fired rifles as a boy in Colorado, he knew that sound too.

"Run," he ordered. The girls ran. They didn't scream, ask silly questions or hesitate, they followed Lewis's commands and directions to keep low. They fled in the direction ordered, straight inside a cafe he'd indicated which sat directly below the sniper's position.

Good thinking Lewis, remarked Travis, watching the boy run into the building behind the two girls. They were safe for the time being, so Travis headed into the building from a side door in the hopes of apprehending the sniper. He needed to navigate the building and locate the roof access without knowing the layout.

Arriving on the roof a few minutes later, Travis knelt at the edge and retrieved the single bullet casing, *Sloppy.* As he rose, he heard footsteps behind him, the sniper wasn't the only one who was slipping. *Shit!* He turned slowly not wanting to spook the person behind him. Any sudden movement could make an assailant with a gun, jumpy.

Lewis Blaine stood there. Eyes blazing furiously. Fists clenched. Face determined. Ready to take down anyone against him. Travis, knowing that posture, raised both his palms in the universal sign of surrender.

"It wasn't me."

"I know," answered Lewis, his voice monotone and dangerous. He recognised this person as the drunken man in Hannah's bar several months ago

"Why are you here?"

What could Travis say? I've been following and tracking you for months? *That wouldn't sound good,* he decided.

"I was asked by a friend of your father to watch over you and yours." It wasn't a direct lie, there was an element of truth in there. Fulwood had sent him on mission, and he was a friend of John Redshaw.

"Really?" Lewis Blaine didn't appear to believe Travis's explanation. "Why did you tell Joni that my momma sent you, then? And why have I only just heard about this friend of my father now?" Travis couldn't think of an answer to that, so he played the dumb card.

"Don't ask me, I was only told to find you. To say hello and keep you safe."

"Why do I need to be kept safe?"

"Search me!"

"So, let me get this straight. A friend of my father sent you to me, not my momma," Lewis stated, his tone disbelieving as he summarized Travis's replies.

"That's about it," confirmed Travis. "He did it because your mother is pulling her hair out over your disappearance. I thought your partners might be more welcoming if I said it was your mother who sent me."

"Who is this friend of my father?" Lewis asked, not missing the fact the man had said partners, meaning he'd been watching them for some time. He'd never heard of anybody connected with his father, John Redshaw. He knew a bit about his father, including that he excelled at karate, and he knew his father was missing. He also had a good idea what he looked like based on his mother's description, though his mother seemed a bit cagey about certain features. Now someone was popping up out of the woodwork eighteen years later, claiming to be a friend. He didn't buy it.

"Does my momma know you?"

Travis could either say he was the private detective as they planned, or he could say something else. He took in Lewis's demeanour and realised the boy, for that is what he was to Travis, wouldn't take being lied to well. So far, most of Travis's comments had held a kernel of truth.

"Your mother doesn't know me, or my boss, but she knows

who we work for. She has known about our organisation since before you were born. Your father worked for us. I understand we rescued her once." Travis, realising he might have said too much, clammed up.

All this was news to Lewis, though it made sense of a comment his grandfather had made some years ago, about being glad his daughter was back home and safe. There was something about her running away, going off the rails when she was younger, before Lewis was born. Maybe these people found her and brought her home, it was possible.

"Say, I believe you. What exactly are you doing here now?" Actually, as a result of the bullet Travis held in his hand, he had a really good reason which he put to the boy.

"My boss says you might be in danger. He sent me to watch out for you."

"You haven't done a very good job so far," muttered a disgruntled Lewis. "We've just been shot at, in case you didn't notice."

"I know, sorry about that. I seriously wasn't expecting a sniper."

"What were you expecting? A bomb perhaps?" Travis's face dropped. *I'm making a right pig's ear of this.*

"Can we at least get off this damn roof?" He asked, noting Lewis's posture had relaxed somewhat since his explanation. "Only it's not the safest place in the world, and I don't fancy being the next person used for target practice."

Lewis wasn't sure he believed the man completely, but his priority was to check the girls were safe, and he couldn't do that on the roof. He nodded to Travis and turning his back on him headed towards the stairs.

The girls were sitting in the back of the crowded coffee shop well away from the windows. There was a Police unit outside, investigating the reported gunfire. Lewis approached the girls with Travis bringing up the rear. Their fearful eyes grew wide seeing Lewis, who smiled. They both jumped out of their chairs and ran to him, throwing their arms around him and kissing him, regardless of how they looked to the other patrons in the shop.

"Lewis, Lewis!" Are you okay?"

"You're not hurt are you?" They both began checking his body for signs of injury.

"When that noise whistled past my ear, I was terrified," declared Joni. Joannie nodded her agreement. Lewis noticed both girls were trembling. He held them close and the three of them returned to the table in the corner, ignoring Travis's presence.

Once Lewis had the girls seated, and ordered coffee, he motioned Travis to join them at their table. Travis experienced a strange sensation. *This boy has power,* he decided, taking a seat opposite the three teenagers. *The three of them look similar too.* He wondered whether any of them had noticed that fact. The two girls, both had long black hair. Lewis's though black too was shorter, just off his shoulders. They all had deep brown eyes, with olive complexions and bizarrely a matching flat mole on their left cheeks.

Once the waiter had served them drinks, and all three had added three sugars to their coffees, Travis realised they were waiting for him to speak. He took a deep breath and began a somewhat doctored story of John Redshaw. He left out all the unbelievable facts, and also the extensive family tree, which caused even Travis St John to blink a few times when he'd heard it from Fulwood.

"Let me get this straight. My father, John Redshaw, who I never met, worked for an international organisation, which you can't tell me about, but you now work for too." Travis nodded. He recognised that it was a lot for the boy to take in and the two girls sitting on either side of him looked like lost kittens. They hadn't got a clue about their parentage.

"So, what's different, why have you appeared now?" That was easy to answer. Travis was starting to get irritated by the boy's superior manner. He needed to be put in his place.

199

"Because you, decided to run away from school like a naughty little boy." The girls turned and looked at Lewis.

Having two girls on call for sex whenever he wants it, is going to his head. Well, one head anyway. He smiled at his own joke.

"What is there to smile about?"

"Sorry, just a personal joke, is all. Regardless, if you hadn't run away, we wouldn't be sitting here having this conversation."

"And what about being shot at? Is that part of this too?"

"No, that isn't part of this. I'm not sure what it is part of, but I know a man who does, as they say in the adverts." That sentence was lost on Lewis, he'd grown up in America and didn't watch English television. Like many people his age, he spent most of his time viewing Netflix or YouTube.

"Where do we go from here?"

"Well, I'm going to do some research on this bullet casing."

Travis pulled the casing from his pocket that he had picked up on the roof earlier. It was a Spitzer round. The type featured a protective copper jacket, capable of withstanding high pressures and velocities that would destroy a plain lead bullet. It was known from its jacket, as a full metal jacket round. Travis knew very well what it was, as he twisted it in his fingers expertly. He didn't want to worry the teenagers unduly.

"It may bring up some information. If there's anything on it we'll find it. Meanwhile, I suggest you and the girls, keep a low profile. The sniper knows where you live. It might be better to move you out. Have you any idea where you'd like to go next?" Lewis Blaine looked at the two girls. The three of them together in unison announced, "Saint Lucia."

CHAPTER THIRTEEN – SÃO TOMÉ

"I SWEAR on my grandmother's crucifix, they all said St Lucia, simultaneously. It was downright eerie, gave me the heebie-jeebies."

"Okay Travis, thanks for the Intel," interrupted Fulwood. "Can you work on them? Encourage them to find somewhere else they would go. Tell them we can't afford to pay for three of them to move and live there. Suggest somewhere else nearby, maybe Italy?"

"Italy's not cheap," Travis replied.

"Some of it may be," said Fulwood mysteriously, knowing Johnson had recently purchased a property near Lake Garda as a summer retreat.

Travis didn't have to push very hard. The following day another shot rang out. This time as Joannie was leaving the apartment to travel to work. It missed her by millimetres, as she too like Lewis before her, appeared to move with lightning speed. The bullet ploughed into the wall behind her, sending shards of concrete flying. Two pieces hit her left arm, slicing through her flesh like it was marzipan. She screamed in shock, the blood running down her arm.

Travis, who'd slept in his car overnight, applied pressure to reduce the bleeding while he waited for the emergency services. She was a strong girl, she didn't faint or have hysterics, but she needed treatment and several stitches at the local accident centre.

By the time Lewis and Joni had arrived at the centre, following Travis's phone call using Joannie's mobile, he had everything under control. Joannie's wounds had been cleaned and dressed and she had calmed down. That was until the other two appeared, and then she burst into tears. They hugged her and kissed her until she stopped crying.

Travis felt uncomfortable with their overt displays of affection. Even the boy Lewis seemed emotional when the girls were with him. He longed to be taken off this mission. If it was a mission and not some kind of bizarre babysitting duty. Shooting at someone didn't really come under the list of things to be careful about whilst childminding. He'd wanted to go after the sniper, but the girl needed treatment. He couldn't leave her bleeding on the street while he chased down the baddies.

Fulwood decided to move the teenagers. Ideally, he wanted them to go voluntarily, but he'd arrange to do it with them sedated, if necessary, he informed Travis. U1 had done it countless times on other missions.

U1 had been investigating the sniper bullet Travis found. The FMJ was worrying. It spoke of a professional hitman, but why? It was only a matter of time before the shooter got lucky. What was more amazing was how they'd survived two attempts, and Fulwood couldn't figure out who would want to try and kill three harmless kids in the first place. His only guess was something to do with Lewis's grandfather, senator Blaine.

"Found something you may like," reported T-cut, entering the Ready Room unannounced later that day. *That's becoming a habit,* noticed Fulwood, looking up from his notes, *and one I'm going to put a stop to soon. It's bad enough that Doc saunters in here like he owns the place. I can't cope with T-cut doing it too.*

Frank Fulwood wasn't a bad boss, or even difficult to get on with. He didn't know if it was because he wasn't as seriously scary as Johnson, but the U1 members seemed to treat him differently. Sure, they listened and obeyed his orders without question. Somehow, though he didn't exude the same kudos as Jeff Johnson, plus in the past, he'd been 'one of them.' To T-cut's way of thinking maybe it appeared he still was.

"Any chance you could knock before you enter, Mason," Fulwood inquired, putting an edge of authority into his voice by using T-cut's last name.

"What and change a habit of a lifetime?" T-cut replied, moving over to sit in Doc's chair. "Nah!"

Fulwood groaned inwardly. *This is going to be a long battle.* While Travis sorted out the teenagers, it appeared the Bucket had other work to do.

The heat haze turned the foliage around Owen Spencer into a tropical Monet painting.

Thinking on it, he wished it were as cool as Giverny in France. He adjusted his position, attempting to remove more sweat from his hands and face and relieve the pins and needles where he gripped the night-vision binoculars. He could hear Davidson's last words in his thoughts now.

"You should take the tripod rest. You may be there hours at a time."

Spencer had scoffed at Davidson's remark, feeling uncomfortable with his teammate's show of concern. With hindsight, he was wishing he'd taken his comrade's advice.

That was over seven weeks ago when he was dropped off by Hutch in the Spade, at the International Airport on São Tomé Island off the west coast of Africa. Posing as a wealthy bird-watching tourist, Spencer was booked into one of the deluxe hotels, his deep undercover role.

His mission, special reconnaissance to discover what was going down at a certain property overlooking the beach on the edge of Ôbo National Park, in the south of the island. The property had been rented by one Jorge Martins; a Portuguese entrepreneur. Checking their database, T-cut found the man was currently wanted for arrest by Interpol. The man in question had yet to make an appearance on the premises.

The park was a vast area of rainforest, sea cliffs and cascades, rich in birdlife and good for hiking. It provided the perfect cover for Spencer to observe the goings-on at the target premises. He understood the hotel owner, one Leumas Sille, was footing the bill for this mission, which was unusual. Spencer wondered if Fulwood was doing an ex-buddy a favour.

The house, situated on land owned by Sille, had developed a shady reputation since his decision to rent it out privately. He wasn't happy about it, but without evidence, he couldn't kick the wealthy tenant out. One negative news report, he'd said, could ruin his hotel's reputation, meaning the high rollers might leave to spend their fortunes elsewhere.

The Bucket, after rescuing the U2 operatives from the cruise ship, had continued up the coast of Africa and was now docked on the island at Ponte Baleia, to the south of Spencer's position. It had been directed there as back-up after Fulwood received contact advising him of movements involving a helicopter. This occurred every Tuesday and Friday evening, and Spencer was sure it was drug-related activity. It was Tuesday today.

The breeze increased around him, brushing the right side of his face and arm, a welcome relief from the early evening's heat. Settling back to his observation duty, Spencer heard an expected noise, the sound of rotating helicopter blades. He adjusted his earpiece and whispered.

"Subject craft on approach."

"Roger that," came the response. Neither said anymore. T-cut in the comms room knew Spencer would continue when there was more to report. Likewise, Fulwood, listening in, would comment if there was to be any change to his orders.

The helicopter, an expensive twin-engine Agusta 109, came in low across the bay. Spencer, situated on a rise to the left of the property which faced the bay, observed its approach. He didn't need to be told to lower his head to prevent his face from being spotted, he did it out of instinct. Stealth missions could fall apart on one point of light reflecting off a piece of pale skin.

The craft hovered in front of the house nestled a few hundred yards back from the beach as if deciding whether to land or move on. Spencer was in motion, seconds after the first burst of a semi-automatic rattled the stillness of the air. Birds and wildlife scattered in all directions terrified by the awful racket. The house windows shattered, the lights going out as bullets found their target. Spencer paused, catching his breath beneath the safety of the tree canopy. The craft remained in place and suddenly, before it swung away taking the same route back across the shadowy water, a body was thrown into the sea.

The U1 operative tore down to the water's edge, ignoring his safety. He calculated the depth of the water at that point realising that if the body, or person, could have survived the fall, they might theoretically, still be alive. Problem was they appeared bound and gagged so death was inevitable unless Spencer did something— like yesterday—within the next few seconds.

Taking a gamble that someone wasn't watching from the receding copter, he raced into the water, striking out long and fast. It wasn't an easy swim, strong undercurrents were pulling at him, and he expected the water to be peppered with gunshots at any moment. In his head, he was trying to triangulate the victim's position underwater. Turning once to check his location from shore, he dived.

The water thankfully was clear. First-time down nothing. He surfaced, gulping air fast. Dove again, keeping his eyes open despite the salty sting. *There! A red shirt!* Grabbing the fabric collar, he surfaced a second time. The deadweight almost dragging him under. Manoeuvring the person around, he secured their chin above the surface not sure if they, correction he, was still alive. The swim back to land, towing the literally dead weight, seemed to take forever. It was hard enough swimming out with the tides.

In between strokes, Spencer relayed his report to base through his fortunately waterproof earpiece.

"On it," came the succinct reply.

"I'm never going to live this down," he muttered, as he proceeded to administer full CPR to the man he rescued, now laid out on the sand in front of him.

Owen Spencer was still working on the man as Hutch arrived with reinforcements. Tobin and Doc took over, using the automatic emergency defibrillator or AED. Spencer sat back on his heels exhausted. Someone thrust a bottle of water into his hand and he drank without even the strength to offer a grunt of thanks. They continued working on the man until at last Doc gave a satisfied sigh. He left Tobin to tidy up the equipment and organize getting their patient on the Spade which had landed on the beach nearby.

"You saved that man's life," stated Doc Williams without any preamble.

"He would have done the same for me." Doc's eyebrows lifted.

"Really?"

Spencer nodded, lifting the top of his T-shirt sleeve as explanation. A rare special forces tattoo was emblazoned on his shoulder—just above his simple U1 tattoo. A vertical Fairbairn Sykes fighting knife, with two blue wavy lines behind it indicating water and underneath the words 'By strength and guile.' Doc guessed if he was to inspect the other man, he would have the same special forces design emblazoned on his upper arm.

"Ahh."

"Saved me in a couple of tight spots." Spencer looked over at Doc. "Do me a favour. Don't tell him it was me that saved him when he wakes up."

It was Doc's turn to nod. He understood these men. They were not just strong, they were fearless. Any show of weakness or obvious care was frowned upon by them. Letting someone know you saved their life, making them potentially beholden to you was just not done. It was bizarre to Doc's way of thinking because they loved each other like brothers and would die for them too.

Despite Spencer's request, the man he saved managed to find out the truth accidentally before the planned debriefing session with Fulwood a couple of days later.

"Good morning, Mr Greenhill. Glad to see you awake. How are you feeling today?" Doc Williams asked as he entered the Bucket's sick bay for his morning duties.

"Much better, Sir," replied Greenhill, his military training instinctually recognizing a senior officer. "And please call me Liam or just Greenhill," he added.

"Good, good," Doc replied absentmindedly, completely missing Tobin's glare from his station telling his Boss to keep it short. "How did you end up in the sea and involved in the Unit One mission anyway?" Doc enquired, forgetting it was Fulwood's job to run debriefing sessions.

Liam Greenhill's eyes widened. He'd heard of Unit One, all special ops knew they existed, but to meet someone who was not only part of it, but an operative within it was extraordinary. Thinking he might have misheard he repeated the call-sign.

"Unit One Sir? The Unit One?"

"Yes, yes," answered Doc dismissively. Then completely forgetting his promise to Spencer, just a couple of days ago, bowled on. "That's not important. What I want to know is how you ended up being thrown from a helicopter. If your old friend Spencer hadn't been on the spot, pulled you out, and administered CPR, we wouldn't be having this conversation." Tobin groaned.

If Greenhill was surprised at learning he was on a U1 vessel, when he heard that Owen Spencer had saved his life, he was officially gob-smacked.

"No!" Was the only comment he uttered.

"Yes."

"No!"

The Doc, recognising he'd let the proverbial cat out of the bag about U1, and in particular, Spencer's specific request not to tell his special forces buddy, tried to backtrack.

"That is to say he radioed for help. Tobin here and myself, we did the necessary to keep you alive." Greenhill turned his head towards the nurse.

At the workstation, Tobin shook his head dropping it into his hands. Spencer was not going to be happy about this revelation to their patient. Not to mention Fulwood, when he discovered Greenhill now knew he was on a U1 vessel.

"Let me get this straight, you're telling me that Owen Spencer saved my life by performing CPR on me?"

Realising his patient wasn't stupid, Doc reluctantly admitted it was true.

Liam Greenhill smacked both his hands on the bed, threw back his head and laughed, but it wasn't a happy laugh, it was a laugh born of vexation.

Doc Williams groaned inwardly. He'd forgotten a cardinal rule. He didn't need to be in the military to know U1 members hated to feel obliged, and it seemed Greenhill felt the same way. He knew what they feared, and he just set up one of his own for a ton of trouble.

At that moment Fulwood entered sickbay. Tobin had politely messaged him, to get his arse down as Doc was digging his own grave. He'd need it once Spencer found out he'd spilt the beans.

"Thanks, Doc, I'll take it from here," Fulwood stated, calmly stepping into the room like he was just passing by. He gave Tobin a nod of thanks and tipped his head to Tobin as a cue to remove Doc elsewhere.

At his commander's unspoken request, Tobin smoothly suggested to Doc that they go over Greenhill's Care Plan and drug regime in the staff canteen whilst having a cup of tea.

The word tea had the desired effect. Reminding himself to thank Tobin later, Fulwood pulled a chair up to the bed. "Is this really Unit One?" Greenhill asked.

Fulwood nodded tersely. "And did Owen save my life?" Frank Fulwood sighed, there was no way around it. He knew Spencer would hate his reply, but Fulwood had made it his mantra never to lie.

"He did," he acknowledged honestly. "But it was a team effort. Without Doc and Tobin, you probably wouldn't be here regardless of Spencer's efforts.

That one word 'probably' decided it for Liam. Owen Spencer had saved his life and now he felt beholden to him. It stung. He never wanted to have that feeling. It was understandable in the heat of battle, but still…

Trying to move the conversation rapidly on to something more positive, and thinking he understood Greenhill's thought processes, Fulwood continued. "I need you to tell me how U1 ended up saving your life." Greenhill stopped short. *Shit, Unit One, that means that son of a bitch is Unit One too! Damn!*

Liam Greenhill told Commander Fulwood everything. How he'd been working for Interpol to follow Jorge Martins, since Gabon, as there was a warrant out for his arrest. This supported U1's earlier information. How he'd been made, on concealed CCTV whilst sneaking around Martin's private rooms in Libreville to install listening devices. He'd guessed his disposal at Martins goons' hands was a regular practice, judging by their efficiency and the way he was bundled up and air-lifted away. He wouldn't be surprised if there were more bodies in the bay, he told Fulwood.

Both men were left with something to think about. Greenhill needed to decide how to handle the news about his life being saved.

Fulwood's concern was growing about the elusive man involved in their supposed recon mission. It appeared their client, the hotel owner Leumas Sille, was playing games. More than one agency appeared to be working the case and that just wouldn't do. He returned to the Ready Room to liaise with Johnson and consider their next move.

✦ ✦ ✦ ✦ ✦ ✦ ✦ ✦

Greenhill was grinning from ear to ear the next time Spencer paid a visit to sickbay to check on his progress. He knew as soon as he walked through the door that Liam knew. Tobin gave him a knowing look, inclining his head slightly to give him the heads up. He approached the bed cautiously.

"Ahhh, Spencer be a pal and grab that mirror, will you?"

Heart heavy, Spencer lifted the small portrait mirror hanging on the wall opposite and handed it to Greenhill. Gazing into the mirror, Greenhill puckered his lips looking at them from various angles. If Spencer wasn't sure before, he knew what was coming next.

"Do my lips look okay to you?" Greenhill asked, lowering the mirror to deliver two air kisses to him. "Only they feel like I've snogged a turtle for seven hours." He stared at Spencer daring him to deny it. That did it.

Spencer threw the pillows, the fruit and the bowl, and the blankets. He'd just lifted the chair to lob it next, when Tobin rushed over and took it out of his hands. Greenhill was laughing so hard it looked like he was going to wet himself.

"Go," ordered Tobin, pointing with his arm. Spencer stood motionless, his eyes hard. "Go now," he repeated and followed this up by frog-marching Spencer out of sick bay. Greenhill lay back on his bed grinning. His outside demeanour, at odds with his feelings, was the only way Greenhill could handle his fragile emotions. Tobin correctly interpreted Greenhill's behaviour for what it was, a coping mechanism to avoid facing, and being beholden to, the man who had saved his life.

The U1 Karate Club had gone from strength to strength over the intervening years. Below decks, in the sports area,

Spencer and Yin were practising with screamer sticks, oblivious to the world at large, as each attempted to decapitate the other. The dojo door opened and closed without either acknowledging the presence of a third party. At some agreed unspoken point, both men lowered their sticks, bowed to each other in respect and turned towards the door to leave.

Greenhill nodded at Spencer as he stepped through the door.

"That was impressive." Spencer shrugged. He'd been avoiding Greenhill since the episode with the mirror. The silence was awkward between them, but Greenhill needed to speak, needed to say how he felt.

"Look, I'm just going to come out and say this."

"You don't need to."

"I know I don't need to. You saved my miserable hide and I took the piss. I'm sorry."

"It's all right."

"No, it's not all right. It was stupid. A stupid thing to do to the buddy who saved me. I was embarrassed. To be honest I thought making fun of it was a better way to manage my feelings. I was sure you'd retaliate. I expected you to plan payback. When you didn't, when you just vanished on board the ship, I knew I'd got it wrong. I'm so sorry, and thank you for saving me."

Greenhill's confession brought a smile to Spencer's face. They didn't talk further. There was no need. They punched each other on the arm where they knew their badge tat was situated. Both roared, "Oorah," simultaneously. It was done.

Greenhill was flown off the Bucket three days later. Liam and Owen had made their peace, and Greenhill had secured a promise from Fulwood to consider him as a future recruit for U1.

Fulwood lifted his head from the pile of documents he had been scrutinizing and motioned for Spencer to enter the Ready Room. Spencer stood at ease; hands clasped naturally behind his back. Fulwood closed one folder and opened another.

"What did we learn from the recon mission?"

"That Martins knew. It was a setup." When his Commander failed to speak, Spencer continued. "Greenhill was left as a calling card, or more precisely a comment on Martins's intention, to kill anyone who gets in his way."

"Agreed," replied Fulwood closing the second folder. "Our next step?" Spencer was surprised at the question, Fulwood was usually the one dishing out the orders. He didn't ask team members for ideas very often.

"To find the mole. Someone on board knew where I was and what we were doing." Fulwood smirked and lifted the phone off its base.

"It's been a few days since I've spoken to Jeff."

"An inside mission? We don't normally do those," stated Fleur, when she was asked to come in the following morning.

"Our reputation is at stake. We need to identify this leak asap," replied Johnson. "We took a job to investigate one person Jorge Martins, and mysteriously he knew our plans. He even threw a body literally, into the mix."

"What is the mission?"

"To gain employment on the Bucket in the hospitality and staff care section."

"What's my role then, and what about your no women law?" Fleur replied frostily, well aware of Johnson's archaic rules.

Her boss had the decency to look uncomfortable, his wife hassled him about his inflexibility over this issue at every opportunity. He declined to respond to Fleur's comment about his rules and continued.

"The Bucket used to have a qualified masseur. Fredericko retired several years ago, and I haven't replaced him."

"How did you know?" She asked warily.

"That you paid for your university tuition by working as a masseur?"

"Yes, that."

"I do extensive background searches on all my operatives before offering them a position, Fleur."

"Obviously, not maintenance and engineering then," she added tartly, pushing her boss needlessly about stereotypes. Johnson recognised women were as capable as men on missions, sometimes even better, being able to go places and do things men found embarrassing. Like going into toilets, male operatives avoided such situations whereas women bowled right in. It was the social complications of onboard romances he fought to avoid.

"T-cut is doing deeper background checks on all Unit staff both at sea and on land." Fleur swallowed nervously, she wondered just how deep T-cut's investigation would go. There were other elements of her life she'd rather not explain to her boss.

"Won't that bring up your mole?" She asked, trying to push her concerns down.

"Maybe, but I don't deal in maybes."

"Let me get this straight, you want me to infiltrate the Bucket, without the staff knowing or finding out?"

"Yes, that should be easy for a person with your many abilities and talents." Fleur arched an eyebrow hoping that wasn't a sexual inference and dismissed it immediately. Johnson wasn't that sort of man.

"What about members of U1, some of them know me."

"I trust the ones that do, to keep mum."

"Really?"

"Stake my life on it. It has to be one of the ship's crew." That was good enough for Fleur and without realising it, she let out the breath she was holding. Johnson said nothing.

"Okay," she agreed. "When do I go?"

"This evening."

"That soon?"

"You will be posing as a trial run for having women on the Bucket. You will keep to yourself. Keep your cabin locked and not fraternise with anybody on board the ship. Is that clear?"

"Yes, but how can I find a mole if I can't fraternise, that's half the fun of it."

"May I speak plainly to you, Fleur?"

"Please do."

"I do not want to hear you are bedding down with anyone onboard. This is a mission pure and simple. Got it?"

"Sir, Yes Sir," replied Fleur, jumping up automatically as Johnson's manner became more authoritarian.

"I didn't know the Martins mission included the capture of the mark," continued Fleur, changing the subject.

"It didn't, but it does now. People do not interfere with U1. We will be chasing down and arresting Jorge Martins and handing him over to Interpol. No one threatens my team."

"Makes sense." Fleur turned to leave.

"Oh, and one more thing." Fleur turned back. "You're gay." Her eyes widened at this statement. After thinking a moment, she replied.

"Short hair Butch?"

"No! No stereotypes just be yourself."

"That might be hard on a ship full of men."

"Harder for them if you're straight," replied Johnson. "Much harder." He smiled wickedly as Fleur left the room. *Definitely sexual innuendo this time.* She grinned.

"So why are we getting a masseur after all these years?" Spencer asked as they trooped out of the Ready Room following their weekly briefing and mission assignments.

"Damned if I know, but don't knock it, till you've tried it,

214

Spencer," answered T-cut abstractedly. He'd been given another mission, the second in recent weeks and he was as excited as a wasp on an open jar of honey. "Personally, I can't wait to submit my body to a professional."

"I bet you say that to all the guys," replied Spencer, fluttering his eyelashes in exaggeration.

"What makes you think it's a man?"

"It's always men. You know Johnson's unbreakable rule. No women on board ship," he sang, in a deep tone supposedly mimicking the man. Then he paused, "Hold on, what do you know that I don't?" T-cut smiled, tapped the side of his nose with one finger and disappeared down the corridor that led to the comms room, leaving Spencer to stare at his retreating form.

Why me? Fleur bemoaned as she stepped down from the helicopter cab. Hutch had almost offered her his hand to climb down like she was his elderly grandmother. She glared at him—daring him. Her gaze threatened seven kinds of hell should he carry out his impulse. José De Silva knew that look. Had seen it a hundred times watching U1 members undertaking missions over the last four years. He was instantly on his guard. *Masseur my arse! She's military.*

After that initial thought, he studied her more closely. Her poise, the way she moved. The way she took everything in, including him, with a discerning eye. *Shit, special forces I'll bet.* This was no masseur with squaddie-basher training in her past. This was a leopard. Mean, lean and looking for someone's jugular. *Or should that be Jaguar?* José smiled at his own joke.

First, he offers me his hand like some Kid Galahad. Now, he's grinning at himself. Probably some private joke at my expense, Fleur speculated, not realising how close to the truth she was, as the pilot escorted her to her assigned cabin.

"Masseur, my arse," repeated Hutch, marching straight into Fulwood's office after showing Fleur to her room.

"Doesn't anyone knock anymore?" Fulwood grumbled, lifting his head to glare at the U1 pilot.

"If that woman is a masseur I'm...I'm...turkey soup!" Hutch announced, unable to think of a clever remark as he stormed up to his boss's desk. Fulwood knew it would only be a matter of time before the U1 team sussed the new Bucket member as one of their own—ex-military. Davidson knew already since he'd been involved in rescuing Atrax and Fleur off the cruise ship. Fulwood was surprised Hutch didn't recognise the woman he'd air-lifted over to the mainland.

The next morning, Fulwood formally introduced Fleur Colton to the rest of U1. He advised them she was a member of U2 and would be staying undercover on the Bucket to dig out the person passing information to Jorge Martins. It's the only way he could have found out that Spencer was waiting for him in São Tomé.

"What about Johnson's no women rule?" T-cut queried, playing devil's advocate, and rudely ignoring the fact Fleur was sitting in the room. Doc shook his head at T-cut's poor manners. "He'll go ape when he finds out."

"Who do you think sent her?" Fulwood almost said 'idiot' but aggravating his men wouldn't help solve their problem. T-cut had the decency to look contrite.

"Look boys," Fleur remarked, turning to face the U1 team. "You're all safe with me, I'm gay." That stopped all the chatter in the room.

"Shame," someone said at the back. Fleur smiled at the compliment.

"Enough," ordered Fulwood, bringing them back under control. "This is the situation, and you know what to do if you don't like it." Every U1 member had open access to Johnson at any time, but woe betide the man who didn't have a bonéfide reason for speaking to him. They could find themselves shipped out without recourse. Only two U1 operatives had been given the heave-ho and it was as if they never existed. Fleur's presence didn't warrant contacting the Boss's Boss.

"And I do a mean massage too." Fleur's comment lightened the air and Davidson was first to put his hand up to book a session.

"This information is restricted to U1 team members only. Is that understood?" The men nodded as one.

"Briefing over," declared Fulwood. One by one they trooped out, several taking the appointment cards offered by Fleur as they left.

CHAPTER FOURTEEN –MALTA

T-CUT stepped out of the lift and onto the marbled roof terrace on the tenth floor. Spread before him like so many seals basking on a beach was the adult-only area of the hotel, or more accurately, the eighteen-plus pool and bar. He wondered briefly whether that meant the dress size, judging by the large amount of skin on show.

"Looks like the Land of the Living Dead," he mumbled. Not one sound broke the silence along the double rows of sweaty red, or walnut-coloured individuals, laying either asleep, reading or listening to music on their earbuds.

Hearing the pleasurable tinkle of ice falling into glasses, T-cut made his way across the roof towards the bar. Here at least there was sound, as the Nepalese bar staff took drink orders, whilst customers engaged in superficial boring chit-chat; the weather, the heat, the food, the heat, the weather, …blah, blah, blah.

Spying several sofas opposite, T-cut chose one with strategic significance, and placing his whiskey on the low coffee table, stretched his arms wide over the back of the beige cushions.

"I could get used to this," he sighed, enjoying the heat of the cushions soaking into his bones. Then, reviewing the slabs of human sausages sprawled around the pool on their loungers, T-cut retracted his statement. "Well, maybe for a little while."

Terrance Mason was, and always would be, a man needing action. Inactivity bored him silly and was the root of his many problems as a teenager.

Conventional schooling hadn't been for him. Primary staff had struggled to contain him and Secondary threw their hands up and washed him away. Home educated from the age of thirteen by his gruff ex-military father, he learnt to build a wall, shape a piece of wood, re-build an engine, and more importantly to him, hone a knife till it was sharp enough to cut air, and assemble a pistol or rifle in seconds.

Regarding academic subjects, apart from learning English, Maths and several languages—Mason couldn't see the point of anything else taught in school. He'd constructed his own computer from parts purchased online. He'd designed and written his own software programmes before the age of sixteen, programme coding being his favourite language.

Despite its innate discipline, when the army called, Mason jumped right in, ending up in covert special forces and making his father proud. Because of his love of blades, his force's nickname naturally became T-cut. The kid no one thought would stay out of prison, fooled everyone. T-cut smirked, thinking of his hard-pressed secondary tutors struggling and failing. Lifting his glass, he made a quiet toast.

"To teachers everywhere and those of us who didn't need them. Thanks, dad."

Mason loved Malta. He often took his shore leave on the island, it's military and Knights Templar heritage called to him. Walking the hot stone-clad streets of Valletta felt like stepping into history. Avoiding the swarming tourists, of which he was often one, he appreciated the high strategically placed battlements surrounding the cities and harbours. He could almost imagine being based here. It was T-cut's type of place.

He had considered buying a property but had yet to take that final step. Properties meant responsibilities and more time spent on land. With that came the dreaded word, retirement, something T-cut was never going to do. He vowed to himself that he'd rather go out on mission.

It was fate too that his last name was Mason. His father introduced him to Freemasonry in his thirties and he was captivated. He attended several social events and meetings as a guest. He loved the comradery, the pageantry, the rules— ironic when he couldn't obey any at school. For a while he attended his father's lodge, learning the necessary lines using his little blue book. Once he joined U1 though, he couldn't attend that many events due to his job taking him all over the world. True, there were lodges in other countries, but it felt intrusive and wasn't something a mason did lightly unless invited. Their values of honour, honesty and humility captured his heart.

He'd been inside the Grand Lodge in London once. It felt both intimidating and like home— a bit like the Bucket. Currently, he was an unattached member. He knew they had a Lodge on Malta. He'd investigated and found the historic building on the road facing the water's edge. However, he wasn't ready to put his toe in that pond just yet.

He thought about Pav Rivera, the boy Johnson had taken on. He was good, and though he wouldn't admit it to Pav, probably better than he was at that age. Pav was today's child, whose first languages were Java, Lua, and Python. He saw the employment for what it was, the Team preparing for the day when T-cut stepped down and relinquished his role. He was training his replacement. He wasn't upset by it, it was life, and he didn't plan to be going any time soon.

Having had enough of thinking about old age, T-cut turned his thoughts to his current location. The rooftop bar where T-cut sat, dominated the skyline, receiving an uninterrupted panoramic view of the surrounding area and St Paul's Bay. For one-hundred-and-eighty degrees, the land reached across the horizon behind the bay. A vista of sky-blue, tan hills, sandstone buildings and eleven haphazard building cranes of various dappled hues.

To the right of his position, an azure bay sparkled, and on the far side, a similar development hunched, staring back in opposition to the construction in Bugibba. Not one cloud of fluff obscured the sun's gaze on the land. Its radiation, disrupted occasionally by a rogue yet persistent breeze, vying for the tourists' attention.

T-cut sat on the comfy sofa, his large whisky on ice in one hand. The bar, the scene for several evening activities including a wedding reception, echoed the landscape in similar colours of cloud, sand and soil. Holidaymakers and ex-pat time-share residents frequented the bar regularly despite, or because of, the watered-down cocktails. T-cut could see why. The height of the building gave it a superior vantage point and made folk feel, for a few short hours, that they were omnipotent, above the humdrum existence of humanity. Worries on hold for a brief moment in time. *Leaving their cares, at the bottom of the stairs.* T-cut smiled at his impromptu rhyme.

His contact was late. It was why his mind was wandering. He didn't like to be kept waiting. Tardiness wasn't a good sign in T-cut's books. He wasn't the usual tourist waiting for a date. Anyone giving him closer scrutiny would have realized that, at least anyone with knowledge of military operations.

He remained on alert, in observation mode. He wasn't here to relax regardless of the impression he gave to others on the roof bar. He was on mission, and if his manner didn't highlight his juxtaposition to the remaining people at the bar, then the tattoos on his right forearm might have left some wondering. Especially, the ex-Gurkha serving behind the counter. T-cut had clocked his Kukri tat moments after entering.

It was pleasant sitting under the canvas awning, listening to ice being poured into drinks and idle chatter about nothing important, but T-cut wasn't here on holiday. He checked his divers' timepiece again. Late, forty minutes late. He'd leave at sixty if no show, otherwise. *No, mustn't think that this isn't like the mission in Palermo, Sicily.* This wasn't a Mafia-run resort with criminals after his head. T-cut shook off the negative doubts and checked the time again.

As he lifted his eyes, he saw her, his contact Daisy Piper. She fitted the description and photo perfectly, which was a change. Usually, the client provided an image five years out of date, the hair changed or gone, the weight variable, and age undiscernible.

He watched as Daisy surveyed the growing crowd around her, then locked on T-cut, he guessed identifying his reserved demeanour in the swelling group of happy outgoing people. Deliberately ignoring him, despite acknowledging his presence, she made her way to the bar. *Why has she gone up to the bar?*

As Daisy crossed the open space between tall potted planters and high bar stools, another person appeared in the doorway. A tail. T-cut caught Daisy's eye again and simply nodded. He watched how her body sagged slightly, relieved that he'd spotted her unwanted guest. The man stopped just inside the entrance to the roof blocking the lifts and stairs. He leant against the wall to the right in what he must have believed was a casual, 'I'm bored' manner. T-cut snorted. He could see him holding his ear as he spoke to a colleague elsewhere.

"Rookie mistake."

"You say something, over?" Came the comment in his ear. Raising his whisky to his mouth in the pretence of taking a drink, T-cut intoned one word, his lips hidden by the glass.

"Tail."

"Roger on that. Go to Plan B, over."

"Plan B," he confirmed, just before he moved the glass again to swallow the entire drink. "Shame, it was a single malt," he spoke out loud. He heard chuckling in his ear, but no apology from Pav. *Bang goes an easy extraction.*

T-cut stood and crossed the now busy bar. His fingers dropped into his right trouser pocket and enclosed around the micro-hypodermic resting there. Palming it, he removed the cover by releasing the clip which exposed the needle. He approached the doorway and in one sudden move, flicked the dart up into the man's exposed neck.

Not stopping to check—he had faith in the Doc's wonder drugs—he slid his left arm around the folding man. Smiling at nearby guests who noticed the incident, T-cut waved them off, on the pretence of his friend having had one too many. Pulling the unconscious man into the elevator lobby and out of sight, he lowered the man to the floor, checking him for weapons as he did so.

T-cut turned, sensing someone nearby, Daisy Piper was blocking the doorway. They froze as the left-hand lift door opened in front of them. It was empty, so T-cut piled the man into the lift. The doors closed as the car was called elsewhere. It was time to leave. Grasping the woman's hand, and apparently taking her by surprise, he instructed her.

"Time to go."

Her eyes widened, and nodding, Daisy let T-cut lead her towards the far end of the roof and the spiral staircase that served as an escape route in case of fire, or in this case Plan B. The staircase ran out two floors down. And left them seemingly stranded on a dead-end landing which jutted out from the main building.

T-cut heard in the distance the sound he loved most, his team coming to collect them. The patrons and bar staff stared in disbelief at the aircraft heading directly towards the hotel from over the bay. The noise became deafening. The wind stirred the scene causing anything not nailed down to either fly into the air, or tumble in anticipation of a new life airborne.

The women squealed, moving away from the edge of the roof terrace, some holding their dresses down to save their embarrassment as panties hove into view. Ironic, when they spent all day on loungers in barely-there G-strings. Others covered their ears at the awful din, again bizarre considering the hours they spent with earbuds in or clubbing.

The Nepalese barman looked up at the approaching tiltrotor and smiled, not bothered one jot. A good memory surfaced for him, of comrades and doing something vital and worthwhile. He glanced down at the glass he was still drying, feeling the heaviness and heartache of a life long gone.

After several minutes the tiltrotor, which had hovered menacingly in front of the hotel, began to rise into the sky. Below it, two people hung suspended wearing safety harnesses. The line they were attached to gradually rose towards the aircraft. The man's colleagues appeared in the rooftop doorway. Semi-automatics raised. Safety's off. They ran towards the rooftop edge.

T-cut watched as without hesitation; the barman 'accidentally' threw an entire container of crushed ice over the floor creating havoc. People struggled to stay upright. The villains floundered, falling amongst the revellers, who were laughing hysterically thanks to the abundance of alcohol. T-cut caught the waiter's grin and saluted. The ex-Gurkha acknowledged the salute by bowing his head in return.

One more to recruit? wondered T-cut, as the Spade took off, out of range in seconds. He hadn't missed the pronounced limp either, which the ex-Gurkha had tried to cover up whilst clearing the tables. Medically discharged, flushed through T-cut's mind. Easy to find.

It was good to be back on the Bucket, T-cut's home. His target, Daisy had been taken directly to the International Airport at Gudja, in the south of the island. The site, known to most military personnel as RAF Luqa, was an important base during the Second World War and the Suez Crisis. From there, she would fly to a destination of her choice and disappear. The statutory witness protection scheme had failed her, but U1 wouldn't. Johnson would ensure she was hidden and shielded from any further harm. Protection was life-long if U1 services were involved.

Lewis and his women had been relocated to Lake Garda by Travis. They weren't happy about it, because they were advised not to get jobs until whoever was after them was eliminated. Most folk would have been overwhelmed to be in a rent-free holiday villa with all expenses paid. The weather was amazing, the food brilliant and Lewis wasn't short of company. They got up late most mornings, ate breakfast then went for a swim, all of them preferring the lake to the pool on the premises.

Lewis was surprised to discover that all three of them were good swimmers and could hold their breaths well underwater. The result was many happy hours spent messing around in the lake and even managing to have sex there as dusk fell. Lewis was pleased to discover he could pleasure both girls easily underwater, away from prying eyes. It was something Madelaine would never know. He grinned, diving for Joni as she squealed with laughter.

Travis watched the three cavorting about, with a hint of envy. He couldn't remember the last time he'd had a woman, regardless of his looks. The job didn't allow time for anything more than a couple of nights here and there, with willing no-strings-attached bedmates. He sat at the waterside bar. *On damn babysitting duty again!*

Travis hadn't discovered anything on the three teens under observation that warranted an assassin contract being put out on any of them. U1 knew the background of each adolescent, right down to their birth weights, which Travis found odd.

Lewis Blaine, born out of wedlock, was the grandson of Senator Blaine so he at least was newsworthy, but Joannie Neem, also born out of wedlock, was the daughter of an ex-prostitute on Saint Lucia. The third one, Joni was born to an elderly couple in Japan. A surprise birth, when her mother aged sixty, thought she'd gone through menopause ten years earlier. The only thing they had in common is that they were all born in the same year. It didn't make sense. There had to

225

be a common denominator if Travis could only find out what it was.

It didn't take long for T-cut to discover who was trying to shoot at Redshaw's children after he concluded his mission and sent Daisy on her way. Four days later, he entered the Ready Room, without knocking as per his habit. Fulwood sighed.

"What have you found?"

"Well, it's not Lewis Blaine they're after," T-cut stated, with a hint of a gloat in his tone.

"It's not?" Fulwood commented, surprised. He'd bet his money on someone finding out about John Redshaw's many offspring and the fact he only sired one male. What better way to disrupt a species in the process of birthing a new population?

"No."

"Who is it then?" Fulwood asked, intrigued now his theory was out the window.

"Joni."

"Joni Miyamoto? The child of the elderly couple in Japan?"

"Yes, it appears her father, though elderly, is quite a figure in the world of the Japanese Mafia or Yakuza. He leads syndicates, in three of the forty-seven prefectures."

"That explains a great deal. I remember Redshaw speaking about the Ninkyō Dantai or Bōryokudan as I believe the Police prefer to call them."

"Seeing as how I'm not from Japan and don't speak Japanese," interrupted Doc Williams, who was ensconced in his usual armchair drinking tea. "Would one of you please humour an old man and translate?" T-cut, fluent in fifteen languages, grinned.

"Of course, Doc," he replied. "The local law enforcement doesn't want the gangsters receiving any status, so they insist the media use the term 'violence groups.' However, the Yakuza which translates as gangsters, or Gokudō, followers of the 'extreme way' as they are also known, feel they are a

226

Ninkyō Dantai meaning chivalrous organisation. They have a strict hierarchy with rituals and rules for disobeying or messing up."

"Thank you, but Travis reported the snipper was aiming at Lewis and Joannie in both the attempts, not Joni," argued Doc. Fulwood sat back letting Doc speak for him. The man still had a mind like a steel trap.

"My theory would be they had orders to take the other two out. Maybe in the hope that Joni, with no one to turn to, would head home."

"Could be," admitted both Doc and Fulwood, nodding at each other.

"Look into it a bit more T-cut. I want to know precisely what activities her father is involved in."

"Will do."

T-cut left the room.

"Travis will be pleased to know there's movement on the case. I think he's getting fed up babysitting," offered Doc.

"It is not babysitting," snarled Fulwood. He was fed up hearing U1 members grumbling about these types of missions. Just because there wasn't any obvious action and bloodshed every minute, didn't mean the work wasn't important. He'd need to have a word with the team and in particular Travis St John. "Its security details, bodyguard status. Make sure you tell them that when they moan to you again."

"He feels its babysitting duty," answered Doc, not one to be cowed by his boss. "Maybe, you should have a word with him, or change the operative. He might get lax if he doesn't see it as important."

"I'll think on it," Fulwood replied, not letting Doc have the satisfaction of knowing he'd already decided to speak to Travis about moving him off mission.

⬥ ⬥ ⬥ ⬥ ⬥ ⬥ ⬥ ⬥

Pav Rivera was enjoying his work on the Bucket. He was pleased to know that he'd never be expected to shoot guns to kill people. Physical violence wasn't his thing, despite being part of a mercenary team. He preferred simpler, less messy ways of ending his victims' lives. T-cut his mentor, was an unusual person but he had to admit he was brilliant. Pav was amazed at the number of programmes the U1 member had invented. Not to mention the activities T-cut was able to carry out using his own designed hardware positioned aboard several satellites circling the Earth. They were ideas Pav wasn't above copying and piggybacking onto his own servers.

He was particularly intrigued about the system the man had installed somewhere in the Ready Room in order to spy on his Boss. One afternoon, Pav's curiosity got the better of him and he decided to use the secret Ready Room set-up. Using T-cut's passwords, which he'd entrusted Pav with, he listened in on a conversation Doc was having with Frank Fulwood about the kids Travis was following. He couldn't understand half of what they were speaking about. Pav lifted his hand to switch off the set when he heard something. He waited, and sure enough, it sounded again. Somebody else on board was listening in. Pav couldn't have that. He didn't like others encroaching on his play. An interesting plan started to formulate in his mind.

"There," he informed T-cut, pointing out the anomaly to him later that same afternoon. They both heard Fulwood moaning about the price of Tiltrotor fuel and airport duties. T-cut was wondering whether their days with personal air transport were numbered.

"You missed it," accused Pav.

"What? I was listening."

"Did you hear it?"

T-cut swallowed his pride.

"No, I was distracted," he admitted.

"Listen." Pav turned up the volume and they waited. Seven minutes later T-cut heard it.

"Shit! Shit, shit."

"See?"

"Yes, I see. How the fuck did I miss that? I'm a real Dick Weasel." Pav sniggered. He didn't know what a Dick Weasel was, but he got the gist of it. There were several seconds when a loud hum undercut Fulwood's words. Someone else was listening in, piggybacking onto T-cut's eavesdropping system.

"What's a Dick Weasel?" Pav asked, playing the innocent man he portrayed.

"Never mind, we need to dismantle the spyware—now," T-cut insisted, feeling upset and guilty that his spying had put U1 at risk.

"Wait," Pav cautioned. "If we dismantle it, we won't be able to discover who is doing it or where it's from, plus they'll know we found it."

"True," T-cut agreed, realising he'd have to come clean with his Boss about his nefarious activities. "We need to tell Fulwood first." Pav nodded, as T-cut bit the bullet.

"Let me see if I've got this straight," replied Fulwood, after he was called to the Comms room. "You've been bugging the Ready Room for nearly twenty years and only now have you realised that someone has been bugging you?"

T-cut had the decency to look shame-faced. Fulwood was trying hard to hold in his humour. It was serious. Both T-cut's activities and also the latest development.

What T-cut didn't know was that Fulwood and Jeff Johnson before him had always known the room was bugged by the IT Team. Johnson had ignored it, and later Fulwood agreed and did the same. Besides, neither had managed to locate the damn spyware despite trying umpteen times—T-cut had hidden it exceedingly well. It was a standing joke between Fulwood and Johnson. They'd even placed a wager on which of them discovered it first.

"We'll talk about your insubordination later. Our most immediate concern is the person spying on us from outside

U1. Pav and T-cut nodding eagerly reminded Doc Williams, who'd arrived with Fulwood, of those wobbly-headed dogs in the back of some folks' cars. He considered commenting on his observations but recognising the serious nature of the situation had the sense to stay silent—for once.

"Do we have any idea where they're based?" Doc enquired, staying on track for a change.

"Has to be inside the ship," advised Pav. Seeing Doc's confused stare, he explained. "To relay the signal. Unless they've access to satellite services, and we've checked the signals from there. They're clear of static and code."

"It was how Pav picked their spying out," continued T-cut, turning to face Doc. "It was too regular a pattern to be accidental. Someone on board has been obtaining information from the Ready Room."

"There's also the possibility of other systems on the Bucket being compromised," interjected Pav, trying to hide his pleasure at T-cut's discomfort. Fulwood glared at T-cut who couldn't make eye contact with the man.

"All the Bucket's computer systems are water-tight," he assured Fulwood. "We have anti-malware and virus software programmes on all U1 equipment including phones. The listening device being Wi-Fi was the weak link in the chain."

T-cut knew he'd done wrong. It was something he started with his best friend Seamark, for a laugh one afternoon, and he never stopped. Even after his friend died. Thinking on that, T-cut wondered how long the link had been in place. How many unnecessary deaths was he responsible for? He shivered at the thought.

"I want you and Pav to do a ship-wide sweep of all the IT systems checking and tracing any unusual signals," ordered Fulwood.

"We can use a wireless signal detector, the same as our hacker must have used to locate T-cut's device initially," advised Pav. Making it clear he didn't approve of T-cut's shady dealings. Another step in discrediting his opposition.

"Good. You need to do this discreetly. If our hacker is on board we don't want them to know we're on to them yet, is that understood? He's obviously an information broker because there's no identifiable link between Travis's mission in Italy, and Spencer's on São Tomé but both were compromised."

"Sir, yes Sir," responded T-cut, turning to leave with Pav.

"And T-cut." T-cut slowed, thinking bad news was coming. He turned to face his boss, back ramrod straight, arms down by his sides, waiting and expecting punishment. "I don't believe this started up until the last two missions, otherwise earlier U1 missions would have been sabotaged."

"Thank you. Sir." The relief in T-cut's voice was palpable as he followed Pav's lead out of the room.

The U1 briefing was transferred the following morning to the Conference room after T-cut had done a sweep with a wireless signal detector to be sure. It wasn't unusual to hold briefings in the room when all U1 members were present, except today they weren't. Travis was back in Italy and both T-cut and Pav were missing. Fleur sat to one side towards the rear of the room, despite being part of hospitality she'd been included in the briefing meeting.

"We have another development," started Fulwood, getting straight to the point.

Every member of U1 was on high alert. It seemed they couldn't trust the ship's crew, or more accurately they couldn't trust one member of it, but as they didn't know who that was, it amounted to the same thing.

Fleur had two avenues to investigate, employees new to the Bucket and those with access to the Ready Room. Of course, it might be neither of these, but it was as good a place to start as any.

She already attended Captain Sallas's weekly crew meetings, but now she had a different focus, trying to get a lead on which of the crew was their mole. Unfortunately, not all the crew attended each meeting. Several never turned up despite it being compulsory. She considered speaking to the captain, to encourage his staff to attend, but she couldn't trust anyone until this was over. Everyone could be bought—for a price. The crew members who failed to arrive were first on Fleur's list to investigate.

A total of four missed meetings regularly, and two of those were no-shows today. She chose to recon those two first. It was tricky because one worked in the engine room and the other in the laundry. These weren't areas a masseur would be expected to frequent in the course of their job. Fleur used it as an excuse to drum up business.

"Hi there, you must be Colin." Collin Beverell, the second engineer on the Bucket, looked up from where he was currently checking a valve on one of the ballast pumps. Seeing the ravishingly beautiful woman in a partially undone pink jumpsuit, leaning provocatively towards him, breasts begging for attention was almost Beverell's undoing. His unexpected erection at her sensual aroma and proximity caused him some anxiety. Fortunately, Beverell was wearing his loose-fitting work coveralls, otherwise, his hard-on might have been noticeable and embarrassing. He distracted his lusty emotions by wondering what on Earth this woman was doing in the engine room, let alone on board his ship, and to avoid any further sexual complications, he told her so.

"You shouldn't be in here," Beverell growled, trying to hide his frustration.

"Oh, don't be like that," Fleur pouted adorably, playing up to her acting role. "I came to see if I can tempt you to come for a massage? I'm going round all the employees," she added, just to ensure she didn't sound too much like a desperate hooker.

"And why in seven hells would I need a massage?"

"To relax you, to ease strained muscles, to reduce stress," she replied smoothly, hoping he wouldn't ask for any more reasons because they were the only three she'd read in the massage handbook.

"I'm fine."

"Are you sure? Only I never see you at Captain Sallas's briefings," Fleur glanced down briefly.

"That's because somebody has to supervise the day's operations. The Chief always attends the briefings. He tells me anything relevant. Though why I'm telling you this I don't know." Beverell turned back to face the faulty valve in the pretence he was still investigating it, hoping if he ignored the woman she'd take the hint and leave. She didn't.

"I don't see why you can't take turns to attend briefings," she insisted, pushing the man. "It's good to feel like you belong." Beverell turned on her.

"I know I belong here. I've been on the Bucket ever since Bailey retired seven years ago and was part of U1 before that. I don't know what you're up to miss, but I don't need some flibberty-jib of a girl telling me how to work. Now skedaddle before I make you regret coming down here."

Fleur made a point of reading each employee's file before she approached them. She'd discovered that as well as being an ex-U1 operative, Colin Beverell was proficient in unarmed combat. She didn't need to be told twice and left.

Fleur's interaction with Hadley the second no-show went almost as bad as Beverell's. She wasn't made to feel welcome in the laundry area where four staff ensured everyone's uniforms, personal clothing, bedding and soft furnishings were kept clean and smart. Fleur decided to enlist Pav's help to narrow her search.

"Do you have anything to report on the sweep?" Fleur

enquired, entering the Comms room where she knew Pav was on duty. Pav wasn't well-versed with speaking to strong women. He found their presence unnerving. They made him sweat.

"Er, should you be in here?"

"I think so, I am the investigator on this case," she replied tartly. Pav swallowed his next question. This woman was far too bold and fearsome for his taste. He liked his women to be quiet, sensitive and demure. Able to take commands. Fleur Colton was an assertive woman of action, something which frankly terrified him. Sensing Pav's fragility, Fleur reined in her forthright manner.

"Sorry, I think I've been taking this role too seriously. I didn't mean to be so intimidating." Without another word or an invitation, she flopped down into T-cut's swivel chair and waited for him to speak.

"You play the role well," he admitted after a few moments. "Scarily well."

"Really?"

"Mmh mmh."

"Maybe that's why I'm not getting any answers or hints." Fleur paused.

They sat side-by-side in silence whilst Pav deftly used his keyboard to review the Bucket's route.

"I was hoping you might be able to help me." She turned her chair towards Pav and waited.

"What is it you need to know?" Pav finally answered, seemingly unaware of the large gaps between their conversation.

"Well, my first two suspects didn't pan out. I was wondering who would have access to the Ready Room?

"That's easy."

"Is it?"

"Yes."

When he failed to elaborate further, Fleur nudged him verbally.

"It would be a great help to know," she suggested, wondering whether all computer geeks were this inept at face-to-face conversations. T-cut wasn't.

Pav gave her an odd look.

"All of U1. The Department Heads. Maintenance and hospitality," he paused. "And catering."

"Everyone then?"

"I guess so, just about," he smiled, realising Fleur had her work cut out for her if she was ever to find her suspect which he doubted. He grinned at the thought.

"It would be easier to count who doesn't go to the Ready Room," she huffed. "I don't suppose you'd be willing to help me cut that list down a bit?"

Pav looked at her. She was a beautiful woman. After another interminable pause, he spoke again.

"You can rule out U1 and the department heads straight away. Also, hospitality."

"Why?"

"Because Mr Kennard, the hospitality Manager oversees that room personally."

"Doesn't that make him a suspect rather than exclude him?"

"Have you read his file? He's been on board for over twenty years. The ship is his life. He'll probably die on the Bucket."

"So that leaves catering and maintenance."

"I'd go with maintenance, catering only attends the room when Fulwood calls them up."

"You seem to know a great deal about everyone's business seeing as how you haven't been here long," Fleur stated honestly. It was the longest conversation she'd had with Pav, and she guessed probably the longest he'd had with most people, other than T-cut.

Pav Rivera was a quiet, like-my-own-company kind of person. As Fleur surmised, a typical computer nerd. Pav gave her another of his odd looks but failed to comment.

"Okay maintenance then," Fleur concluded. "Who have we got working in that department, my Font-of-All-Knowledge?" Pav's eyebrows raised at the sarcastic title Fleur had given him and failed to offer a reply. Realising she'd overstepped the mark again with him, and aware she needed his help, Fleur back-pedalled.

"Sorry, I got carried away there again for a moment."

Nothing. No reaction from Pav whatsoever. He ignored the woman to concentrate on his keyboard once more.

"Look I said I'm sorry, my mouth sometimes comes up with things my brain doesn't approve of but by then it's too late." That made a smile appear on Pav's face. He liked it when his women apologised.

"Is that a smile? I'll take it."

"The Bucket has two electricians, one plumber, one carpenter and one Joat on board," answered Pav, resuming their earlier conversation as if it hadn't stopped.

"What on earth is a Joat?"

"Jack-of-all-trades. He does everything from laying carpets to painting."

"Yes, I know what a Jack of all trades is. Why the… Forget that, mouth speaking again." Pav smirked at Fleur's reply. The woman was learning her place.

Fleur checked her list. One of the electricians was down as one of the four who regularly missed briefings. What better way to move around the ship than when the majority were in a meeting? Especially, if U1 were off ship on mission or the Bucket was docked for R and R? Fleur went back to her cabin to re-read Fischer's file.

Larry Fischer had joined the Bucket at Port Everglades in Fort Lauderdale two years ago. He had not been called to account for his workmanship in all that time, in fact, he'd received several commendations from the Chief engineer for the high quality of his work. As a member of the crew though, he wasn't a very sociable person, it was only his work skills that kept him in post. Fulwood reviewed the employees' files every six months and together with the Chief, his line manager, concurred that not everyone was the life of the party. It appeared Fischer was an obsessive computer gamer. In his downtime between eating and sleeping, he played. It wasn't uncommon for single young men to become engrossed in the gaming network, but Fischer was forty and another reason he got the job was he had no attachments on land.

An only child, his single mother had died young, leaving Fischer, then fifteen, to survive in foster homes until adulthood, where he was cast adrift from the care system. Fortunately, with the state backing him, he'd secured a scholarship for a good technology institute before leaving care. After completing his apprenticeship and journeyman levels, he obtained his Master's electrician qualification by passing his National Electrical Code exam.

The following two days were busy for Fleur. Her jaunt down to the crew areas hadn't gone unnoticed and soon she was booked solid for massages via her online booking system. Fischer wasn't amongst those listed. His profile didn't fit a man who had massages, but she hoped he might bite.

She thought about bugging his cabin, but if it was him, he'd probably check his room daily—she would—and then he'd know they were on to him. Instead, she had to settle for secreting a camera in the air vent a little way down from Fischer's door, in the hope she could track his movements and sneak a peek in his room. Employees were responsible for keeping their cabin and showers clean, putting any litter outside their doors weekly.

It didn't work out as Fleur hoped. It was almost as if Fischer knew, or he knew where he would put a camera if he wanted to spy on someone, because he never opened his door wide, and went in the opposite direction every time he left his cabin, rather than past Fleur's camera. She put two more cameras up along the opposite passages and still wasn't able to spot his coming and going. It was like he didn't exist. *Back to the drawing board.*

"I need your help again, Pav," Fleur muttered, as she walked into the Comms room to discover both T-cut and Pav present.

"What do you mean again?" T-cut asked confused. Fleur looked at Pav, and T-cut looked back and forth between them. *Pav hasn't told T-cut of my earlier visit. I wonder why?*

"Never mind. Can you help me?"

"Go on," advised T-cut, not wanting to get into a discussion over why Pav didn't tell him about Fleur's visit.

"Okay, so I have a suspect." T-cut rubbed his hands together. He knew where this was going.

"I bugged the air vent in the corridor outside his cabin, so I'd know when he left. I wanted to check his room, but he always went the opposite way. Next, I placed two more bugs on the opposite corridors, but he still seemed to dodge them. I discovered him two corridors away last time." She paused, wondering if the next idea sounded a bit unethical. "I want to search his room, but also leave spyware."

"But naturally you don't want to alert him," replied T-cut, jumping straight to the conclusion. "He's either got sensory equipment in there, or he'll do a sweep and find your stuff. If, he's our man."

"Right."

"Right," added Pav.

"So, you want us to do a sweep to check first."

"Yes," replied Fleur, pleased that T-cut got the gist so quick.

"Problem," interjected Pav. T-cut nodded.

"Problem?"

"If he is your man, I mean our man, and we sweep even outside the room, he'll know," declared Pav.

"How?"

"Well, if it were me. I'd set up sensory devices which would identify any detector devices sending out sweeps."

"You can do that?"

"Easily. So far we have only done sweeps around U1 and Bucket equipment, not around personal stuff. If we do a sweep of the cabin, he'll know and clear everything away. Probably chuck the laptop overboard. No equipment, no proof."

T-cut hadn't heard Pav speak so much in the last seven days. He obviously had the hots for Fleur. Letting Pav keep the floor T-cut stayed silent.

"You're better going in blind."

"Huh?"

"What Pav means is during an electricity blackout," interrupted T-cut, unable to stay silent no matter how good his intentions.

"So how do I achieve that? Fleur asked.

"You don't, we do. We need to get Fulwood's okay first. It happens sometimes. We have to close down the generator and re-boot operations."

"There's one snag in your plan," Fleur added. "My suspect is the Master electrician."

"Shit."

It had taken a little while for Fleur to come up with another plan for getting into Fischer's cabin. Pav had helped to secure the equipment. She only hoped it would work. It was this or her last resort, lowering a camera down on a fishing line to peer in through the porthole. She sincerely hoped it didn't come to that Tom and Jerry idea.

The tastefully designed boxes had been individualised for every member of the ship's crew, lovingly provided by the Bucket's new masseur. They contained an assortment of massage creams, scented candles and incense, together with massage rollers for those crew who'd failed to accept her service.

Fleur sailed into the canteen loaded up with armfuls of treasure and began handing them out to those crew members she had got to know first. She ensured Larry Fischer's had his name emblazoned across the top like everyone else, then sat back and waited. The remaining boxes she'd left in the canteen were gone when she returned to check the following day. Of course, she couldn't know whether Fischer had taken his, or whether someone else had picked it up. She hoped not, it was why she provided one for each person, that, and it reduced the likelihood of looking suspicious.

"Anything?" Fleur asked, popping her head into the Comms room that evening.

"No, nothing so far."

"Damn."

"Don't worry, it might still be in the box or against a wall," Pav reassured her. They'd decided to go with a security micro-camera which fit inside the point-eight-centimetre screw head on one end of the massage rollers, with the tiny battery inserted inside the centre. It was a bit risky, but they were transmitting at irregular intervals and then only for a minute, each minute being recorded.

Bizarrely, at two in the morning the camera activated and though they couldn't see a thing in the dark—something Pav failed to factor in— even more strange was why Fischer would be opening the box and removing the roller at that time. It was unusual for off-duty crew to be up in the middle of the night unless they were engaged in night-time pursuits. Anything was possible, Johnson's rule of no women—till Fleur—had not changed, and lonely men could always seek out company.

"What's he doing?" Pav asked as they sat viewing the previous night's recordings together the following morning.

T-cut fiddled with the brilliance setting and managed to obtain a grainy grey image of Fischer moving around his room. He'd opened Fleur's box of massage goodies and was examining each one. Surprisingly, the next recording showed him using his laptop with a candle flickering somewhere nearby. The massage roller must have been on the bed next to him.

"Who knew," T-cut commented.

"What?" Pav asked. T-cut looked at Fleur over Pav's head and raised his eyebrows in mock surprise.

The deep dark web was a place most sensible people stayed away from. It was notorious for covering and containing many illegal activities but mainly identified with the sex trade. The recording showed Larry Fischer ogling his screen and using a box of tissues to good effect.

"Yuk! Turn that off!" Fleur and Pav growled simultaneously, turning their faces away. T-cut grinned and cut to the next recording. It was still dark, the candle guttering, giving the cabin an eerie vibe. There was no sign of Fischer on the bed, or at his computer. They concluded he was either out of shot in the on-suite or prowling the Bucket.

When he failed to turn up for his work shift later that day, the chief engineer knocked on his cabin door. With no reply, his cabin was unlocked and entered. Fischer was on the floor—dead. His laptop missing.

CHAPTER FIFTEEN – KHAO LAK

Doc Williams sighed as he lowered his old bones into his favourite armchair in the Ready Room—after helping himself to an enormous whisky. Fulwood ordered T-cut to remove all his spyware from the Ready Room, regardless of their assumed watcher being found dead. The U1 team undertook a ship-wide search, while T-cut and Pav swept the entire vessel for Fischer's laptop and any other spyware.

It appeared they had a murderer on board, though why Fischer had been killed was a mystery. No signs of physical violence had been found on his body. Doc, with his pathology qualification, had completed an autopsy in the hope of shedding more light on the cause of death. He would present his findings and register the death at their next port of call.

Fulwood waited, while Doc collected his thoughts and enjoyed his drink. He deserved it.

"Not something you see every day." Fulwood's eyebrows rose. "I put the time of death between Pav's recording at two a.m. and the next at three a.m., based on their recordings and the rigour Mortis level."

"Unusual death I take it?" Fulwood enquired, eager for Doc to continue now he'd started.

Doc didn't rush, he took another sip enjoying the whiskey burn down his throat.

"Very," was his enigmatic reply.

Fulwood wanted to shake the old man but he was well used to Doc's ways and could wait it out. Fischer wasn't going anywhere. He was on ice in their personal mortuary.

Deaths happened at sea from time to time. The ability to

complete autopsies and store bodies was a godsend on a ship whose average speed was equivalent to twenty-five miles per hour.

"The candle had been doctored of course."

"Of course."

"Contained enough concentrated opium to put a small army into a state of rapturous oblivion. World War Three could have taken place outside Fischer's door and he wouldn't have noticed. The Chief was so overcome by the fumes when he opened the door, that Tobin had to keep him in sick bay for the afternoon. I ordered the room ventilated using full BA."

"Good call, Doc. Was that his cause of death?"

"Heavens no. Bleach."

"Bleach?"

"Yes, bleach. Injected into the left jugular, based on the needle puncture mark I discovered."

"Bleach, my god!" Fulwood was appalled. Bizarre when the man used violence for a living. Yet, he would never have imagined using bleach to kill a person.

"Two hundred millilitres of sodium hypochlorite with concentrations as little as three per cent can be a lethal dose."

"So, we have a murderer on board."

"It would seem so."

"Johnson's going to love this."

"I don't believe those were the words he used when I called him."

Fulwood realised belatedly, that Doc Williams would of course have informed Jeff Johnson directly in such a case. He didn't hold it against the man, he was only doing his duty as he saw it. It would have been nice to capture the felon and have it all wrapped up before phoning his Boss though.

"I think I'll join you in that drink, David."

✦ ✦ ✦ ✦ ✦ ✦ ✦

Fleur and T-cut were discussing the murder in the canteen.

"I feel awful. That box I put out with his name on it gave the murderer the means to kill him."

"You don't know that," T-cut responded, attempting to reduce Fleur's guilt. Her eyes were brimming with tears she was trying to hold back.

"I do. I handed him Fischer on a plate. I'm as much to blame for his death as the villain who killed him."

"Hold on, you didn't put the narcotic in the candle, nor the bleach in his system. You're not to blame. We didn't know we had a killer on board as well as an eavesdropper."

T-cut was feeling awful too because he'd rigged up the spy camera in the massage roller. He couldn't understand how it could go so wrong. They'd identified a possible suspect that only Fleur, him and Pav knew. Who would be waiting for an opportunity to kill Fischer and know when to do it? What possible motive could they have?

"All the death has done is confirm we have a mole, and that mole is capable of murder, which makes it even more crucial we track him down."

"We don't even know if Fischer was the mole now. The first mole. Oh, this is too complicated," Fleur stuttered, as the tears tipped over the edge of her eyes and fell down her cheeks. "He could have been innocent. We didn't find anything in his room. I'm responsible for the death of an innocent man."

Davidson chose that moment to come in search of lunch. Grabbing a tray and piling it with food, he joined Fleur and T-cut at their table uninvited. T-cut ignored Davidson's presence and continued speaking.

"No, you're not. He was up to something dodgy, or he wouldn't have ended up dead. And where is that damn laptop? The man hardly ever left his room except to eat and work."

"I guess he or the murderer chucked it overboard, as Pav suggested."

"Of course, Fischer could have been working with a partner," interjected Davidson, as he began eating his burger and fries.

"What?"

"A partner, he could have had a partner who did the deed."

"Why didn't I think of that?" Fleur groaned. "It makes sense. Fischer might have been taken out because we were getting too close. Would that be enough of a motive to kill him?"

T-cut and Fleur looked at Davidson for an answer since he already offered some good insight. Davidson held his palms up.

"Look, I don't know all the answers, but my guess would be that the man was worried Fischer, or more likely his laptop, might incriminate him."

"Of course." Fleur buried her head in her hands in frustration, while T-cut stole one of Davidson's French fries off his plate, almost losing a finger in the process.

"Hey!" T-cut complained, checking out his index finger for fork puncture marks.

"Never touch another man's fries," Davidson warned in mock threat, a grin plastered across his face, his fork raised menacingly.

Fleur looked up.

"What did you just say?"

Davidson shrugged.

"Never touch another man's stuff?"

"That's it!" Both men looked at Fleur like she'd lost the plot.

"What if, Fischer piggybacked onto T-cut's spyware in the Ready Room, and realised someone else was already spying on U1? Maybe he found T-cut's camera whilst doing a detector sweep or something. Then he started his own investigation to find the hacker. Especially, if he learnt, via his spyware, that two U1 missions were jeopardized recently. If he'd been listening, it could be possible. Remember the crew didn't know I was undercover, but Fischer may have known."

"Not partners then," agreed Davidson, concurring with Fleur's conclusion. "Fischer just happened to get caught up in the game. Unfortunately, the man he crossed is playing one far more dangerous."

"Whoever it is, has to be aware of my investigation, and knew I was close to nabbing Fischer and his laptop. He must have thought Fischer had something on him and took him out of the picture to keep his own identity a secret."

"The only people who knew you were from U2, were U1 members." T-cut and Davidson stared at each other.

"It's not me!" They both announced simultaneously.

"Who does that leave on board?" Fleur asked, ignoring their outburst.

"Fulwood, Doc, Tobin,…"

"You can cross those three off for starters. All of them have been in U1 over twenty years," muttered T-cut.

"That leaves Yin, Spencer, and Hutch."

"Who?"

"De Silva, the pilot," answered Davidson.

"And Rivera," added T-cut.

"Really?"

"He's part of U1," he replied, by way of explanation.

Just then Pav Rivera appeared in the canteen doorway. He glanced at the three U1 members sitting together but didn't step inside, continuing on his way instead. "My money's on him," announced T-cut, when he was sure Rivera was out of earshot.

"You're just worried he's your replacement."

"No, I'm not."

"Are so."

"Okay, what if I am. He could still be the one."

"T-cut's got a point." Fleur agreed. "He knows everything, even helped with accessing Fischer and he made several comments, which make more sense if you consider the events of the last twenty-four hours."

"Like what?" Davidson queried.

"He didn't tell T-cut he'd been helping me."

"That's not a crime, more a lapse in memory."

"He used the wrong turn of phrase when speaking about U1 men."

"Again, not a crime and English isn't his first language. What else?"

"He seems to have made it his business to find out who everyone on board the Bucket is, from the cleaners to the engineers."

"See my previous answer."

"What if Fischer, discovered Rivera listening in to the Ready Room, via T-cut's spyware, and threatened to report him?"

T-cut's mind was reeling as he listened to Fleur and Davidson hash it out, but he detected something.

"Hold that thought. What if…"

"What if, Rivera found Fischer's piggy-backed system first and realised someone might have guessed he was the person selling U1 information. Rivera could have been searching for the culprit, worried he'd spill the beans."

"That's a helluva big what-if, T-cut," interrupted Davidson.

"Yes! Rivera used my investigation to find the man. Oh my god, I led him straight to Fischer." Fleur gasped. "I did kill him."

"You couldn't know Fleur. He's supposed to be one of us."

"Now what?"

"We go to Fulwood."

"We can't, we've no evidence. Fulwood employed the man for God's sake."

"Then Johnson."

"And how do we do that with Rivera in the comms room twenty-four-seven."

247

It was Hutch's turn to arrive in the canteen for food, and with his arrival, Fleur realised she had an opportunity to get information off the Bucket without being suspected because frankly, everyone on board was a potential next victim if they were correct. Fleur had to fool Rivera into believing he'd won.

At briefing the following morning, Fleur announced that she had concluded her investigation. Rivera sat in the briefing silent and grinning, his expression noted by the three comrades. Fleur told the team she believed the murderer had left the Bucket shortly after Fischer's death, either using a pre-arranged set-up to depart, or hidden in the back of the Spade when it left to go to the mainland for supplies.

Hutch protested hotly at such a suggestion, arguing that no one could access the Spade without his knowledge let alone hide in it, but T-cut proved him wrong when he appeared on deck, after stowing away in the back of the cab that very afternoon. Hutch was forced to concur.

Fleur left the Bucket in the Spade the day after.

Pav Rivera was feeling very proud of himself. He'd fooled the silly girl and disposed of the irritating fool who'd discovered his spying. He hadn't planned on killing Fischer, but the stupid man had put spyware in his room—who does that? He'd caught Rivera in the act of taking the laptop and confronted him.

The laptop which now resided somewhere at the bottom of the South Atlantic along with the hypodermic syringe he'd utilised. Rivera grinned at his cleverness; he'd actually told the idiots that. They hadn't got a clue. With no incriminating evidence on board, Pav went to bed very content that night.

Fleur returned to the Bucket as a stowaway in the back of Hutch's cab, much like T-cut earlier, after speaking to Johnson from the mainland. She was mindful of all the spyware Rivera could have set up around the Bucket, which he'd probably lie about existing. When she was sure Hutch had secured his craft for the night and gone inside, she waited a short while longer, then climbed out. In her hand, she grasped one of the tranquilliser pistols kept inside the tiltrotor.

Fleur stalked the corridors to Rivera's cabin, knocking lightly on T-cut's door on the way. Together, they reached Rivera's door without meeting anyone. Using a master key, held by Doc for emergencies, which T-cut had purloined, he unlocked and opened the door. Fleur shot Pav Rivera twice in the thigh at point blank range without hesitation, while he lay sleeping, an S & M porno magazine lying across his lap.

"Good work Fleur," declared Fulwood, at the debrief later. He was slightly irritated about being kept out of Fleur's investigation regards Rivera. He'd hired the man and realised it didn't say much for his judgement. As if he could read his thoughts, Johnson piped up from his end of the conference call.

"You couldn't have known Frank. He fooled us all, as was his intention. The checks we ran proved to be bogus, set up by Pav himself. Mason?"

"Here."

"We need to tighten our IT and security from today."

"On it."

"If you need to bring in consultants do so." T-cut nodded. Forgetting Johnson couldn't see his face from where he sat.

"Sir, yes sir," he answered.

"So, what have we done with Rivera?" Johnson asked.

"Handed over to the authorities in Cape Town along with Fischer's corpse," replied Doc Williams. "Tobin found the bleach used in Rivera's cabin. Sloppy clear-up by him. Same chemical composition as that used to kill Fischer, and not one used on the Bucket. Open and shut case according to local Police, carries a minimum fifteen-year sentence.

"I'll see you back in England, Colton."

"Sir Yes sir," replied Fleur.

"What no more massages?" T-cut muttered under his breath, a big grin sat on his sloppy face as Fleur threw him a dirty look and middle finger in return.

"Did you feel that?"

"What?" Joannie asked, floating calmly on the surface of Lake Garda next to Lewis.

"The feeling of someone stroking the back of your neck."

"Should I?

"I don't know. It's weird. It's the same feeling I got when I saw you, and then Joni for the first time.

"You mean there's another person, here, in the lake?" Lowering her feet to the sandy lakebed, Joannie turned and scanned the immediate area.

"Not here at the lake no, but close."

"Lewis, I don't know if I can cope with any more than the three of us," Joni remarked truthfully, in her heavily accented Japanese, as she also stood observing the nearby shore.

"I know and I'm sorry." Lewis knew Joni disliked being in large numbers of people. "I don't know what's going on either. You know, you both mean everything to me."

"Yes, we know," they answered in unison, Joni moving over to put her arms around his waist and hug Lewis tight.

"I feel it here, like a pressure on my heart, when I think of either of you." Moving closer as she spoke, Joannie placed both her hands over her heart. Then she placed her left hand over Lewis's heart and her right one over Joni's. Lewis closed his eyes sensing their unique oneness. He knew there was something different about him, about them.

Is this why my father vanished? Is he the same? Is he like me? Did he feel this way when he was with women? Lewis suspected there was a strong possibility.

He hadn't mentioned anything about his father, his words had raised both girls' anxiety levels enough. They didn't feel safe in the water now despite the deep sensation of security it normally gave them. They'd spoken at length before about moving on to a new place, aware of the keen pair of eyes watching their every move. Joni and Joannie's pregnancies weren't that far along. Lewis wanted them to leave Italy before anyone suspected they were carrying his children. He had a suspicion that once the girls' condition became obvious, they wouldn't be left alone.

The heat of Khao Lak in Southern Thailand was oppressive, the temperature reminding Spencer of Libya. *What is it with Fulwood sending me on missions where the heat threatens to kill me?* He was situated a few miles south of the national park of the same name.

Even sitting in the shade, sweat covered his body. From his scalp, it ran down his forehead and temples, causing him to wipe it away every few minutes with his forearm. At the back of his neck, it collected between his shoulder blades, then trickled lazily down his spine. Another time, in another place, the feeling might have been sensual, but Spencer was trying to maintain his focus.

Taking his hand off his tranquillizer rifle, he wiped his sweaty trigger palm on his camo fatigues. The rifle contained a special cocktail of drugs designed specifically by Doc. It was Doc William's latest pride and joy, seeing as how there were no other 99% safe drugs listed globally for tranking felons via sniper rifle. Tested on U1 members first, naturally.

Neither the Police nor military used such a gun on felons, as they couldn't be sure of the safest dose or side effects for each individual, preferring instead to use taser devices on civilians. How long the formula would stay exclusive to Unit One was anyone's guess. Currently, it remained the property of U1 until such time as Johnson saw fit to release it to the pharmaceutical companies. Several were aware of U1's research innovations, thanks to Doc and Tobin's past endeavours. They would snatch up further products quicker than you could say, 'take two aspirin and go to bed'.

251

Spencer smiled, they'd come a long way from shooting their targets outright, and that was good to his way of thinking. Things could get very messy and complicated when blood was involved. He'd heard the stories of their in-house assassin John Redshaw. He was glad they'd never met, though the older team members spoke about him with something bordering on hero-worship and awe.

Following a lead, Fulwood had sent Spencer to catch Jorge Martins. Now that the leak had been found aboard the Bucket, U1 was free to act. These types of missions were why Owen Spencer had been recruited into the team. He was good—amazingly good—at long-range sniper work. He shot things, both stationary and moving, from objects to animals and people. He was experienced in using a vast array of weapons including crossbows, slingshots, and blades. His hundred per cent record stood. He had never missed a target he aimed for—ever.

Jorge Martins came into view as he stepped out of the rental house he had transferred to after leaving São Tomé. It was the first time Spencer had set eyes on the mark. He wasn't what Spencer expected. He'd seen photos but scrutinizing the man in real life didn't compare. He oozed confidence, in his walk, in his manner, everything about him asserted his dominance. And there was something else, a frisson of evil hung about him. Spencer had only ever witnessed such sensations during active combat. Hate, a disregard for life—all life. A being who considered themselves above humanity. It made his flesh creep and the hairs on the back of his sweaty neck rise. *The sooner this villain is put away the better.*

Spencer leaned down into the shot, his shoulder fitting snugly against the butt of his adapted PAX-22 rifle. It was almost an intimate relationship. People would have thought him odd if he expressed feelings towards his guns. It was no different, in Spencer's mind than loving your car or motorbike, and plenty of folks admitted to doing that. His current baby, back in the Bucket's armoury, was an SVLK-14 Sumrak rifle made by the Lobaev Arms Company in Russia, able to hit a target almost two miles away. He'd managed to obtain one prior to international release, thanks to Johnson's contacts. He spent hours lovingly disassembling, cleaning, and reassembling the gun. He knew every component better than his own body, and the gun oil… took him to another place. Combat.

"Go away T-cut. I don't want to hear any more." Fulwood clasped his hands over his ears and closed his eyes.

"Okay," responded T-cut a little too smugly, backing out the door. "You don't want to hear that Spencer took out the mark in Khao Lak, then?" Fulwood took his hands down and opened his eyes.

"That is good news."

"Yes, and Interpol have collected the goods."

Fulwood smiled with relief.

"Sorry about that."

"It's fine. Oh, and one other thing," T-cut added, sidling towards the door. "Six more trackers have landed at Leonardo De Vinci airport in Rome today."

As the door closed behind him, T-cut heard a large object hit the other side. He sniggered all the way back to the comms room. *Things are about to get a whole lot more interesting in Italy.*

CURRENT UNIT ONE MEMBERS

Frank Fulwood aka *The Boss*, aged 54. Runs the Bucket and U1. Active commander since Johnson's semi-retirement. Surveillance and recon specialist, fluent in over twenty languages.

Terrance Mason aka *T-cut*, aged 44. Communications and IT expert. Fluent in fifteen languages.Second in command of bucket. Ex-covert special forces.

Michael Davidson aka *Texas*, aged 43. Height six-foot-four. Jet pilot and explosives expert. Stints in Afghanistan, Bosnia, Iraq. Weapons officer in Unit One. 3rd Dan black belt in Kyokushin Karate.

David Williams aka *Doc*, aged 78. Bucket's medical officer. Eminent plastic surgeon. English

Michael Tobin aged 47. U1's charge nurse practitioner and paramedic. From County Cork, Ireland. Trained by the military. Experienced in active war zones and field hospitals. Capable of minor surgery to intensive care. Holds qualifications as a registered sports physiotherapist and counsellor.

José De Silva aka *Hutch*, aged 28. Pilot on U1 last four years, second cousin of Lola. Speaks, Spanish, French, Aymaraian. Born in UK.

Fan Yin aged 22. Been with U1 since aged nineteen. British but of Chinese descent. Later years, before U1, spent in Cornwall. Recruited by Fulwood in Rome. Three black belts.

Pav Rivera aged 24 yrs. Filipino. IT guru, 3rd Dan jujutsu Born to a Filipino mother and older English father. Father died, when Pav was eight. Mother died of AIDs when he was fourteen. Put into care.

Travis St John aka *Swoop.* aged 38. Fourteen years in army on active service. Two years in Police SWAT. Medically pensioned after taking a bullet in the back. Expert in Filipino Kali martial arts. Been with U1 two years.

Owen Spencer aged 34. Sniper. Ex-member of Special Boat Service (SBS). Royal Marine Commando. Was in Libya in 2011.

UNIT 2 MEMBERS

Jeff Johnson aged 63. Unit Two Leader and overall Commander. English. Married to Vivienne Oakwood. Two children.

Thomas Seamark aged 47 land-based with Johnson. Marksman, second helicopter pilot and forger. Wife, Lolita De Silva

Lolita De Silva aka *Lola.* Joined U2. Does missions alongside husband on occasion. José in U1 her second cousin. Born in England of Peruvian descent.

Fleur Colton aged 32. ex-RAF pilot. Ex Member 21st Regiment British Army.

Baptiste Estefan aka *Atrax.* Aged 35. Of Greek descent. Spent two years in U1 before transferring to U2

EX-UNIT ONE MEMBERS

RETIRED. James Franklin aged 56. Tour in Afghanistan in 2006. Demolition expert, aeroplane and helicopter pilot and engineer.

DECEASED. Gavin Sureswift aged 37. Died on mission five years after Redshaw vanished. U1 electronic expert and paramedic.

MISSING IN ACTION. John Redshaw. Aged 56. No contact for the last nineteen years. Weapons and tactical officer, Martial arts expert to 6th Dan Kyokushin, Northern Shaolin, Aikido and Gensieryu. Mother died when he was four years old. Sent to military boarding school. Dad, John Redshaw Senior, military officer.

ACKNOWLEDGEMENTS

DAVID & MICHAEL SALTER, my son and husband respectively, who make my life worthwhile in so many ways. They are my heart.

GEOFF FISHER, my brilliant formatter, who I finally managed to meet up for lunch. We got on famously and I look forward to undertaking many more projects (and lunches) with him.

JOZANE GRAY, Account Manager at Book Printing UK, for supporting and assisting my publications.

KAREN HUTCHINSON – for her insight and knowledge in wordcraft.

LUCIE at PEGU DESIGNS, for continuing to put up with my everlasting changes and creating beautiful covers.

AUTHOR BIOGRAPHY

 Carol M. Salter offers this her long-awaited sequel, to Aquasapien Metamorphosis—**Aquasapien Prodigy.** This is her sixth independently published full-length novel and the third in the Aquasapien saga.

Carol still works full-time as a school nurse, since retiring from the NHS in 2014. In 2022, she was proud to be chosen to receive the Queen's Award for Voluntary Service after volunteering her time during the Covid Pandemic.

Carol continues to practise Kyokushin karate and achieved her long-term goal, passing her 2nd Kyu brown belt grade. She continues street dancing lessons, adding more moves to her repertoire.

"Above all these things she reads, and when she isn't reading—she writes..."

You can find more about Carol's writing and follow her blog on:

carolmsalter.com

Subscribe to her podcasts on; YouTube Channel
Carol M. Salter

In addition to Waterstones, and Amazon, you can purchase hard copies of all Carol's books and related merchandise on Wayside Publications Estore at:

Authors survive by reviews. If you enjoy Carol's novels and stories, please leave her a rating and/or review on Amazon, Goodreads or the Estore.

Inspiration Writers Group (IWG), the group Carol founded in 2010 continues to survive regardless of Covid and several recent changes. They are currently working towards *Indigo*, the next anthology in their Rainbow Series, and members were judges in the national anthology competition this year. You can find out more about IWG at:

https//inspirationswritersgroup.weebly.com

PUBLISHED WORKS

NOVELS

WITCH ON THE WARPATH, (2015) is a full-length urban family fantasy novel for all ages. It introduces the adventures of Onk, a London city troll. Set in London, Kent and Thanet, it chronicles the events following Onk's rescue of an unborn fairy babe and a witch who is desperate to kill her. Published by Wayside Publications.

   ISBN 978-0-9933174-0-8. It is also available on Kindle.

GRISTLE'S REVENGE, (2018) is a full-length urban family fantasy novel for all ages. The follow-on novel from *Witch on the Warpath,* this story is about the kidnapping of Purity, a dual heritage fairy, and niece to Onk, the city troll. Published by Wayside Publications.

   ISBN 978-0-9933174-6-0. It is also available on Kindle.

QUEST FOR COURAGE (2021) is the final book in the *Witch on the Warpath* trilogy. It follows Purity's search for her brother. Will Gristle be at the heart of their troubles once more and will they ever defeat her? Published by Wayside Publications.

   ISBN 978-1-9993528-8-2

AQUASAPIEN – METAMORPHOSIS (2017) *Limited Edition*. The complete story is an **adult 18+** military adventure Sci-Fi novel set on present-day Earth. John Redshaw, a member of an elite mercenary team codenamed Unit One, is genetically altered by an alien lifeform. Will he bring destruction or salvation to the people of Earth? Published by Wayside Publications

ISBN 978-0-9933174-2-2 Also available on Kindle.

AQUASAPIEN – METAMORPHOSIS, BOOK ONE – PART ONE (2021) **18+** Published by Wayside Publications
ISBN 978-1-9993528-3-7 Also available on Kindle.

AQUASAPIEN – METAMORPHOSIS, BOOK TWO – PART TWO (2021) **18+** Published by Wayside Publications
ISBN 978-1-9993528-4-4 Also available on Kindle.

AQUASAPIEN – PRODIGY, BOOK THREE (2022) **18+** Published by Wayside Publications
ISBN 978-1-9993528-5-1

WHAT IF? (2021) A full-length contemporary fantasy novel. Kate Wadlow discovers the life she knew is a lie. People are trying to capture and kill her. Will she survive? What if she doesn't? Published by Wayside Publications
ISBN 978-0-9933174-9-1

SHORT STORIES

UNDERWORLD, (2012) a short dystopian fantasy story published in **Broken Worlds Anthology** by Firedance Publications.
ISBN 978-1-909256-11-8 Also available as a stand-alone story on Kindle.

THE MOTHER I DON'T KNOW & MY SELFISH WAYS (2013) in **Tellers of Tales Anthology** Published by Canterbury Soroptimists.
ISBN 978-0-9926171-0-3

BLOOD, and SCRUFFY MAN WHO WORKS IN THE CHIPPIE VAN, (2017) Two short stories in **Red Anthology** *from Inspirations Writers Group.* Published by Wayside Publications.
ISBN 978-0-9933174-4-6

BOTH ORANGE, (2017) a short story, in **Orange Anthology** from Inspirations Writers Group. Published by Wayside Publications.
ISBN 978-0-9933174-5-3

A TIME TO..., & LIFE ISN'T FAIR, (2018) short stories in **Yellow Anthology** from Inspirations Writers Group. Published by Wayside Publications.
ISBN 978-0-9933174-8-4

THE VANISHING MAN (2019) short story in **Green Anthology** from Inspirations Writers Group. Published by Wayside Publications.

    ISBN 978-1-9993528-2-0.

FIGURES (2021) short story in **Blue Anthology** from Inspirations Writers Group. Publication by Wayside Publications.

    ISBN 978-1-9993528-7-5

COMPETITION WINS

LIFE AFTER COVID (2020) short story. **Winner of the Faversham Eye Essay Writing Competition.**

GREEN ANTHOLOGY (2019) from Inspirations Writers Group. ***Winner of the Denise Robertson National Anthology Award 2021***, sponsored by the NAWG.

NOVELS IN THE MAKING

A SACKFUL OF DRAGONS - What can possibly go wrong when two orphan children discover a sack full of baby dragons in an alley? A work in progress.

BETWEEN WORLDS - Someone from Hell is trying to kill Arianne, but who, and why? A work in progress.

CHICKEN WIZARD – full-colour picture book about a magic cockerel. Aimed at 5- to 8-year-olds. Due for release in 2022/23